An Accidental Pope

A MYSTERY IN FIVE BOXES

James Casper

PEQUOT LAKES, MINNESOTA

James Casper/Farhaven Press
4612 Hemlock Lane
Pequot Lakes, MN/56472
www.farhavenpress.com

An Accidental Pope is a work of fiction. Names, characters, places, and incidents are a product of the author's imagination. Locales and public names are sometimes used for atmospheric purposes. Any resemblance to actual people, living or dead, or to businesses, companies, events, institutions, or locales is completely coincidental. Its theology is not represented as being consistent with accepted teachings of the Roman Catholic Church, nor does it claim adherence to Vatican prescriptions in the event of a pope's death and the election of his successor. The opinions of its characters are not necessarily those of the author.

Book Layout and Cover Design ©2018 Kate Casper/
TipTopWriting.com

An Accidental Pope: A Mystery in Five Boxes/ James Casper. –
1st edition revised.
ISBN 978-0-9994715-1-7 (Paperback)

For my beloved son, Jon Nathan Casper,
who left this broken world
of a fallen Paradise
as this story was being written

Contents

Box One: A Box of Crackerjacks

Box Two: A Puzzle Box

Box Three: A Jack-in-the-Box

Box Four: A Box called a Confessional

There are known knowns; there are things we know that we know. There are known unknowns; that is to say, there are things that we now know we don't know. But there are also unknown unknowns—there are things we do not know we don't know.

—DONALD RUMSFELD

BOX ONE

A BOX OF CRACKERJACKS

Not everything that rises must converge.

—VINCENT VESUVIO

CLIPPINGS

TWIN RIVERS DAILY CLARION
May 7
Body Discovered Behind Hotel Paradise

During a routine patrol of the derelict Hotel Paradise, Twin Rivers police and Paradise County deputies discovered the body of a young man in an alley near the hotel fire escape.

While an investigation continues, the area is being treated as a crime scene. Identification is being withheld pending notification of next of kin.

No further information is available at this time.

May 7
Note on East Pendle Street apartment door near Notre Dame University

Phil, all your friends are looking for you. Nobody seems to know anything. Mock Trials begin next week. Let us know where you are. Jake and Brian

TWIN RIVERS DAILY CLARION
May 9
Foul Play 'Ruled Out' in Hotel Fire Escape Fatality

May 10
Note on East Pendle Street apartment door near Notre Dame University

Phil, if we don't hear from you by tomorrow morning, we are calling the police. Brian, Jake, and Paula

1

Porky and Harriet White

Wilbur and Harriet White were one of Twin Rivers' most conspicuous couples. Apart from separations during work hours, one would seldom be seen without the other, pushing grocery carts, sitting on benches in the mall holding hands, on the same side of a café booth, and out on a dance floor together wherever a band played. Sunday mornings were an exception: Harriet attended Mass at St. Callixtus and sang in its choir. Wilbur, a determined atheist, would meet her in front of the church afterwards, and off they would go to a café for breakfast.

Whoever thought of calling cops *flatfoots* did not have Wilbur in mind. For that matter, whoever nicknamed him Porky did not have Porky in mind. He was as trim and nimble as a champion welterweight boxer. In another world than Twin Rivers, instead of wearing a police badge, he might have worn gloves and won by a TKO in the third round. He might have donned tights and been a ballet dancer. When he twirled Harriet around on a dance floor, other couples would drop out to watch and applaud when the spectacle was over. Add to this Wilbur's skill as an amateur juggler, good enough to entertain at community events. Here was somebody who wasn't the typical town cop and wasn't a typical guy nicknamed Porky.

When he wasn't twirling Harriet and lofting beanbags for local Scout troops and fundraisers, Porky used his dancing skills and juggler's coordination in police investigative work. In place of Harriet, he twirled suspects and suspicious situations. In place of beanbags, he had three or four questions in the air at once, barely handling any of them longer than it took to flip them around in his investigative mind—or in a suspect's face.

Harriet White worked in the background of her husband's investigations. Credit for her crime-solving deductions went to Porky. Personal satisfaction came her way. She thought of detective work as a hobby: untangling a mystery was like filling in the last gaps of a jigsaw puzzle, or reciting old jump-rope songs to the rhythm of Porky's juggling. The steady rhythm helped her think. In the public world of Twin Rivers, she was the soprano soloist in Bernard Passmore's 'award-winning' St. Callixtus choir. Otherwise she worked as a veterinary assistant at a local pet clinic. As a victim of epilepsy subject to occasional seizures, she was unable to drive. She depended on Porky to ferry her from point to point in daily routines.

Recently, she discovered a new hobby in writing the history of St. Callixtus Church for its sesquicentennial celebration. The church archive had become yet another ferry point. The archive held mysteries of its own, some the equal of those Porky encountered and brought home.

Women with first names of three or more syllables often wind up with nicknames. Harriet insisted on being Harriet, no matter how many times it was spelled wrong. Only Porky got away with something else. In private, he often called her Wren. No one loved to hear her sing more than Porky did. It was almost enough to make him a churchgoer.

2

Rain or Shine, Suicide or Murder?

On a mid-spring Saturday morning of the sort requiring both sunglasses and an umbrella, Porky White's eyes were riveted skyward to the fifth floor of The Paradise, a derelict hotel. His thoughts wandered between suicide and murder.

Fifty feet above him, another Twin Rivers, Minnesota officer outside an open window leaned over the railing of a rusty fire escape. The two of them had been in this alley several times during the past week, each time with the same questions flipping around in Porky's mind.

This was his first time there with his juggling beanbags, which, at his direction, were being dropped and tossed in various ways from the fire escape's zigzagging stairway. It was a curious sight, two cops appearing to play with beanbags behind a dilapidated brick building boarded up on its lower floors and with broken windows on its upper ones.

In fact, the scene had attracted an audience: a man watching the game from a red roadster parked beyond the alley; another man, of substantial girth, pacing within a grove of honey locust trees between St. Callixtus Church and the hotel. The man in the roadster expected to be noticed. The man in the trees thought himself concealed. Porky knew and was known to both.

Sitting in the roadster was Dusty Dwyer, owner of the Purple Palace, a strip club as old as its hotel neighbor. Half hidden beyond the trees was Bernard Passmore, St. Callixtus' choir director, of burgeoning silhouette, unmistakable as any thumbprint. He appeared to be reading a book, a church hymnal held upside down as he cast sideways glances down the alley.

Each colorful beanbag lying scattered about in the alley marked Porky's attempt to answer one of his questions:

First, was it possible either to jump from there or be pushed and land where the young man's body had been found?

Second, if he had been pushed, were his injuries consistent with a body colliding on jutting parts of the fire escape in its plummet to the alley below? The coroner's report had been inconclusive.

If he leaped, how far to clear the fire escape entirely? Porky removed his sunglasses to study a yellow, chalk-painted form on alley pavement. The form looked washed-out after several spring showers this past week. Its location bothered him. None of his beanbags were close to where the body had been found.

The suicide note had also missed its intended mark. Carefully folded and tucked into a jacket pocket, it looked like a fake.

Suicide notes were supposed to resemble messages scrawled on restroom walls or left as last-minute reminders under magnets on refrigerator doors. They always had at least one spelling mistake. A torn corner, or a dog-ear would clinch it. Porky had seen a number of such notes in his investigative work, last words scribbled by people angry, raging, half out of their minds, and revenging themselves on the world for screwing up their lives.

Carefully printed in block letters, Phillip Fowler's read like a rehearsed speech in act three of a high school class play. It used indented paragraphs, and even included a bit of Latin legal lingo, as if somebody had tried to imagine what a law school student would say at such a critical moment. Here was the fabrication of a perfectionist with tunnel vision.

"And about as convincing as those done-up pooches at a dog show," Harriet had said as he dropped her off for an early morning shift at the pet clinic. Her eyes twinkled as they always did when she imagined something amusing.

In the hotel alley an hour later, Porky said, "*It's about as convincing as a done-up-pooch at a dog show.*"

Officer Charlie Cook nodded, pretending to understand. He was used to it. Porky's analogies, as an old saying goes, often went in one of Charlie's ears and out the other without gaining much traction.

Also too contrived was the blue windbreaker jacket bearing the victim's monogram draped over the open window casing as if the victim had removed it to dive into a swimming pool, not fifty feet into an alley.

"A swimming pool?" said Charlie.

"You can bet on it," said Porky.

From where he stood, everything pointed to a murder contrived to look otherwise. Whoever killed the young man had both a high opinion of his own intelligence and a view of police work bordering on mockery. In taking too much care, the killer had been careless.

Other thoughts Porky would keep to himself. For the time being, this would officially remain a suicide case. Thinking he had pulled it off, the killer would become complacent. A criminal thinking he got away with something was a cop's best friend.

Having run out of beanbags, Charlie had trundled down the fire escape, and was looking down on his boss from its last step.

"Do you want to try it again?"

They had gathered the beanbags twice before, with Charlie, overweight and breathless, struggling up the fire escape to send them down in various ways.

"I've seen enough," said Porky, without revealing what he had seen. "I need to ask that priest Vesuvio a few more questions. The funeral is today, isn't it?"

Charlie looked at his watch. "In about two hours, except Vesuvio won't be here for it. Another padre was sent in."

"What's that all about?"

Charlie shrugged, hung by his hands from the bottom of the fire escape, and landed in the alley, several yards from where the body had been found.

"You're too old and too fat to be trying that stunt, Charlie, but my point exactly—a guy simply lets go; he lands where you are. If he is pushed or makes a flying leap, he lands somewhere in this area." Porky waved a black baton hanging from his belt. "No way does he land there. You can bet on it." He pointed to the faded, yellow chalk form.

"Maybe someone moved the body," suggested Charlie. "Maybe he crawled that far."

"Dead men don't crawl. This guy died instantly if we can believe the coroner's report—'blunt force trauma consistent with a fall of more than twenty feet.' Of course, our county coroner should have retired twenty years ago, and lately it's like he earns his living by making mistakes. Keep that to yourself, Charlie, like I never said it."

And Porky kept to himself the suspicion that Phillip Fowler had been killed somewhere else, with his body dumped in the hotel alley, staged to look like a suicide.

"Charlie, you're a Catholic, right?

"Right!"

"Is the coroner a Catholic?"

"Yup. He and his wife sit three pews in front of me and my wife every Sunday."

"By the way, did Corrie get over those migraines you mention now and then?"

"She's doing all right. Thanks for asking, Porky."

"Right," said Porky, casting sideways glances, two or three, a skill known to lawmen in detective novels.

Having gorged himself on a youthful diet of such novels, Porky was an encouraging example of a man who grew up to become exactly what he dreamt of being. He knew that great detective heroes always knew more than they said, and sometimes said things they knew to be false just to cast a net for the unsuspecting and complacent criminal.

Like those detective heroes, he also noticed things that ordinary folk missed, but he would wait till the right moment to say something about it, that moment being when everyone else's attention had drifted away. He glanced toward the church apse beyond the rangy locust trees at the end of the alley, then the other way toward the parking lot of the strip club.

"And I would like to know who's been circling around here overnight on a motorcycle." Porky pointed to loose gravel displaced on the perimeter of the crime scene and darkened by an early morning shower. Any alert detective would have noticed.

"Somebody colorblind who can't read." Prior to this, Charlie had not noticed, but whenever he partnered with the redoubtable Porky, he had to pretend. He picked up a fallen section of yellow crime-scene tape and wrapped it around an orange traffic cone as if all along he had been thinking about the motorcycle.

"Or somebody with something on his mind," said Porky. "—Speaking of which, I'm going to have another word with the guy who runs that strip joint. Guys who run dives like that always know more than they say the first time. You can bet on it. You go over to the church and check around. Maybe the new padre will be there by now. Maybe somebody will know something. But, if you happen to run into him, ignore the fat man who's been keeping an eye on us from those trees. He's my wife's choir director. I wouldn't want to rile him. He might keep me waiting for her while she sings solos after Wednesday practices. I hate eating late. Makes my stomach hurt."

"An ulcer?"

"You might say so." Porky loped down the alley toward a nightclub called the *Purple Palace*. Too many unanswered questions also made his stomach hurt. He had a few for the choir director, but those could wait.

3

A Slippery Fish

"Looking for me?" said the man in the red roadster, rolling down his window as Porky approached.

Wearing a white turtleneck beneath a dark blazer, sunglasses propped atop his head, Dusty Dwyer might have been an advertisement in a men's magazine from forty years earlier.

"Dusty, I hope you enjoyed our little beanbag fun," said Porky who fancied having the exceptional peripheral vision of all legendary detectives.

"Reminds me of an act I staged in Chicago before I bought this joint years ago. *All My Sins* was the name of my Chicago club."

"Sins?" Porky knew he was in big city territory with that one.

"Yeah, sins, if you know what I mean, like honey for flies, or a corpse for maggots. You wouldn't have heard of All My Sins, but it was big in Chicago, very big, mortal sins you might say. I wanted to give this Purple Palace joint the same name when I bought it years ago, but subtlety is the way things go around here. As an old choir boy, I know purple is the color for Lent, Advent, and penitence. This town is forever in Lent or Advent or feeling bad about something, so I thought the name Purple Palace would catch on, if you know what I mean."

"Has it?" Porky retreated a step as if the mere thought of all those sins might be radioactive.

"Not really. With so much raw porn available on internet, strip shows are about as enticing as PTA meetings. Pouring booze is what keeps me in business these days."

"You were a choir boy?"

"Yeah, I can get quite nostalgic about that part of my life, growing up in Chicago. Ask me about it sometime. My church, run by a fusty old mugger of a priest, kept using Latin years after all the other churches used English. I don't know how he got away with it, but I really enjoyed that old Latin Mass hocus-pocus—had a musical ring. I can still recite some of it, and sometimes do when I can't sleep—stuff like *juventutem meam* and *mea maxima culpa*. I like the sound of it. Beats counting sheep, if you know what I mean."

"Can't sleep?" Porky made a mental note about a guilty conscience.

Dusty was ahead of him, reading the cop's mind. "No, not because of anything I'd done that might get me thrown in the clink, but I have restless leg syndrome. My legs keep kicking under the covers just about the time I'm nodding off.

"—Anyway, as I was saying, sins are sins wherever, and there's good money in sin. Sin is like a currency you can spend anywhere, even around this hick town. All the cops knew about my Chicago club. A lot of mafia types hung out there, not the chief honchoes, but the heavy-lifters who took out contracts on squealers, and did protection racket hits, extortion and all that stuff. They weren't the brains. They just did what the brains higher up told them to do. I don't suppose you run into much extortion and protection racket stuff around here."

Dusty glanced down the alley toward the locust tree grove and the church. He made it sound like a question whose answer lay in that direction.

This was enough to convince Porky that Dusty knew something. Porky had a competent lawman's knowledge of getting people to talk by not saying much. He stayed silent. His face said nothing. He could appear to follow when he was leading. He could play dumb. All this aside, getting Dusty to talk was easy; the hard part was getting him to say anything that went anywhere.

Dusty seemed to be enjoying himself.

When it came to playing games and baiting hooks, he was more than a match for what he regarded as a small-town cop with a fantasy life. He launched into a lecture for Porky's benefit:

"You know how the protection racket goes.... If somebody has 'the goods' on somebody who has a lot to lose if the secret ever gets out, the guy with plenty to hide gets squeezed, if you know what I mean.

"Pretty soon desperation sets in, especially if someone even bigger has a lot at stake, and 'bigger' knows about the guy's secret. If a guy has a family on one side, and on the other, something else he cares about a lot, like maybe his career and reputation, he gets split right down the middle. Then anything can happen. It could happen here. It happens all the time in Chicago. It's like being drawn-and-quartered. You know, tying horses to a man's legs and arms, and running them off in different directions. Lots of blood gets splashed—I knew a man in Chicago ... these days they use motorcycles instead of horses, works the same way. Ask me about him sometime. All My Sins makes this place look like a kiddie show."

"The Purple Palace, a kiddie show?" Porky glanced down at his badge. It seemed to have become a plastic prize in a box of something like Crackerjacks, the large economy size.

"Yeah, a kiddie show, if you know what I mean. But I was ready for a change of scenery, so I sold out and moved here. This is just what I was looking for, a quiet, small town with lots of fresh air, only an occasional murder, and people easily shocked.

"If I did the stuff here that was our main attraction there, you'd shut me down, officer. In Chicago, I even had a couple of cops who worked part-time as male strippers, off duty of course. That's Chicago. You could never be sure what side of the law anybody was on, and sometimes they could be on all sides at once.

"We ran acts seven nights a week, the Sabbath and all that. Sunday nights could be our busiest. People, guys and gals, would come piling in after the big football games. You would have sworn they were on their way to church.

"–Speaking of which, would you believe that the pope showed up at our Chicago church when I was a choir boy? I got to meet him, along with the other kids in our boys' choir. Then my voice changed, but anyway the pope blessed all of us choir boys on the spot, and you can't get a blessing that beats that. I think it still does me some good, brings luck, if you know what I mean."

Dusty spewed facts and stories like a device bubbling air in a fish tank.

Porky made mental notes—*blood, choir boy, Latin, a pope, the fake suicide note*. Dusty moved up a notch on his suspect list. Guys like Dusty always talked in riddles, but once in a while, they let something slip.

"Latin, you say? You know Latin?"

"Yeah, years ago." Dusty grew wistful.

"Lawyers sometimes use that stuff, don't they?" Porky pretended not to know for sure.

"Yeah, lawyers, priests, and thugs—they all know Latin. Thugs especially like *habeas corpus, corpus delicti*, and *cherchez la femme*—of course that's French. We choir boys never got to say *corpus delicti* in church, but around Chicago gangsters it has a sweet sound. Without a body, there's nothing to pin on anyone, but sometimes even if there is a body.... Lots of bodies wind up in city landfills. That's one of the reasons gangsters are so much into running garbage collection businesses in places like..."

"Chicago?" said Porky.

"Yeah, Chicago," said Dusty. "Up here in Twin Rivers, there's nothing but amateurs where bodies are concerned. Like that one in the hotel alley."

"Are you saying that was a crime?"

"*Caveat emptor*—buyer beware! Any con-artist recites that in his sleep with a smile on his face. –But you're the inspector. I'm just a next-door neighbor, from Chicago. As I was saying, things are one way in Chicago, another way here, but I've never seen cops playing with beanbags before, so I figure you must be onto something."

Porky glanced back up the alley where his sidekick's elongated shadow had melted into a portion of the locust tree grove adjacent the church parking lot.

"You don't happen to own a motorcycle, do you?"

"A Harley," said Dusty.

He squinted at Porky, the sort of narrow-eyed squint that was his specialty from long experience, sizing up a situation. He had two bikes, one he rode and one he kept for old time's sake.

"And an *Indian Classic*, officer, in case that rings a bell with you."

"This reminds me to ask if you ever heard of a young Indian woman named Melody, last seen in Chicago?"

Porky had just made one of his fastest interrogation moves ever. Though a shower was beginning, he lowered his sunglasses over his eyes. Professional pride gleamed there. It was Porky's turn to squint.

"Melody, yeah, a great name for a stripper—Melody. I've known one or two who went by that name, back in Chicago, part of their acts of course."

Dusty was equal to a cop's best moves. He could sprint like a jack rabbit in a greyhound race. He never said no when there was a way of saying yes. He never flinched at a clutch moment in the game. He had been the star pinch-hitter on his choir boys' baseball team. He had met cops climbing through windows with a drink in each hand, while other cops—off duty—scrambled out windows in the back. He had faced down mobsters who might take out contracts on his head, and outlived them in the end. He had passed well beyond the meaning of fearless and cool as a cucumber.

Any of his strippers might have agreed as they shuttled between Chicago and Twin Rivers. In their worlds, Dusty knew every rope; he was safe harbor, haven, a future, and as good as a one-way bus ticket to college.

"The name Melody reminds me of something else about Chicago. Ask me sometime—when it's not raining, maybe while your wife's at her choir practice. There might be a show on—lots of interesting types on display during my shows—no charge for you of course, on the house."

"Are you talking about your strippers, and maybe an Indian girl now and then?"

"No, it's the guys who show up to watch—that's the real freak show. Ask me about it sometime—like I said, when it's not raining."

"I intend to." Porky, jaw set, managed a steely-eyed look.

The shower had stopped, two minutes ago.

Porky pivoted on his heels and danced away toward the hotel.

As a parting shot of Latin, Dusty left Porky with this: "You probably know *errata* means mistakes, a list of mistakes, officer. Us choir boys had one list for the confessional; another list for surviving out on the streets. Word gets around, you might say. Ask me about it sometime."

"You can bet on it," said Porky, over his shoulder and two steps down the alley.

Choir practice? How did he know Wren sings in the choir? The guy knows more about me than I know about him, and I've questioned him twice.

Among other things, Dusty had given him new respect for Chicago cops juggling suspicions in a city full of slippery fish like Dusty Dwyer.

4

Aloysius Brandy 100 Proof

Father Aloysius Brandy's name had high alcohol content. The old priest himself had never been known to be tipsy, despite parishioners' repeated efforts in that direction whenever he was invited to a wedding reception or a Knights of Columbus gathering. Throw in Father Brandy's broad facial features, a bit of a pug nose, dark-rimmed glasses, hair on the furry side turning white, and he could be imagined as an Alpine dog with brandy cask rescuing travelers lost in blizzards.

While the name Brandy fell off most lips with the smoothness of a worthy cognac, his given name proved tricky to spell and pronounce. Since almost no one could say Aloysius, as a youth he was known simply as Brandy. Even his parents called him that. Whatever they had intended, the name Aloysius led him into a lifetime of annoying difficulties, too small to be worthy of complaint and too inevitable to ignore.

In his many years as a parish priest in the sprawling northern Minnesota diocese of North Port, he was bound to become peevish from so much pronouncing and spelling of *Aloysius* every time a parishioner murdered it or a secretary needed it for a church bulletin. Nor did it help that Aloysius rhymed with delicious, suspicious, auspicious, vicious, and doing-the-dishes, none of which were spelled the same as Aloysius or—except for his church soup kitchen work—fit a life better described as *steady, dutiful, and determined.*

And so it came to pass, on a brisk spring morning, His Eminence Norman St. Claire, Bishop of North Port, with scant explanation, sent him on the road at half past three....

With his mongrel Fred in the back seat of his timeworn sedan, Brandy began a trip of almost two hundred miles into western Minnesota, Ojibwe Indian reservation country, his destination Twin Rivers, the Parish of St. Callixtus. He had last been there as a young priest. Forty years having slipped by, he had never been back. St. Callixtus had become a distant world beyond several horizons and a lifetime of experience.

At about the same time, pigeons roosting overnight on St. Callixtus Church ledges took flight toward a river and then circled back to shelter once more on its illuminated façade. Far below them, what might have been a cannonade quieted to the imagined purring of a large jungle cat. A rectory garage door lifted, and a black motorcycle emerged, paused while its black-clad driver adjusted his helmet strap, and then moved slowly down an alley toward a circular barrier of traffic cones and yellow tape bearing the words *Crime Scene Do Not Cross*.

The words, repeated in sets, had been there for several days. Yet the driver, who had seen them before, seemed to read them as if for the first time, and as if, illuminated by his cycle lights, they contained a different message. He dismounted, removed his helmet, and stood with head bowed over a human form outlined in chalk on the alley pavement and sand. It might have been someone he knew long ago, a memory fading into memories yet more distant.

Five minutes passed before he turned away, circled the scene on his motorcycle, parked in front of the church, and took a skeleton key from his pocket.

The empty church shuddered as its heavy main door closed behind him. He made his way in darkness down a familiar aisle. His hard-soled cycling boots echoed on its granite floor. A few vigil lights flickered their last from banked rows on a cast-iron stand. In the cavernous darkness, a red sacristy light had been for him the last light of yesterday and first light of another daybreak. Minutes later, he came out a church side entrance, leaving that door unlocked as well.

A BOX OF CRACKERJACKS

Mounting his motorcycle, Father Vincent Vesuvio sped east under a morning sky starlit between patches of fleecy, gray cloud.

5

How Many Roads, Cardinal Crackerjack?

Lake Superior lay at Brandy's back under a blue-grey fog-bank from which solitary North Port City shore lights glimmered. Then the highway took him over a ridge, away from the lake, and across the southwestern portion Minnesota's Mesabi Iron Range, folk-singer Bob Dylan's country.

Ahead of Brandy were familiar towns not far from where he and Dylan were born—the same year—hard-faced mining communities, now asleep with their traffic signals blinking over empty thoroughfares, and their town cops parked in front of all-night cafés, scenes from Dylan's songs Brandy knew by heart. He sometimes hummed to himself, *Blowin' in the Wind*. Brandy couldn't carry a note, but that never bothered Dylan fans.

A waning crescent moon settled behind clouds of an approaching front. In his rearview mirror, the sky began to brighten with the purple and mauve tints of early dawn. Halfway to his destination, he turned on his car radio, with weather in mind. He had by then driven into scattered squalls rushing east to meet him. Rain splattered on his windshield, became more insistent, stopped, and then started again. He had forgotten to bring an umbrella, but undertakers always had umbrellas.

Instead of the local forecast for northern Minnesota, the radio brought a familiar voice from long ago, that of his grade-school classmate Jack "Crackerjack" Cudahy, now the formidable Cardinal John Cudahy stationed in Rome, seven time zones and what seemed a lifetime away, with singer Bob Dylan somewhere in between.

The three of them had once shared the same obscure life on Minnesota's bleak Iron Range. With decades behind them, Brandy alone remained obscure. Dylan still looked like a youth wearing funny hats with hair hanging in his eyes. Jack wore a cardinal's hat with an eye on his future. Brandy had once seen a picture of Crackerjack, as an archbishop and not yet a cardinal, sharing an outdoor stage with Dylan, holding Dylan's guitar upside down and pretending to play it. Jack had a great smile; Dylan had a great frown.

Now, Crackerjack was a close confidant of popes, with Rome some days seeming upside down. Dylan had just won the Nobel Prize for Literature. What could Crackerjack do to top that? Brandy, on the road to Twin Rivers, could think of only one thing.

Fred awoke with a bark and pressed his nose between the front seats. He must have known something was up. Indeed it was, for the pope had died overnight, and Cardinal Cudahy was being interviewed from the Vatican for his reaction.

Jack's voice, once bantering on a school playground, now brimmed with authority and self-confidence of the sort great stature affords. Brandy had never gotten used to the idea, because Jack for him remained as he had always been when he last saw him, a madcap boy nicknamed Crackerjack whose tousled, red hair flew in the wind.

Whatever could or could not have been imagined back then, whatever may be believed or doubted, Jack had raced up the Church ladder two rungs at a time to become known as the *Iron Cardinal*, one of the most important of that flock. Now, with the pope deceased, and a papal conclave days from beginning, Cardinal Cudahy was among the few whose views would be newsworthy.

The reporter suggested that the Minnesota-born cardinal himself might be a dark-horse candidate to be elected the next pope.

"No horse in the world could be that dark," Cardinal Cudahy laughed. "The Church is fortunate to have a number of highly-qualified men to choose from as this conclave begins. Protocol prevents me from mentioning names, but we can all be confident that the Holy Spirit will guide us as a worthy successor is chosen."

"Thank you for sharing your views with our listeners, your Eminence."

"Eminence, perhaps, but far from *imminent*," said the Cardinal with a parting chuckle.

And the same old Jack, quick as a whistle and quick with a laugh, thought Brandy. Jack had always been smooth with words. He could even whistle better than any of the other boys. And it was Jack's old laugh, perfectly at ease with his shoelaces untied, unchanged since their days in a schoolyard thirty miles and fifty-some years from the road Brandy now drove while listening.

How many roads does a man walk down in a lifetime, Cardinal Crackerjack?

How much do old friends change?

Dylan had not yet announced whether he would accept the Nobel Prize.

6

Both *It* and Both Crazy

An hour later, while parked in a highway wayside rest area, Brandy listened long after his boyhood friend had spoken. His voice seemed to reverberate from a radio turned off. He went through Jack's words from beginning to end; and then from there back to an earlier beginning, when he and Jack Cudahy as boys first met during a school recess in the middle of a year, more than half a century ago.

As an awkward boy with an awkward first name, Brandy had been slow on his feet and slow of reflex.

In his first years at All Saints School, before he knew what was happening, with his hands in his pockets, he had been tagged and became *It*. The other boys were faster in every way.

He stayed *It* for the next five years. Without a break, he raced around church and school chasing classmates always dodging and darting just out of reach. Since the school had no playground, sometimes recess games spilled out into the immediate village. Steps leading to the church's main entrance were a haven where no one could tag or be tagged. Brandy could often be found there breathing hard and catching his breath before resuming his hapless chase.

This taught him more patience than most boys his age. He developed the circumspection and dogged determination discovered in some old men in the last years of a long lifetime. He learned to live within his limitations. He learned to think of a church as home, where he could recover from a futile race.

Then out of nowhere Jack Cudahy showed up to challenge much that he had learned. As a prominent cardinal assigned to the Vatican, he was still doing it.

"You're *It*!" Brandy tagged Jack at the beginning of the next noon recess.

"Let's both be *It*!" Jack laughed and tagged him back. Who would have thought? From the very beginning, Jack was always doing the unexpected.

His parents had seemed to move in while the village slept, appearing as if at daybreak, from nowhere, without notice, fanfare, or explanation. They sent—what everyone thought to be—their only child to its Catholic school without themselves joining the parish or connecting themselves to the community in any other way.

Their wealth was evident from the estate they purchased on a hillside whose contours were outlined by high fieldstone walls, too high to peer over. Once the private kingdom of an iron mine owner, its brick mansion, servant's quarters, horse paddock, and tennis court were hidden within a leafy grove. At all hours, expensive cars with deeply tinted windows came and went through heavy, wrought iron gates. The one taking Jack to school and bringing him home at day's end appeared to be driven by a chauffeur who would step out gingerly to hold the door for him.

All this led to talk and speculation of the small-town sort. Some people thought Jack's family came from California, while others thought Pittsburgh with its steel industry. Some thought Jack's father had invented something important, or perhaps owned a fleet of iron ore boats, or maybe he was a gangster lying low. Somebody heard that Jack's mom was pregnant.

None of this mattered to Brandy. He soon learned not to ask Jack questions. He would hear too many answers.

But Brandy had been *It* for so long that he could not imagine being anything else, so at Jack's suggestion, they teamed up. Even when they cornered and tagged a classmate, they insisted on remaining *It*. "You can't be *It*. We're *It*," they shouted, whirling away to begin the chase all over again, while their remaining years at All Saints flew by, happier years for young Brandy, all because of Jack.

As the months passed, Jack became known as Crackerjack, so amazingly fleet of foot, so good at dodging and darting, that no one in the class could keep up with him. This might have suggested to an onlooker that Jack, from the beginning, had been capable of more, much more, than he let on, and that Jack in fact had been faking all along.

Onward to their last day at All Saints School, they both were *It*. They ran and ran till their hearts throbbed in their throats. Then as sometimes happens in the lives of school friends no more than age fourteen, they found themselves on separate roads, and never met again.

One road led to a seminary for a youth who had seen that goal far enough ahead that he thought it okay to mention his secret to his tag team friend.

"Become a priest? I can't imagine it. It's pure magic," said Jack, evidently musing. "How would that be?"

They were in the village park near its fire station, beneath its water tower, after school. The other boys had all run away. Jack faced him in sunlight, squinting, as if trying to imagine how it would be, something as mysterious as water in an old water tower never freezing in Minnesota's sub-zero cold. He shook his head.

"If you ask me, I'd say you're crazy. I could never do that."

With those words, Jack wandered over a horizon and vanished for years, suddenly a stranger again, at least until a letter arrived when Brandy had been no more than a week at seminary.

Brandy's mother had the most amazing news. Word had trickled back to his hometown that his old grade-school classmate had entered an East Coast seminary and was studying for the priesthood somewhere near Philadelphia, or maybe it was Boston. Little could be more surprising as far as Brandy's mother was concerned, for as she put it, "I thought his family were just a pack of atheists." She underlined *atheists*.

Brandy folded her letter, slid it back into its envelope, and gazed out a window of his seminary room overlooking a tree-lined quadrangle where one of his teachers in a cassock strolled in the late afternoon reading his breviary. He held the letter in hand no more than a minute, but it took him back eight years to the day Jack told him how crazy he was. An unseen hand seemed to have tagged the two of them.

Now we're both crazy, Crackerjack, said Brandy to himself.

After all, God played tag. They both were *It*, or so he thought.

From that day forward, the lives of two boys who had once played tag in a schoolyard took remarkably different directions, diverging ever more as years went by.

Their lives as priests could not have been less alike. Jack—known these days as the "Iron Cardinal"—traveled a Roman road whose destination was selection of the next pope. Brandy for no apparent reason was heading toward a funeral for a young man he never knew. Next week, Brandy would hire a new church janitor with the approval of a parish lay committee. Brandy obeyed Bishop Norman St. Clair, no questions asked. Bishop Norman obeyed Jack, no questions asked. Jack was sometimes pestered by photographers and insistent reporters who *did* ask questions, while Brandy fended off deerflies and wood ticks in making his parish rounds.

As Cardinal Cudahy, Jack authored books widely reviewed in the Catholic press. He was quoted in footnoted essays, was seen on television and heard on radio. He had acquired a hint of an Italian accent. Brandy appeared at parish picnics, and sometimes was seen in soup kitchens. Irish to the core, he nonetheless sounded like a singsong Minnesota Swede.

Had he once truly known the great Cardinal John Cudahy? He himself sometimes wondered if it had been no more than a crazy-quilted dream—as so many dreams can be—about an obscure parish priest in a humdrum northern outpost and a great Cardinal sweeping past Swiss Guards at ornamented porticos.

Meanwhile, battered Iron Range communities wondered if Bob Dylan would bring tourists their way, doing for them what Elvis did for Memphis. Jack could seem as much an entertainer as the two of them. Anything could happen.

7

Vincent Callixtus Vesuvio

Birds chirped as the rising sun flamed through a breach in dark gray clouds. Strips of ruddy sunlight flared between eighteen-wheeler trucks reflected here and there in glinting pools of rainwater. A long shadow shot across Brandy's path as he guided Fred through a wayside parking area. A blinding swatch of horizontal sunlight burst between two semis parked at the end of a row. The shadow bolted forward, and an instant later Father Vincent Vesuvio of St. Callixtus in Twin Rivers stepped from what might have been a gap in the universe.

Fred barked.

"It's only me, Fred, old boy," said Vesuvio in thundering voice, sufficient to rouse any truckers asleep nearby and not already awakened by his motorcycle.

A tall figure in black leather, Vesuvio was exactly as his name suggested. Brandy was among the few who knew that his middle name coincidentally was the same as his current church assignment. His imposing stature and fiery disposition called to mind volcanoes, worlds of molten lava and brimstone, scorching deserts, blazing seasides, and the Old Testament mountaintops of Isaiah. This impression was reinforced by his red hair and beard, sufficiently deep red that it might have been the bed of embers beneath flames.

There could not have been a parish priest more striking, a presence more heart-stopping with a voice full of portent, occasion, and what seemed to be its own echo. By his mere presence, he dominated every room he entered. Even out of sight somewhere, he seemed to take over by simply being nearby. To stumble upon him in the setting of dreary gatherings at diocesan meetings was sufficiently electrifying to bring the whole place to life, simultaneously turning an engaging bishop into a shrinking violet. In an era other than this one, he might have been the most intimidating of grand inquisitors, a Torquemada to make Torquemada tremble without so much as asking a single pointed question or pointing to a burning stake.

In a parking lot, with idling diesel behemoths all around, he seemed to be the largest thing. He altered vanishing points by stepping into a scene. In the redrawn perspective, he became its dominant entity, even without his leather jacket and boots and sitting astride the black Harley-Davidson motorcycle he drove in weather tamer hearts would have avoided.

Vesuvio's familiar voice boomed. "By the Lord, Aloy, if this doesn't beat all. You heading to my church. Me heading to yours. Priests passing in the night like ships. Is that it? And you even brought your hound along."

Fred growled.

"He doesn't like being hauled around in the middle of the night," said Brandy.

"None of us do," said Vesuvio. "Can't blame him either. I myself feel like growling. A complete mystery, what's going on here—you and I switching churches for a funeral on my end and another on yours, with almost eight-hundred miles of driving between the two of us, and neither of us likely to get home in time for the Saturday vigil. Bishop Norman brings two more off the bench for that. The whole diocese has been turned inside out and backward, and I for one would like to know why."

"I just heard that the pope has died." Brandy had spent enough time with his colleague to have discovered the value of sudden shifts. To be with Vincent Vesuvio long was to perch on the edge of a cauldron. A change of subject, even in the direction of a dead pope, could be a step back.

"I am sure that doesn't explain it, though on second thought perhaps it does. Our Iron Cardinal has one foot in Rome and another here, and Bishop Norman has career aspirations. He does not mind having an iron foot stepping on his toes." Vesuvio stroked his beard. "Well, not much surprise where the pope is concerned. He had been in failing health, and names of possible successors were already being bandied about. As for us, many more days like this, and we will soon be following our Holy Father. You can bet we won't have a crowd of cardinals gathering to send us on our way with talk of canonization soon after. Just a few shovels of dirt will suffice. Speaking of such, that funeral you are taking today will be quite an affair. I ought to be thankful to have gotten out of it, yet I am not. I feel as if I have been forced to shirk a responsibility."

Brandy glanced at his watch. "Mine should be routine, an old parishioner who had been in a nursing home for years and has outlived almost everybody who knew him. I left you a few background notes on a table in the sacristy just in case you wanted to include a few personal remarks."

"Kind of you, Aloy. I like to do that—but as long as we have run into each other, there are things you ought to know. We're both ahead of schedule. I didn't leave you any notes, and I should have. I imagine Bishop Norman himself doesn't know the whole story. It's been seeping out, and it's a disturbing one to walk into blindly. Give me five minutes."

8

A Horror in Paradise

Those five minutes of a chance encounter on the road between North Port City and Twin Rivers stretched to almost fifteen in Brandy's car. Rain had begun again, more earnestly than ever, with large drops drumming overhead. Alongside, Vesuvio drummed on with equal insistence, ignoring both time and the weather. His breath fogged windows.

"Like all men, I have my pride. Nothing like this should happen. If someone requests a special priest for a wedding or as in this case, a funeral..."

"Someone requested that I be the celebrant? Vincent, who on earth? Are you sure? How do you know that you weren't requested on my end? My old parishioner at one time was a prominent civic leader—all mentioned in my notes. There might be a connection you have overlooked."

"Nice try, Aloy, but it won't work. Do not ask. I cannot say more. But this much you can trust: Bishop Norman did not just pick our names out of his hat, or in this case, his mitre."

"After all these years since I was last at Twin Rivers, I find it hard to believe that anyone would want me there in your place."

"Well, *I* have never been stationed at St. Norbert's, so that discounts your theory about who wanted whom. Look, Aloy, there is much here that is hard to believe—too much these days—but my point is that in the normal course, such a request should lead to both of us in the picture. The home priest is not simply booted out for the day and sent packing on a road trip. I have spent the better part of two days attempting to explain it to first one parishioner and then another. The best I can do is prevaricate."

"You can't tell them the truth?"

"If I knew it, or if I could say what I knew. Even a lie might accidentally turn out to be true. All I can suggest is that because of the shortage of priests throughout the diocese, I have to fill in for you."

"That might be the truth." In the darkened interior of his car, Brandy could not see his companion smirk.

"I doubt it. These are strange times in these parts, and nowhere stranger than in Twin Rivers. That promising young man dead at the bottom of a fire escape, in an alley behind the hotel—you remember the hotel next door to the church?"

"Of course, Vincent, the Hotel Paradise. The fire escape? God forbid! What was he doing there?"

"No one knows. If someone asked what *I* was doing there, as I was this morning before I left, I would be flummoxed and subject to no end of suspicion.

"Phillip Fowler was not the sort to be hanging around that grim representation of Paradise after the Fall, gossiped as a warren of thieves, drug dealers, and prostitutes before the county condemned it and boarded it up. You will soon see for yourself that the Hotel Paradise is far from a paradise—abandoned, and reputedly haunted, no longer even offering cheap rooms to questionable characters.

"How young Fowler managed to get in there would be the first of several mysteries. What he was doing there, the second. Why someone with a life so promising would come to such an end, the third. His body was discovered a week ago. At first he was thought to have slipped and lost his balance while climbing down from the top floor where a window had been left open."

"At first?"

"It gets worse. A suicide note was found in his jacket pocket, so you can see what you're up against attempting to find perspective and consolation in all that. Bishop Norman has not done you a favor, sending you into this funeral, and I should probably thank him for keeping me out of it. You did not know any of this?"

"Only that the young man was a hometown hero, with much to live for. The bishop described his death as 'under troubling circumstances'. He did not say more."

"He may not have known more, but troubling for sure. The police have been tightlipped, a sure sign that something is up. The alley where the body was found is still closed off a week later and treated as a crime scene. The Paradise County Sheriff's Department chief investigator—a slender man whose first name is Porky—has as good as set up shop there. Meanwhile, Bernard Passmore, my choir director, a blowhard and bully—I don't mind saying so—sniffs around the fringes like a bloodhound on the prowl. What is there about this that interests him so much? What is there to investigate about a suicide and a suicide note? What is it that would take a week if there were not more in the picture than meets the eye?

"Then, for no apparent reason, the bishop boots me out and brings you in. Cardinal Cudahy is somewhere behind this if you ask me—but don't ask. He has the whole diocese equally dancing to his tune, Bishop Norman included, a trusted protégé. Your old school chum is everywhere and into everything these days."

"He was just on National Public Radio, interviewed from Rome. Some think he might become the next pope."

"An American? Fat chance of that, unless the world is about to end, which some days I think it is. But your old grade school chum, the so-called Iron Cardinal, pulls many strings and plays his favorite tunes, even in our own backyard, wherever and whenever he has an interest."

"An interest? Cudahy? Do you think so?"

"Maybe Cudahy heard something as far away as Rome. I suppose even cardinals have ears and hear a Confession now and then. We old-timer priests heard lots of things before confessionals were as obsolete as fountain pens and inkwells.

"There has always been idle speculation about young Fowler's mother—you know how inbred and gossipy Twin Rivers can be. A comely young woman moving in from 'somewhere out east' with an infant son, Delores Fowler bought a fashionable home and traveled out of town a lot. She was bound to attract speculation, and made a point of not being the least bothered by it. You know how it goes: the Eighth Commandment is no more observed in Twin Rivers than anywhere else. With winters around these parts as long as they are, people need something to shrug off boredom. What's better than malicious gossip? I have been hearing Confessions now for over forty years, long enough to become disillusioned. If I circled the days on which somebody kneeling the other side mentioned gossiping, backbiting, and character assassination, I would have no more than a month of circled days out of the entire forty times fifty-two weeks. What about you, Aloy?"

"I try not to keep score, Vincent. Confessions give me a headache as it is, but you and I have seldom agreed on the subject."

"And never will," said Vesuvio firmly. "Well, anyway, as my late, beloved grandfather used to say to his gaping grandchildren, 'The whole world knows who your mother is, but only God knows who your father is.'"

"Your grandfather actually said that?"

"Not only said it, but seemed to enjoy saying it, to me especially. Of course, he had a point, at least until DNA analysis came along. —But to get on with my story before we bolt off to do Bishop Norman's bidding: Delores Fowler registered as a widow in the parish about twenty years ago. Her boy was confirmed there. He turned out to be a sports hero and a brilliant student, a small-town *wunderkind* with a prom queen, Ojibwe beauty girlfriend. After high school, he snagged a fistful of scholarships and enrolled at Notre Dame, in his last year at law school there at the time of his death, and by all accounts distinguishing himself. Then with classes still in session, he shows up dead in Twin Rivers. No one seems to know anything."

"His mother?"

"She was not home at the time. According to a parishioner neighbor, she was traveling somewhere in Italy—Rome, Naples, Capri. Of course, even that might be gossip—I ought to have left you some notes."

"No matter, Vincent, Bishop Norman sent me a prepared homily, 'just to be helpful given the short notice'—that's how he put it. He doesn't expect me to say anything, and as far as I can tell, the less I say, the happier he will be."

"More than likely he doesn't want either of us to say anything. Your homily may have come straight from the shadow of St. Peter's and a Vatican email account. Cardinal Cudahy's hand is in this somewhere, even though the rest of him is leagues away. Bishop Norman never makes a move without him."

"I can't imagine it, Vincent—my old classmate has better things to do than play games with our bishop and put words in my mouth."

"In this instance, perhaps not—but again I will have to leave it at that, except for this little item sent to St. Callixtus three days ago. It's a copy of the homily you have been directed to read today, and a complete departure from the role of a priest. We are supposed to be pious and circumspective at funerals, are we not? But that's not the half of it. This isn't like reading a letter from Bishop Norman. Are you supposed to pretend that these are *your* words? Or do you begin by saying, 'An anonymous source sent me this to read in place of what I might have said'? A panic-stricken schoolboy could have come up with a better plan than this."

"Of course, Vincent, of course, but 'Ours is not to reason why...'"

"Somebody should have put that on a sign at our seminary entrance."

"Would it have made any difference? I think most of us would have entered regardless."

Vesuvio shrugged, not the easiest thing while sitting in the front seat of a car several sizes too small for him. "Well, anyway, this homily is intriguing, in view of what I know about your childhood games with the great cardinal. I presume you have read its last sentence."

"I have, Vincent, and of course it's coincidental. It has to be."

Vesuvio pulled his copy from a jacket pocket and read the last sentence: "'God sometimes plays tag, tapping us on the shoulder when we least expect it, calling us away.' Hardly a coincidence, my friend. Cardinal Cudahy wrote this, and this was his way of letting you know. He wants you to know—that's my guess. You're *It*, Aloy!"

"Call it coincidence, and let sleeping dogs lie. I am glad Vincent Vesuvio is about the only one I ever shared that story with."

Vesuvio wrinkled a brow. "Is that so, Aloy? I am flattered. You and the Iron Cardinal playing tag makes for a very good story to keep so much to yourself, but your secret is safe with me. I too keep secrets well, sometimes too well."

"It is not exactly a secret, Vincent, but it takes someone like you to believe it, and of your sort there are not many on this earth. I have often thought the same about the Cardinal John Cudahy that I knew as 'Crackerjack'. I still think of him as a schoolboy. I have not seen him since then—almost sixty years ago now—except on television or in a newspaper picture. You know how people stay in one's mind a certain way, never seeming to age as the years go by. His pictures tell me that his hair is still red, though with traces of grey in it now, quite like yours. His voice commands attention, much as yours—actually, except for your beard, the two of you could almost be brothers."

Vesuvio laughed. "I myself have never seen the resemblance. It's the red hair, I think. People are distracted by that similarity and overlook obvious differences. All the same, if we both need a day off, maybe I could wear his red hat, and he could explain to my parishioners what the devil is going on in our diocese. We could change places, and no one would catch on. Everyone somewhere in this world, they say, has a *doppelgänger*. It is one of the reasons I grew this beard. I got tired of people asking if the great Cudahy and I were related. My obvious answer was that we are all the children of Adam and Eve, brothers and sisters in the eyes of a Creator who *knows* who fathered us. Still, I resist playing Cain to the Iron Cardinal's Abel."

Brandy glanced at the clock on his car's dashboard and switched off the windshield wipers, the rain having stopped as suddenly as it had started. The sun, still very low in the east showed signs of flaming through a cloud gap once again. In the back seat, a sleeping Fred began to stir. Vesuvio showed signs of eruption or perhaps thundering prophesy.

"I long ago learned that sometimes it is better not to look deeply into certain things. I'll drive you back to your car, Vincent. We'll both be late. I'm sure there is an explanation somewhere."

"I brought my Harley. Didn't look like rain when I left. Anyway, whoever or whatever is at the bottom of this, don't bet on us ever knowing it, no matter how far down or up we look, and I am not talking about the hotel fire escape." Vesuvio slammed the car door and strode off to the parking lot's other end, striding almost as fast as Brandy could have driven him.

He rolled down the window on his side and pulled up alongside. "Be easy on my flock, Vincent. They scare easily."

"So do I, when things get this murky."

Resting his hands on the rolled down window, he leaned in to speak a few inches from Brandy's ear. "It is as if I know something I do not know I know, or am not supposed to see something, or something or someone on hand is not supposed to see me. Inevitability flies before us, irrevocability sweeps behind, and Hell is knowing we can never change what happened—every blessing, Aloy."

He looked up as if in disbelief from a personal, too easily imagined cauldron into which he was slowly descending. A look of enormous sadness swept over Vesuvio's face, temporarily dousing every magnificent fire burning within him. No one seeing that fleeting expression could ever doubt that Hell was about more than mere flames. All this had been said in his best attempt at a whisper, but nonetheless his voice seemed to echo.

"By the way, I should have mentioned something else about the local lawman with the unlikely name of Porky White. If I am any judge, there is no more Christian man in Twin Rivers, Old Town or New. He interrupts his 24-7 work to chauffeur his epileptic wife Harriet to Mass at St. Callixtus; to choir practice, and volunteer parish duties; to Mercy Hospital's clinic for medical appointments; and to her part-time work at the other end of Old Town. He entertains kids with his juggling and comic acts. He has shared with me his idealistic plan to open a billiard and ping pong game room for Old Town kids who have no place to burn off steam with innocent fun..."

Brandy saw something coming without knowing what, as Vesuvio strode away.

"An atheist," shouted Vesuvio over his shoulder, "and positively one of the most *Christian* men I have ever met!"

He slipped between the two semis from which he had first appeared. The lights of several parked nearby came on as if a signal had been given. The world stirred from its stupors in Vincent's turbulent wake.

Following the red taillights of his Harley in his rearview mirror, Brandy nearly rear-ended a school bus stopped at a railroad crossing.

9

Outsiders on the Inside

Some friendships can be a mystery. That of Brandy and Vesuvio was one of those. Anyone knowing the two would never have predicted it. In some ways, they seemed more likely to have become adversaries.

Brandy went by the book; Vesuvio tore pages from the book, and at times seemed to chuck it entirely. More than once, Brandy had half-seriously labeled him a heretic. Nothing pleased Vesuvio more. “Lord have mercy! Aloy, why not think of me as a pious skeptic, not terribly pious, and distinctly a skeptic?”

The two had always been outsiders inside the diocese. Vesuvio with his motorcycle, his blazing hair and beard, and his brazen ways could be an iconoclastic hell-raiser of the sort sufficient to cause strokes among pious old widows who forgot to turn down their hearing aids whenever he preached.

No one would have tried harder than Vesuvio to meet pastoral challenges head-on; no obtuse theological question could have mattered as much as duty. His personal physics never quite reached escape velocity: his destiny was to revolve in an oblong orbit whose extremities were a martyr’s faith and brooding doubts. Even had he become an atheist, even were he an anti-pope, he could not stop doing what he had committed himself to do all along. His generosity and sense of duty overrode even faith or the lack of it.

When he wasn’t clad in motorcycle leather, he might have been seen as Mephistopheles in a broad-brimmed black fedora wearing a cape. Tell him that you saw him as such, and he would laugh. He would raise one eyebrow and then another. His features would gleam with amusement. “What is better, to be a priest taken for the devil, or a devil taken for a priest?" He had had run-ins with more than one bishop.

Brandy was a priest of an almost forgotten school of discipleship. If he had ever in his life come to a bishop's attention, it might have been at his confirmation as a sixth grader when he flubbed a question the bishop directed his way for no better reason than that his last name began with the second letter of the alphabet, placing him first among the bishop's list of confirmation candidates.

"Can anyone else explain what is meant by *false gods before thee*?"

Jack Cudahy, next in the alphabet, of course, stepped in and got it right.

Except for Brandy's Roman collar, he resembled a door-to-door bible salesman in a rumpled suit and battered hat. Bred to be dogged, intent, duty-bound, determined, pugnacious, and irascible when necessary, he would not have minded the comparison. He might have said that Christ's disciples would resemble traveling salesmen, were any of his disciples around today. In those early days, no disciples had a church. When there were no churches, Christianity was about roads seldom traveled and villages seldom visited. What better than a rural road for a true missionary?

Brandy, Vesuvio, and Jack Cudahy were each on his own road. It would take more than Brandy's Roman collar, Vesuvio's black cape, and Cudahy's red socks to get to the bottom of it.

10

Bernard Passmore Bound to Please

An hour after meeting Vesuvio and well before the funeral, Brandy neared Twin Rivers. For the last ten minutes of his four-hour journey, the twin towers of St. Callixtus shifted north to south along the horizon as the highway formed elongated curves through wooded hills surrounding the city. The church's north tower bore a gold cross; its south, an angel blowing a trumpet, designed as a weather vane and symbol of heaven announcing Christ's birth in all the world's lands. The trumpet pointed east, a harbinger of unsettled weather.

In the more than forty years since Brandy had been stationed at St Callixtus, Twin Rivers had become two cities. It had also become two states of mind and spirit. These were known locally as New Town and Old Town, joined by bridges over the two rivers meandering between them.

New Town and Old Town had postcodes ending respectively in 01 and 02. One or the other had become the difference between pride and humiliation. To amble through Twin Rivers crossing its bridges had become a journey through time across whatever divided presumption from despair. This division recently had grown more pronounced on the despair side when unemployment and then homelessness became an Old Town epidemic.

St. Callixtus Parish was also one in name only: two church congregations using the same name, the same Mass schedule, the same Sunday bulletin, and listening to the same homilies from the same pews delivered by the same succession of priests, while having nothing else whatsoever in common.

Wealthy businessmen and professionals of New Town and the increasingly impoverished, working class Old

Towners had given up pretending. Divisions, now seen as inevitable, led each group to segregate itself into different sections of the church. Old Towners and their supporters hunkered down in back and along the capacious church's side aisles.

Even the church's parking lot showed signs of segregation, with distinct clusters of the latest models on one side and rusted jalopies with worn tires on the other. An accommodating priest attempting to manage social disparity should have designated Sunday Masses for the rich and for the poor respectively, the destitute with their ragtag urchins and crying babies at eight o'clock in the morning, and members of country club and professional societies at ten. In the long run, though, nothing would have worked. A journey to St. Callixtus had become for New Towners a bridge too far; for Old Towners, a bridge too near.

Institutional divorce suggested a way forward. An organization had formed to build a second church and create a new parish in Twin Rivers' affluent north. A retired banker had contributed land; plans had been drawn up; funding secured. Bishop Norman's approval was needed, but the bishop had yet to be persuaded. The Sunny New Future Association began as the brainchild of Bernard Passmore, St. Callixtus' choir director, himself a resident of affluent New Town where he lived in splendor well beyond the means of ordinary church musicians. Ask Passmore about the condition of St. Callixtus, and he would declare that not even bats would nest in its twin belfries. "It's a piffle dump," he would say with the confidence of a man who knew a good thing when one crossed his path.

Apart from stray signs of weathering forty winters, St. Callixtus appeared much as Brandy remembered it. He could even park in his usual place. At his back, beyond a grove of ancient honey locust trees, towered the blackened brick carcass of the Hotel Paradise, a dark and brooding horror show. Four decades ago, though still open for business, it was well past the era when it hummed with traveling salesmen, lumber barons, north country entrepreneurs following timber money, and tourists from north and south brought in by passenger trains making daily journeys between St. Paul and Winnipeg. The abandoned rail line was now a snowmobile trail leading into a brush-strewn prairie once an aboriginal forest.

Already, as long ago as Brandy's day, professional wrestling matches were held in the Paradise's former ballroom. Its elegant breakfast lounge had become a pool hall; and its street side hair salon, a pawnshop. Now, even these sure signs of decline were hidden beneath sheets of graffiti-smeared plywood.

A moment of reverie mingled with revulsion as Brandy studied both church and hotel for signs of change. This ended with a tapping at his car window. Fred barked.

A sheriff's deputy flashed an ID. "A question or two if you have a moment, Father."

"It will have to be brief—I hope I wasn't speeding."

"Nothing of that sort, Father. At least, I wouldn't know. Cruising highways is not one of my duties."

Charlie Cook followed the priest into St. Callixtus as far as a vestibule stairway leading to its choir loft. On the way in, they passed framed photographs of Cardinal Cudahy and Bishop Norman either side of the main entrance. The half-lit church was empty except for a woman placing flower arrangements below the altar table and on both ends of where the open coffin would be positioned. From the choir loft, a few notes boomed beneath Bernard Passmore's fingers, then stopped. A mirror on the organ console offered a view of the enormous church's nave, its crossing, and its sanctuary above which hung a gigantic cross hewed by axe from northern white pine.

As his fingers danced among organ stops, Passmore could eavesdrop. Charlie's questions flowed toward him up the stairway, the very ones Brandy and Vesuvio had been asking themselves an hour ago. *Why was he here instead of Father Vesuvio; and why had he specifically been selected to fill in for him? Did he know of any connection between himself and the victim or the victim's family*?

"Your guess is good as mine, Officer. You might try asking Bishop Norman St. Claire. I just do what I'm told."

"Same with me. My boss asked me to ask you about it. If you think of anything that might connect you with the victim, give me a call. Ask for Charlie Cook."

"Charlie Cook. Yes, by all means ask for faithful old Charlie! "A thunderous voice echoed above them. The church music director lumbered down the stairway with his shoulders brushing both sides. Ignoring evident sarcasm, Charlie nodded in Passmore's direction, and excused himself.

"An irritant, the police hanging around here all the time with their inane questions—piffle!" A hand that might have spanned a third of an organ keyboard enclosed Brandy's as a monstrous oyster might have trapped a minnow. "A word about the music and occasional music, if you please, Father. Just to let you know, I am a non-traditionalist where liturgical music is concerned, fair warning, funerals hardly excepted—though I try to honor a family's desires as far as tradition and my music conscience permit. Today you will definitely *not* hear Mozart's *Ave Verum* or Franck's *Panis Angelicus* sung by Harriet White, our best soprano. The usual piffle stuff for the usual funeral will not be heard. I will join Harriet at points in a duet of hymns much more up-to-date and relevant to the occasion."

"I look forward to it," said Brandy, retrieving his hand with a distinct grimace.

"You will not be disappointed," said Passmore in a voice more like a command than a promise. "You are bound to be pleased."

Back in the choir loft, he settled again in front of his keyboard, a man large enough to make even an organ seem small. He had one word for the old priest. It turned out to be a word he often used. "Piffle," he muttered. He chirped a second piffle for Bishop Norman St. Claire. "A lot any of them know. Piffle."

He glanced up. "Good morning, Harriet. I happened to spot your husband in the alley behind the hotel again this morning. Nothing serious going on back there since the young man's suicide, I hope."

"I'm sure it's just routine," said Harriet, removing her hat, while tucking her handbag under a chair. Standing up, she adjusted wire-rimmed glasses already well positioned on her nose. "Wilbur is a detail person, you know."

"The same with me," said Passmore. He appeared to study her for a sign of something. Harriet's face might have been a music staff without notes; Passmore's a fishbowl in which a variety of species mingled. "Let's run through a bit before the mourners arrive," he said, striking a key and hitting an organ pedal. He could make a pipe organ sound like a beerhall calliope.

The bleating organ and Harriet's vibrant *bel canto* descending upon him as Brandy wandered about a church interior much changed since he was last there.

A massacre of the old statuary had taken place, some of it leaving empty niches. Gone were Saints Patrick and Boniface, patrons of the church's pioneer Irish and German communities. The missing St. Boniface, a replica of the one in the cathedral in Mainz, Germany, was especially inexplicable. Long ago, in a time before Father Brandy arrived on the scene, it had been carried through Twin Rivers streets in procession each year on June 5, the saint's feast day. How could St. Boniface be banished? Gone also were the angel candelabra stationed at the ends of the Communion rail. Gone as well, the Communion rail. The hand-carved Stations of the Cross, the work of a Swiss parishioner, were still intact. An ancient statue of St. Callixtus had also survived, though now in a less prominent position, in a corner at the rear of the church near a side entrance once used by students of the primary school.

The creaking of hinges and shuffling of feet announced the arrival of Phillip Fowler's body. The church began to fill with mourners. Brandy retreated to the sacristy whose battered old cupboards and closets remained as before along with the aromas of old cloth, moth cakes, candle wax, and incense lurking in corners.

11

Even Bishops Cannot Plan Everything

St. Callixtus' pews filled till people stood in aisles in an atmosphere especially somber, as it is at funerals for the young and promising, suddenly swept away. The overnight death of a pope did little to overshadow that of hometown hero, Phillip Fowler.

Taken together, this made Vesuvio's absence all the more inexplicable, to the point of embarrassing, and Brandy's presence equally the subject of speculation, to the point of resentment evident on the faces of parishioners. Jack Cudahy, in his schoolboy heyday, could have faced down the throng. Brandy plunged forward like a man eager to put it behind him.

"'God sometimes plays tag, tapping us on the shoulder when we least expect it, calling us away.'"

He read as directed, be it homily or eulogy, whether written by somebody he knew or by a stranger. He concluded Mass with mention of the pope's death, and a prayer request for cardinals gathering to elect his replacement, and prayers especially for Cardinal John Cudahy, 'Minnesota's own'. Brandy's words, carrying with them unspoken memories, seemed like funeral flowers, the drying arrangements left on graves.

After an interment service in a riverside cemetery, Brandy shook hands and swapped stories with a few old parishioners who recalled his earlier tenure there in what struck them all as another lifetime. In their twenties and thirties when he was last at St. Callixtus, they were old men with grandchildren in high school, some of whom had known the deceased. A grouse-hunting partner asked if his aim was any better these days. How many dogs named Fred had he had by this time?

"I still cannot hit the broadside of a barn twenty feet away with a twelve gauge. I am now on my fourth Fred, this one an old mutt—sleeps all the time—waiting for me in the car, so I will have to be off soon."

The few who remembered him were as surprised to see him as he himself was at being there. Only that hurried interlude felt natural, engaged as he was in getting through polite formalities while easing his way out of a scene that would end as funerals so often did, in the church undercroft with goulash, sheet cake, and coffee forming a transition from death to life going forward. Bury even a pope from St. Callixtus, or from any other Midwestern church, it would end the same way.

Bishop Norman's instructions included, "Leave promptly afterward," underlined as if he were being urged to flee a crime scene and might be implicated if he lingered for long. The bishop had not added, "Make up an excuse if necessary." This was self-evident, and in view of the curiosity surrounding his presence, seemed prudent.

Brandy had rehearsed several quick exits while driving from the church to the cemetery. Most of them involved having his dog along. Dogs were always good for an excuse in a world of men without children. As it was, some polite formalities could not be avoided.

One of the pallbearers, a lanky man with thinning, unruly hair and a gray-flecked moustache, stepped forward, prodded by his wife, and extended a hand.

"I'm George, George Cobb. This is my wife Phyllis, and this is Whisk, or rather this *was* Whisk." He pointed to where a boy had been standing the moment before. "Well, that's why we call him Whisk. My Indian workmen call him No-See-Um. Now you see him; now you don't. I think it's because he is part Indian, and isn't sure where he fits in."

"Don't be ridiculous, George," said Phyllis. "Father, we call Whisk our foster-foster child because we look after him when his foster parents don't, which is most of the time, so we brought him to the funeral."

"Phyllis was in the choir today, singing with Harriet White," George volunteered. "Phillip worked for me summers, for my construction company, when he was in high school and then at the university before he left for law school. Phyllis and I got to know him."

"And thought of him as family," said Phyllis, "along with Jane Blue, an Ojibwe girl, Phillip's girlfriend back then—she was here somewhere this morning."

"I saw her just a few minutes ago," said George glancing around. "Phillip was at the top of the class. Forty years ago, I was at the bottom." George spoke with the evident pride of a self-made man his teachers might have thought a moron.

"Don't brag," said Phyllis. "You weren't even that high up. Father, you probably baptized Phillip. He was born about the time you were here last."

"—I'm sure I was here longer ago than that. There were three of us priests back then, the parish had a school, and the hotel ... well, I guess it was already going downhill, but at least it was open."

George lit up at mention of Brandy's memories. He grinned and offered his hand for the priest to shake a second time, as if recalling the parish's primary school deserved congratulations. He began recounting his days there. His class had been the last before it closed. He pointed toward the distant church towers whose shadows in certain sunlit seasons fell on what was now a weedy, vacant lot. He pointed toward the hotel as if it too could be seen from the cemetery hillside a half mile away.

"My company was just awarded the contract to demolish it," he declared. "We're going to blow it up this summer. Should be quite a show."

Brandy raised both bushy eyebrows. "Blow it up?"

"Actually, blow it in, from the inside out. It works this way, Father: There is *ex*plosion, and then there is *im*plosion."

At that point Phyllis intervened. "Not now, George, I am sure Father Brandy doesn't have time to hear you split hairs."

"Implosion," George managed to say before she yanked him away.

To be with George and Phyllis Cobb for more than a minute was to have a ringside seat in the middle of a verbal boxing match of few rules and unlimited rounds.

Next to approach was Delores Fowler, standing apart and awaiting this formality. Watchful as a parrot, she fixed him with a knowing gaze as she thanked him for his services. With her tiny hand trembling in his, Phillip's mother smiled woodenly, the way people do after they have been to a dentist and had Novocain, two shots.

"Your son accomplished so very much in the time given him. A great loss. You must have been very proud of him. All the people here today, a tribute to his memory."

It was the worst part of any funeral, the attempt at consolation, doomed to flounder, and put on life-support by small talk and feckless changes of subject. Brandy mentioned Father Vesuvio filling in for him; the shortage of priests in the diocese; the good fortune of a showery morning not leading to yet another shower.

"I hear you were in Rome recently."

Mrs. Fowler looked away, removed her hand, slipped an envelope into his suit coat pocket, and excused herself, there being others she needed to thank.

She knew why her son's funeral had been tossed in his lap. Of this Brandy was certain. It had nothing to do with a shortage of priests. Her eyes and her abrupt departure said as much. Far from making no sense—diocesan musical chairs, as Vesuvio had described it—it made too much sense: something or someone connected him to Phillip Fowler and his mother. Had she revealed it in so many words, Brandy would have agreed. He could have made some sense of this day making no sense. Vesuvio, cynical and evasive, probably knew what it was, but would not suggest more than that his old friend Crackerjack had a hand in it somewhere.

What was Vesuvio hiding?

Suddenly, as if a door had opened and a gust of wind blown it shut, Brandy was alone. No more was expected of him. He headed to his car, parked on a distant lane where lilacs budded near a cemetery groundskeeper's shed. Parked in the same lane was a red roadster whose driver stepped out as he approached.

Dusty Dwyer introduced himself. "I run the club on the other side of The Paradise, Father. Me and a couple of my dancers were at the funeral today. None of us knew the kid, at least not directly, if you know what I mean, but he came to a bad end right next door, so we thought we should be here to pay our respects as neighbors."

"Neighbors?" said Brandy, between startled and amazed.

"Yeah—the Palace, The Paradise, the church, all in a row on the same street, next-door neighbors. I sometimes get church mail at my place. Padre Vesuvio tells me that every so often, stuff meant for my joint winds up in the church's mail, same zip codes, or maybe just a mailman with his thoughts elsewhere. The church even gets a fan letter now and then, addressed to one of my strippers. —By the way, you should do something about this tire before you get on the road. I happened to notice that it's nearly flat. Do you have a spare? —We'll help you change it."

Dusty hailed two women parked in a car yet farther down the lane. "Let me introduce Rita Fajita and Amorous Laetitia."

Rita strode forward to shake Brandy's hand. She laughed. "Nothing to fear, Father. Rita is my real name. The rest is made up. I'm not even Hispanic. My parents named me for St. Rita of Cascia..."

"Her feast day is just around the corner," ventured Brandy looking at his hand.

"May 22," said Rita. "The patron saint of abused women."

"And I'm known as Amorous Laetitia these days" said a young woman wearing what resembled a private school's student uniform. "I thought of it when the last pope issued his encyclical. Dusty knows Latin—he helped me get the spelling right."

"Ask me about it sometime, but not before that tire goes flat," said Dusty.

And so, Brandy's day ended yet more strangely than it had begun, with the owner of the Purple Palace and two of his strippers jacking up his car, mounting a spare tire, and getting him on the road, laughing all the while, the four of them.

Even bishops could not plan everything.

12

Remains of a Day

Beyond Leech Lake Reservation villages, miles of jack pines and birch flowed like an unbroken, divided stream either side of Brandy's car. Reflections upon a day offering more darkness than light rode along with Brandy. He seemed to be both fleeing from and racing toward something he could not see, either behind or in front. Pools of ground fog from the day's showers formed in shallows; a deer stood at the edge of a cedar swamp; somewhere he and Vesuvio must have swept past each other, each heading home.

The long shadow of Brandy's car hurtled ahead of him as the sun lowered over Twin Rivers, now far behind in a west turning fiery orange. Slowly, the highway seemed to climb as if approaching a ledge, and then without warning, Great Lake Superior sprawled inky black far below him, with North Port City aglow at its feet.

Brandy had just begun wondering if his old friend Jack Cudahy, in those thoroughly incensed and candlelit Vatican chambers, ever felt as much an outsider on the inside as this day had made him feel. Had Jack ever been a functionary brought in to punctuate an occasion, and then in the next paragraph, left behind in someone else's story? The vast, dark lake rolling out from beneath his feet, oceanic in its reticence and miserly of its secrets, had nothing to say.

Brandy had been on the road more than nine hours total for the round trip and would be arriving home almost thirteen hours from the time he left. He had acted out his assigned role in what might have been a play, and which like any artful production, had its surprises, its ironic twists and turns, and seemed less real as hours went by outside the theater.

Contributing to this sense, as Brandy well knew and had experienced firsthand, was the public's diminished confidence in priests in the wake of Church scandals. Priests were not as trusted as they once had been, and this sense of being viewed with suspicion had encouraged a sort of defensive roll-playing. Priests could not be themselves. They were regarded in the same light as car salesmen, used cars at that. Any day now he expected to see a medal worn around somebody's neck reading, 'I am a Catholic. Please call a used car salesman'. This joke had gone around. It was almost that bad. He had first heard it from Vesuvio.

St. Norbert's, his home church on the south side of North Port City, was dark when he arrived. His Saturday Vigil Mass had been celebrated by a fund-raising missionary whose parish visits had been switched around to have him at St. Norbert's two weeks before his announced appearance.

A scattering of 'special collection' envelopes lay adrift upon vestibule ledges, the remains of a day.

A restless night lay ahead.

13

"We call it Narcissism when people adore themselves..."

Having forgotten to reset his alarm clock, Brandy was awakened again around 3:00 a.m.

Unable to sleep after that, he turned to a Sunday newspaper left at his front door. Its front-page lead story about the deceased pope included a photograph of Cardinal Cudahy kneeling, head bowed, outside the locked papal apartment. He might have been asking to be let in, while a beardless Vesuvio looked up at him reflected in marble floor tiles. No wonder Vincent had cultivated a beard to fend off comment, even though he himself could not see the uncanny resemblance—or so he said.

Narcissus had mistaken the vision cast upward from a mirrored pool, fallen in love with himself, and therefore drowned. Long ago, one of Brandy's All Saints teachers had recounted that myth for the benefit of Aloysius, Jack, and her other young charges: "And so today, we call it narcissism when people adore themselves." Jack, in the desk behind him, laughed. "And since you find this so amusing, Jack Cudahy, spell narcissism if you can." Jack, of course, spelled it perfectly.

Brandy opened weary eyes having closed upon the memory.

He fiddled with his homily for the three Sunday Masses mere hours away before letting Fred out to lope around the parish grounds. While watching him sniffing about in shadows cast by St. Norbert's façade lighting, he discovered the envelope Delores Fowler had slipped into his coat pocket at yesterday's funeral. It contained a thousand dollars in ten, crisp hundred-dollar bills held together by a paperclip, nothing else, not a word of thanks or explanation.

Back inside, while sitting on his sofa, Brandy looked for something he had missed. He traced his journey to St. Callixtus, slowly counting the hundreds to ten, the hours to more than a dozen, the miles to almost four hundred, and his steps to the hundreds. Nothing added up to a thousand bucks—a funeral stipend like none he had ever received, for a funeral like no other.

Perhaps Cardinal Cudahy flying in from Rome would have expected such an offering. Perhaps such things were routine in a cardinal's life with its knee-high, red socks. Fifty dollars, a cut square of cake, and leftover parish hot dish were Brandy's usual pay. The common blackbird was getting a taste of a cardinal's pie.

It felt like a kingly bribe, bringing to mind something Vincent Vesuvio once said: *It is as if I know something I do not know I know, or am not supposed to see something...*

"Well, anyway, Fred, I guess we can use a bit of this money to perk up your suppers. You were on the road all day too, and maybe know a bit more than I do." He eyed him closely. "But you are almost as reticent as our talkative Vincent, aren't you, old boy?"

He picked up a tableside book given him by Vesuvio who had been much taken with its theology. On its front cover glowed a star-filled universe in the middle of which a spiral galaxy spun; on its back were these words:

> No matter what else anyone chose to believe, the world of the New Testament was, and will always remain, the world as it is. Timelessness is one of its messages.
>
> Evolution might be indisputable scientific principle, but with respect to human nature, it is an illusion. Change is like the full moon racing over a landscape viewed from the window of a speeding car. Nothing has changed in two thousand years. Nothing will ever change.
>
> The throngs of ancient Palestine's dusty streets are the rabble and proud townsfolk of anywhere and anytime. It had all been there and will always be there on any other day in any other place: the echoing footfalls, the jeering

> mob, the trickster, the innocent accused, the unforgiving and the not forgiven, the Samaritan and the Sadducee.
>
> Christ and Christ's world was a river flowing through time. Repetition was destiny. The generation described as 'this' had yet to pass away and ultimately was as timeless as salvation itself with the fripperies of moment peeled back to expose the flesh of eternity. Christ is still here in the crowded byways, among the sullen and the sullied, challenging men clutching stones, shaming them with his off-the-cuff retorts, and framing their hypocrisy with mysterious marks drawn in sand with a stick…

"And so it is," said Brandy to himself. "When Vincent has not the words, he always finds them elsewhere, just like Jack at All Saints."

14

Full Stop, and Then Full Speed Ahead

Bishop Norman viewed himself as a man of action. He harbored ambitions of the sort propelling men of action. He not only harbored ambitions, but he drove them from port into turbulent seas. He relished storms. He saw opportunity in conflict. A well-read man in a selective way, he knew what sent Hannibal across the Alps, Caesar across the Rubicon, and Columbus across the Atlantic. He relished the declarations of leaders who said things like, "Damn the torpedoes! Full speed ahead!"

Had it not been out of keeping with a bishop's public image, Admiral Farragut's immortal words would have been on a poster in his office. He also knew how to cultivate and feather nests, and to be both admired and feared. He had set his sights on becoming a bishop or even an archbishop in a major city or perhaps on having an appointment in Rome. He scoffed at the gullibility of laity who think ambition absent from the souls of apostolic men. "There are abundant opportunities in the Church today," he had said to many a young man contemplating the priesthood." They of course thought he referred to the saving of souls. He knew his way up the professional religious ladder, and whom to please along the way, Cardinal John Cudahy foremost among them. He would have described himself as the Iron Cardinal's *protégée.*

Saturday's word of papal death wiped away all thought of Brandy and Vesuvio switching places for funerals at opposite ends of the North Port Diocese universe. While the two mystified priests had been traveling over rural highways betwixt and between, hour upon hour on Saturday, Bishop Norman's thoughts roamed higher and higher, vaulting other barriers than those death had thrown up in a dark alley near St. Callixtus Church.

If Cardinal Cudahy would ever have his moment in sunlight on the Church ladder's top rung, this was it. If ever Bishop Norman would be pulled up by the seat of his pants, this was also it. Still, the circumstances were far from perfect: an unpopular pope had had bad timing; he might have picked a better day to breathe his last. Instead, he expired on a weekend with diocesan offices closed. Masses and a complicated week loomed in opportunity's way. A dead pope could not have been more annoying. Lucky thing for him that Bishop Norman was too far removed to disturb the pontiff's eternal peace.

What could a bishop do but pace along empty corridors where his slippered footsteps echoed? His team was all tied up at weekend Masses, or sound asleep, from auxiliaries to janitors. He was caught between Communion and a part-time, weekend receptionist who spoke broken English and fielded transposed number requests for take-out pizzas. Monday morning seemed as far away as Israel and Rome where Philistines might already be at work undermining ladders.

Still, Monday would come as Mondays would, to be followed by a Tuesday and a Wednesday. Bishop Norman's was only a temporary paralysis allowing his brain to teem with fretful strategies and vague regrets: after all, his was the world of Church administration, not exactly what apostolic succession was designed to be.

Given a bit more time to think, he might have been prayerful. As it was, church weekends could be hard enough on one's soul, stretched as they were between prophets and profits, between redemption and church collections. He had always meant to be a saint, in the ordinary sense.

And so next week would come with its unpredictable weather and its predictable church candles and office lights. Meantime—still thoroughly Saturday—he paced and strategized: North Port, both diocese and city, would have a splendid memorial service to honor the departed pontiff, and a successor on the tallest ladder. Meetings need be postponed, and pastors notified. Parishioner buses should be chartered; the choir of that insufferable Bernard Passmore invited to sing. Invitations would go out to civil dignitaries near and far. Press releases would fly like paper airplanes. Digitally-encrypted communiqués would zip to Rome.

A telephone rang downstairs at the part-time receptionist's post. What the woman lacked in the way of English was backfilled by her lack of ceremony.

"It's for you, Norman," she shouted upstairs. "Some cop named Cook. He 'ants t'know what gives with some guy named Brandy replacing that kook Vesuvio at St. Canixticus!"

15

Juggling Theories

In Twin Rivers, Porky White reviewed at home what he had for evidence and suspicions in the Phillip Fowler case. His weeklong investigation had added little: an unconvincing suicide note; a routine DNA sample taken from the body and stored for future reference; a report from a coroner who should have retired years ago; a chatty, local strip club owner with two motorcycles and a smattering of Latin; an inquisitive choir director; a substitute priest brought in without explanation; and a bishop who had yet to return Charlie Cook's call.

"I need a motive," he said, repeating what Harriet had said as she breezed by him while dressing for choir rehearsal. "Without a motive, this is going nowhere. You can bet on it."

"Actually, Wilbur, you need two or more motives. We do not yet even know how many motives. The first, for our victim being in Twin Rivers, with law school classes in session and his mother away in Europe. The second, for his murder. I am sure he didn't come home intending to get pushed off that fire escape, or whatever happened to him. There is more. When I get back, I will tell you about discoveries in high school yearbooks that made their way into our parish archive collection. They could provide clues, at least for the first motive."

"Do I have to wait?"

"Waiting is half the fun, my dear. Meet me in the parish archive after rehearsal. It's all there. No, on second thought, just wait for me in the church parking lot as usual. I'll bring everything home—it's better that way. No, on third thought, the archive should be okay, but Bernard Passmore may be hanging around."

"And why is Wren so indecisive?"

"I hate giving in to fears and suspicions. They usually lead to something really stupid and pointless, but Bernard Passmore..." Harriet left her sentence unfinished.

Two hours later, arranged on a table in the parish archive, were two Twin Rivers High School yearbooks, photocopies of various newspaper articles, and a hymn she needed to rehearse with Phyllis Cobb.

"Our choir has been invited to provide music for the deceased pope's memorial service at North Port City, so Phyllis and I need to work on this, pronto. We just got started tonight. I don't know how Bernard manages to wrangle these invitations. We're good, but not that good, yet somehow, he does it. Word is that we may be heading to Rome and the Sistine Chapel next month, once a new pope is chosen. Don't look so worried, dear, I am sure you can come along, and you won't even have to sing."

Porky was already leafing through one of the yearbooks. "Phillip Fowler is everywhere here."

"Notice the girl he is with for both his junior and senior prom. I have bookmarked the pages—Jane Blue, strikingly attractive, and elected prom queen despite local racism. Next notice the newspaper items retrieved from a computer search of Twin Rivers *Clarion* back issues. They may explain what young Phillip was doing in Twin Rivers when he was supposed to be attending law school classes."

Both items were from a *Clarion's* feature called "News from the Res." The first mentioned an automobile accident in which Jane had been injured and admitted to the Turning Wind Reservation hospital. The second, two days later, announced her giving birth, to a baby girl, "both mother and daughter doing fine."

"Wren, I'm afraid you've left me behind on this one. Is there something to connect the dots? Are there even any dots?"

"So far, Wilbur, only dates, not dots; an old saying in detective work, *cherchez la femme*; and this *Clarion* photograph of Phillip Fowler's graveside service. Notice the young woman to the left holding a baby and standing behind Delores Fowler as she visits with Father Brandy. A bit older, and a bit sadder, and lovely as ever, but there's no mistaking her—it's Jane Blue!"

"And?"

"Well, it is not exactly speculation at this point, Wilbur. *The Drumbeat*, Turning Wind's tribal weekly newspaper, has been archived at our Paradise County Historical Society, just around the corner from your headquarters. I walked over there to have a look yesterday morning and made some copies. *The Drumbeat* has a playful, gossipy feature full of teasing tidbits, innocent and playful as the Ojibwe are. It turns out that Jane has made several trips to the Chicago area and to South Bend, Indiana, Notre Dame territory. The author of this Ojibwe gossip column is tittering about it: 'We wonder what our reservation beauty finds so fascinating there.' I myself wonder, but putting the pieces together, connecting the dots as you say: the yearbook prom pictures; our supposed 'suicide' victim's sudden trip here after Jane's accident; the graveside photograph of Jane and baby at Delores Fowler's side..."

Porky interrupted. "Wren, I can see it as plain as day! — Jane and Phillip Fowler's high school romance followed him into law school. She became pregnant with their baby. After he heard of her accident, he rushed back to be with her. Delores Fowler is now a grandma, you can bet on it!"

"Wow! Brilliant deductions, my dear Wilbur, you are so very good, but slow down. There are many missing pieces in this puzzle picture. Here's a teeny bit more, just in case you're interested, a story about Melody Stillwater, that poor reservation girl apparently caught in the Chicago sex trade, remember? The authorities were trying to..."

"ID her, Wren! They requested our help."

"Right! And the reservation police got there first with her name."

"The Res police were on the inside track with that one," said Porky. He frowned while perusing Harriet's *Drumbeat* clipping. "It's about Melody's murder as a victim of assault, no mention of her pregnancy."

"The Ojibwe are far more refined and discreet than their white Twin Rivers neighbors. They would never have mentioned prostitution, sex trafficking, her pregnancy... —She may have crossed a pimp by getting pregnant. The one-way bus ticket from Chicago to here—you were told about Chicago authorities discovering that."

"On her person," said Porky, thinking he had something to add.

"In a jacket pocket at the scene. But, Wilbur, *The Drumbeat* mentions something that Chicago missed: Melody Stillwater planned to return here to enroll in our community college. A fascinating twist for a young woman trapped in the sex trade and pregnant, don't you think?"

"I questioned Dusty Dwyer about Melody. He either played dumb ... or didn't know much."

"Stick with 'played dumb,' Wilbur. There must be more to this. Young women like Melody do not just apply to college and get up and walk away from the sex trade enslaving them. She may have been courageous, but she had to have support and encouragement from somebody who understood things from the inside. Somebody in this picture was willing to take chances on a rescue mission. Once trapped in this life, these girls seldom get out. This may have been a one-off that failed, or maybe we're looking at a sort of sex slave version of the underground railroad in pre-Civil War days; one gets free for every five that don't. Still, the rescuer keeps trying. The idea gives me chills, even while it seems far-fetched, and I will tell you sometime why it might not seem farfetched."

Among Porky's other childhood interests, trains were prominent, in this instance a distraction. "We haven't had a train running to Twin Rivers for decades."

"A bus will do, and these days, passenger records are kept. Maybe you could pull a few strings to give me a look at them. What if there tuned out to be other women like Melody who actually got here or somewhere, anywhere, on the bus?"

Porky volunteered something Harriet already knew: "Bernard Passmore owns the passenger bus franchise on this end."

"What doesn't he own? I would rather not involve Bernard," said Wren.

Porky was suddenly in his element, juggling facts Harriet tossed his way. They spun in a circle before him, just as his beanbags did at home. Harriet would feed another, and yet another his way. She spoke through arching possibilities, adroitly passing through Porky's hands, left to right, up and over. "—It's only a theory, but let me add a last, fascinating *Drumbeat* contribution to our investigation: Melody Stillwater and Jane Blue were cousins."

Harriet removed her glasses, much as if she and Porky were in their living room at home with his beanbag total at five in the air. She too was in her element, calm, focused, and intent. With her ideas flowing smoothly in an invisible arc nearing the archive's vaulted ceiling, she noticed a nondescript, dark object not quite imbedded in an ancient oak beam.

"Wilbur, all this amounts to one theory among many, and we still don't know who killed Phillip Fowler, staged his suicide, and why? We need a motive, maybe more than one, remember? We need to get Melody's, Jane's, and her baby's DNA, if she will cooperate. Maybe she knows why somebody killed her baby's father. She might be afraid, very afraid; even more so with her pregnant cousin murdered in a Chicago alley."

"She would have every reason to be," said Porky. "Somebody in this picture is playing for keeps."

"And complicating things further, I have just heard from Father Vesuvio that 'Grandma' Delores had a stroke the day after the funeral. She is comatose and almost as silent as her buried son. Lots for you to piece together here, my dear hubby, but of course I am suggesting things you already are pursuing. Let me know if I can be of some small help. I think I will stay here a while longer, plugging away at my church history, an hour or so. Pick me up on your way home."

Harriet's eyes gleamed with a mixture of intensity and mirth.

"I am on it, Wren. You can bet on it," said Porky. They kissed, and Porky—with Harriet's customized, investigative roadmap in hand—danced out the door.

Alone once again in the archive, she pondered Bernard Passmore's presence in the parish center hallway as Porky slipped past him. She resumed her parish history notes, often pausing between entries to gaze out a window at the honey locust trees, the Hotel Paradise, and then up over her back at the archive room's vaulted ceiling.

I need a flashlight. The backside of that vaulting beam is always in shadow. An oak knot or not *is the question a stepladder and flashlight will answer.*

Closing of Box One

BOX TWO

A PUZZLE BOX

Alloy:
A mixture of two or more metals combined to create a desirable characteristic, such as resistance to corrosion or tensile strength

16

The Iron Cardinal Rises Again

Two days after first word broke via newswire services around the world, the cause of the pope's death was reported as an 'apparent heart attack'. In keeping with Vatican rules, no autopsy had been performed. Speculation was rife.

Within hours, the usual hoopla, subtle conjectures, and clichés were erupting around the vacant center of "nothing new to report": the next pope would be chosen in an atmosphere of mounting crisis; calms moved in ahead of storms; no one knew what tomorrow would bring; history was being made—in this case slow-cooked. While headlines blared, pundits predicted, and the non-pontifical pontificated, helicopters joined aimless gulls cruising the Tiber from Piazza del Popolo to Trastevere before circling St. Peter's. In what could only be described as a TV vacuum, the close-cropped shrubbery of Villa Doria Pamphili vied for attention with an orange tree in a Vatican convent garden.

A constant presence in all rumor and report was the name Cudahy, the Iron Cardinal, who seemed to be everywhere.

The prescribed fifteen-day interval between a pope's death and the beginning of a conclave to elect his successor was now in its fifth day. A Thursday morning of flaming Minnesota sunrise happened to be a rainy afternoon seven time zones away in Rome. The Piazza San Pietro had become a sea of dripping umbrellas, breathless expectations, and childhood memories for Brandy watching from afar on an old television while half-absorbed in childhood memories....

Years ago, on wintry days of sub-zero cold at All Saints when the boys were kept inside and could not play tag around the church, Aloysius and Jack would commandeer a classroom corner to play Pig in a Poke. Sitting opposite each other on the floor with tablet paper between them and pencils in hand, each drew a line in turn attempting to trap each other's pig, a dot somewhere on the page. Jack, a master strategist, always won, except when he seemed to let his friend win, maybe once in the course of a day's recesses. At such times, an indulgent smile would play across his freckled face a split second before a grimace appeared. It was his way of saying, *Of course, I let you*. It was all part of Jack's game, pretending to lose, knowing he might have won any time, allowing himself to appear defeated.

Jack Cudahy was a born actor.

One year, the sisters picked him to provide animated commentary for the school's annual Nativity Play. Aloysius was a silent shepherd standing head bowed by a stable entrance. Sixty years later, with Jack in Rome and Aloysius in northern Minnesota, it remained that way, affability on one side, silence on the other....

Cardinals were gathering from around the world, some photographed departing from aircraft at Leonardo da Vinci airport. The inevitability of papal succession was in the air along with the rumored inevitability of Cardinal Cudahy. Some commentators thought his time had come. Others resisted, arguing that turbulent times called for the election of a younger man less encumbered by long involvement in Vatican politics and intrigue. Still others embraced the possibility that the Iron Cardinal, considering his age, would not be around for long. This naturally led to thoughts about the value of his insights and experience versus his reputation for craftiness, guile, and climbing over bodies and men of stature on his way to the top.

Brandy nodded in the direction of his television: Jack was still good at tag, darting and dodging, always out of reach, but never far away.

Behind the scenes there were even childish mutterings about Cudahy's red hair—"dark ginger," as some detractors described it, yet more the color of smoked paprika—colors in medieval superstition associated with Devil's Spawn and stolen souls. No one would have dared mention this publicly. It was insinuated in utmost privacy by the Cardinal's whispering enemies. It was like a dust mote dancing in a gilded Vatican hall beneath impressive chandeliers. Ginger was simply in the air somewhere. No one could be quite sure where, and of course balloting in the Sistine Chapel would be anonymous. Still, the Sistine's painted walls and ceiling had many painted eyes and ears and here and there a secret. Enemies of great men, as Michelangelo knew, cannot be too careful.

Someone once said of secrets, even the most well-kept: everyone will tell one other person. No one knows where; no one knows whom for sure. Sometimes that other person is a priest in a confessional, but the priest is supposed to tell no one. The Seal of Confession is said to be stronger than bank vault or cathedral door. All priests know what it is like to be locked inside such a fortress.

17

A Rome Weather Report

Under an umbrella, obviously not held by him, stood Cardinal Cudahy while speaking to an American Public Television reporter. The reporter was positioned outside Bishop Norman's North Port City residence, on the bishop's sunlit front lawn affording a view of Lake Superior. The split-screen television transmission displayed faces of both the Cardinal and the reporter.

A familiar, indulgent smile played across the freckled face of the man once known to Brandy as Crackerjack. It seemed to say, "I can win whenever I want; I can lose when I choose to lose; win or lose, the game is always mine."

"There are many good men, more so than ever," said Cardinal Cudahy, deliberately vague. "The keys to the kingdom will be held by capable hands. A trustworthy shepherd will bar the gate." He mixed a metaphor or perhaps likely candidates.

As before, a reporter suggested that the cardinal himself might be one such.

This elicited a well-timed, jocular chortle at once dismissive and accepting.

Brandy could not but admire the show. What a great performer Jack was, always full of fun and trying to make the world laugh. Did people ever change, or did they just get better at the roles they were given to play? If anything, over the years, Jack had gotten better at performance; Brandy at silent witnessing.

The reporter, having done his homework, knew the right words, though he pronounced *papable* as if it were pulpwood in a Minnesota paper mill.

The Cardinal also knew the right words, and feigned surprise at being asked about his prospects. Ever a soft hand at the right moments, perhaps long acquired from playing schoolyard tag, he discreetly handled the reporter. He denied any personal ambition. "*Im-papable* and impossible!" It was Jack's old laugh, now with a hint of a quiver in it. He had grown old. An umbrella bobbed across his face. The cardinal shoved it aside and issued in Italian a stern reminder not meant to be heard. In Rome, among his assistants, he was iron turned to steel, *nessuna sciocchezza* (no nonsense), and never to be monkeyed with.

Undeterred, the reporter delved into Jack's youth in Minnesota, so long ago and about which so little was known that over the years it had become no more than hearsay.

"I hardly recall it myself," said Jack with another velvety laugh. "It seems like another world," he said. He changed the subject to Roman weather. "If your listeners could see me here in the Vatican rotunda, they would also see my umbrella."

"I can hear the rain pitter and patter," said the reporter. "But we're also on television, your Eminence. They *can* see you!"

Cardinal Cudahy, adroit as always, brushed the lofty title aside with the same laugh Brandy knew so well. "Well, in any case, call me Eminence if you will, but not *imminent* when it comes to the Chair of St. Peter. That I can tell you." He was as quick as ever, though it was his joke repeated from an interview only days before. He may have forgotten already using it, or perhaps he had lost count from using it so many times over the years. "But when it comes to pitter-patter, were you speaking of me or of the rain?"

They both laughed this time. Crackerjack's Minnesota past had devolved into a Rome weather report.

Brandy turned off his television and closed his eyes upon yet another memory.

For recess on rainy days, the teaching sisters brought out jigsaw puzzles of a thousand pieces spread across folding tables in the school's tiny gymnasium. No rainy period lasted long enough for any puzzle picture to be completed. Even stored safely intact as far as the students got with them and brought out for the next rainy day, the fragmented puzzle scenes never seemed to become whole. Crackerjack, as usual, had been the best at jigsaw puzzles: he always managed to find the piece everyone sought. Still, even with eagle-eyed, nimble-fingered Crackerjack on the scene, no puzzle became a complete picture.

The one Brandy, Jack, and the others attempted, a panoramic scene of the Piazza San Pietro on a rainy day, sepia-toned as if taken from an old photograph, might still be there with holes and gaps and a pile of pieces to one side in a box lid, forgotten on a back shelf of a school storage room. No one, through fifty years of indoor recesses had ever put it all together.

Jack, in Rome during a rainy recess, was still trying.

18

Texas Hold'em and Cheroots

Bishop Norman had few choices when it came to scheduling the deceased pope's memorial service. As ruling prelate, within his domain he had 'wiggle room' when it came to the common run of feast days, but Pentecost Sunday in the immediate vicinity was as untouchable as holy fire. Hemmed in by a fixed liturgical calendar and papal succession timelines, he was limited to two possible dates.

His grandiose scheme envisioned a crowd larger than the capacity of his cathedral. Though St. Stephen's would be an alternative in the event of rain, he set his sights on leasing North Port City's sports stadium. When it came to that, its superintendent proved to be a tough nut to crack. The bishop knew he was in trouble when he introduced himself and the superintendent replied, "I'm not a Catholic, what did ya say yer name was?"

"Bishop Norman."

"I knew a guy named Joey Bishop years ago when I lived in Toledo. You aren't by chance related, are you?"

With clarity at least achieved, the superintendent proved not to be awed by conversing with a bishop. His first date coincided with a scheduled painting of stadium restrooms; the second ran head-on into a local junior high school marching band using the stadium's playing field to rehearse maneuvers.

"Could you shift things around a bit?

"No way, José!"

"The marching band could use our Catholic high school athletic field for the day."

"No way, José! They need to practice in the stadium where the games are played."

"Could the painters come in later in the day?"
"José, no way! I'd have to pay them overtime."
"The diocese would be happy to reimburse you."
"No, José. I don't accept bribes."
"I don't mean you, I mean pay the painters."
"Too confusing."
"The pope has just died. This is important."
"So are my stadium restrooms."

Daunted but determined, Norman turned to North Port's mayor, a shark when it came Texas Hold'em poker. The bishop had reason to know, for he was not shy about having a night out with the 'boys', with its bluffs, its cheroots, its talk of who was in and who was out, and chatter about an old girlfriend or two. At the table were North Port City elite, among them a banker, the harbor master, and the owner of a pizza factory. When Norman shared a blind-date story from his high school years, he was ever after "a regular guy." Poker nights showed up on the blank underside of his Vatican-inspired desk calendar. Furthering his acceptance was the revelation that when it came to drawing a straight or a flush, God took everyone's side against the bishop.

The mayor, of course, accepted Norman's invitation to a front row seat at the memorial service while bluffing his way to fifty dollars with a pair of nines, mostly at the bishop's expense. The superintendent, not one of the guys and out of the game, had no chance whatsoever: the service would be held the week before Pentecost, on the third day after the pope's funeral in Rome. The mayor would see to it.

The road to success, as Bishop Norman saw it, was paved with good connections.

19

None Dare Call Him Jack

A highlight of the diocesan service was Cardinal Cudahy's eulogy by closed-circuit television from Rome. Among the throng of clergy and public officials at the memorial service were those present more for the sake of the Iron Cardinal than to honor the unpopular late pope's memory. The name Cudahy was once more on many lips, not only because of his televised presence, but also because a papal conclave would begin in seven days.

Some claiming to have known him in his Minnesota mining-country youth spoke of him familiarly as "Jack" and as "homegrown" as aviator Charles Lindbergh and Nobel prizewinners Sinclair Lewis and Bob Dylan. In fact, little was known about Cudahy's secretive upbringing. No one knew much, not even Brandy, and no one to the cardinal's formidable face would have dared call him Jack.

Others were curious onlookers, eager to be in any grand scene made all the grander by the presence of a prominent cardinal rumored to be a possible papal successor. A television network helicopter circled overhead trailing a microphone. Someone thought they saw a drone. Word of this rippled through the assembled throng.

As an outdoor Mass went forward with Bernard Passmore's award-winning St. Callixtus choir in full throat, many necks were craned skyward, not from reverence or love of modern church music but from curiosity and a sense of great occasion. Could they be seen on television? Were they being watched by a drone? Harriet White and Phyllis Cobb performed a soprano-alto duet, but not even hovering angels could have been heard with the helicopter likewise hovering.

Afterward, in the milling crowd outside the sports stadium, Brandy chanced upon two of his old grade school classmates, now aged well beyond recognition. He would not have known they were chatting at his elbows except for their mention of All Saints School and Jack Cudahy, their classmate. There was enough vainglory in the story of his childhood friendship with a great man to make him anticipate one of them calling it to mind as he eavesdropped, but the name Brandy went unmentioned. Not even they remembered how he and Jack had teamed up to chase them around the schoolyard. It was as if Jack had been there at a time when young Aloysius was not, or even when together playing tag, they had been in different worlds when they thought it was the same world.

"Did you know him, Father?" one of his old classmates asked when he turned to confront them.

"We were both *It*," he growled, "playing tag in the same grade as you. We chased you around during recess, just in case you have forgotten."

The classmates had forgotten. They threw a bewildered look his way and tottered off, leaving him in a reverie of the sort brought on by reunions with old friends with whom ties had been long broken and now seemed to be a dream.

Then came a hand upon Brandy's shoulder, and a booming voice from behind. "There but for the grace of God, Aloy," said Vincent Vesuvio. "We might have fallen in that Holy Land instead of this unholy one."

(The pope had died while on a pilgrimage to Israel.)

"For us priests, Vincent, it is all the same land, holy or not."

"Indeed, it is—by the way, one would think that our great cardinal in more obscure times was not your classmate. I am surprised no mention was made of this, with you right here and Cudahy, larger-than-life, on television just a few minutes ago." He gestured toward the stadium with its gigantic television screen, now darkened. "Not even your old classmates seemed to remember—I could not help but overhear."

"It's all too long ago, Vincent, and is best forgotten."

"You might be mistaken on that point, or you might be right. Cudahy's games on the playground with young Aloysius Brandy might have been among his happiest, most memorable days. Perhaps he thinks of them still, in an hour of need. Even great men have hours of need. You never know what memories Cudahy clings to in his lonely moments when his thoughts turn to your humble All Saints School—as now and then they surely must—what cherished things he might have left behind."

Vesuvio stepped closer and lowered his voice as if revealing a secret. A chill breeze rose toward them from the lake, an inland sea large enough and cold enough that even late spring had the smell of winter in it. Vesuvio's breath steamed over a paper cup of coffee he held without sipping. He had a way of elevating his eyes when he was thinking of something he could not say.

"Ahem—by the way, the St. Callixtus Church choir was in great form today, if you could hear them with that damnable helicopter buzzing about. Better than anything the cathedral has to offer. Still, I do wonder though how Bernard Passmore succeeds in inveigling his way into every important occasion, some much farther away than North Port. Rumor has it that his choir might soon perform in Rome, in the Sistine Chapel no less. I am not sure they are that good, but Harriet White is as talented as they come, almost an opera-quality soprano. You have to wonder where that inquiring mind and sublime voice come from in a frame so petite.

"If Bernard Passmore's gifts were proportionate, considering his elephantine girth, he would be the next Pavarotti and Twin Rivers would soon be called Passmore Town, which might happen anyway. His influence grows like that of a dragon invading our complacent midst. Harriet, ever alert and deliberately oblivious, is busy writing a sesquicentennial history of St. Callixtus. She has practically taken up residence in our parish archive, which reminds me that we haven't had a chance to visit about how last Saturday's funeral at St. Callixtus went."

"As well as could be expected, Vincent. I have been attempting to thank Mrs. Fowler for an extraordinary money gift, but she does not answer her phone."

"Don't tell me how much money—I'll be envious. Delores Fowler has money, lots of it—from what source she alone could say. She was for many years a most prolific traveler. That takes money, and naturally attracted attention around Twin Rivers where most folk seldom set foot outside Paradise County. In years past, she would speak about her travel adventures at the community college and at various local service organizations looking for an after-dinner program. I went to one or other. She was quite good, attractive, knowledgeable, articulate, and informative on the Mediterranean especially—Spain, Italy, Sicily, and Greece."

Vesuvio cleared his throat and stared into his coffee as if reading something there. By this time, an ebb tide of onlookers had swept them into a shadowy parking lot corner where a wild grapevine dangled from a concrete wall. He bent low over his friend and lowered his voice again.

"You never know who may be listening, Aloy. These days even walls have ears. As for Mrs. Fowler, she has always been a most private person—to the extent that anything is private in Twin Rivers—but of necessity now more so than ever. She suffered a stroke the day after the funeral, brought on I suppose by the stress of losing her son. That is why you have not been able to contact her. No one can. She has lost the use of speech, with her mental faculties likewise impaired. She appeared befuddled and semi-conscious yesterday afternoon at the hospital when I administered Last Rites and attempted to speak with her. She is not expected to live much longer. No surprise there, by the look of her, so much altered since the funeral, scarcely days ago."

He tossed among the grape leaves what remained of his coffee. Both men stood silently by, watching it drip from leaf to leaf earthward, until Vesuvio spoke again.

"I am scheduled to meet with Bishop Norman in his office later this afternoon, a meeting delayed while this pious shindig spun ahead. I will use the opportunity to ask him for next week off, to tend to some important personal matters coming up on short notice. On Bishop Norman's side, my guess is that he will banish me to the furthest corner of his diocesan kingdom, the St. Brendan's Indian Chaplaincy, North Port's version of Siberia. I don't at all mind. The fringes have always been my comfort zone. I can get into as much trouble as ever, but attract less attention doing it. The Indians won't object either. They fancy a show. But, as for you, given the evidence of an unseen hand somewhere in recent events, when you meet with Bishop Norman next week, I would not be surprised if you were sent to Twin Rivers. Let us hope I am mistaken. St. Callixtus is no place for you to wind up on your way to pasture. How long till you retire?"

"Do not remind me, Vincent. I think I have a few more years in me. I am more afraid of the pasture than I am of St. Callixtus. Do you really think I might be sent back there?"

Vesuvio edged closer to the parapet. With his face framed by dripping grape leaves, he looked like a Roman god staggering from a feast. "Look, old friend, it's more than a bit messy in Twin Rivers these days. In the midst of all that messiness, nothing beats having in place a reliable, old warrior. It may have been a long time ago, but you left a permanent impression on our Iron Cardinal. Phillip Fowler's funeral should have told you that much."

"You bring up Cudahy again!"

Vesuvio nodded as if to say, *Who else?* "As I said when we met on the road Saturday before last, 'even cardinals have ears'. Who knows what news reaches from here to your Crackerjack and from your Crackerjack to here? Rome and St. Callixtus these days are no farther apart than the two of you sitting opposite each other years ago playing Pig in a Poke. And, who knows when any of us priests are circumscribed? The dead pope and the living Cudahy began as priests, and likewise Bishop Norman. We are all bound-and-gagged and hemmed in by promises, sacred or otherwise, made one way or another. Bishop Norman sometimes expects us to take notes for sharing with our congregations. Don't try bringing a clipboard or a recorder into the confessional with the same thing in mind."

"Vincent, I am losing patience! Quit playing games. Why bring up things you don't want to talk about? Why Cudahy and promises and why Confession?"

"I do apologize, Aloy. I am not being fair. I bring things up because I want to talk about them, and cannot. My lips are sealed. I have begun to envy Delores Fowler who cannot talk at all. We would all be better off dumbstruck. I have gotten inside-outside or outside-inside of something. I am not sure which, but nothing has been the same since young Fowler's body was found behind the hotel." He gazed over Brandy's shoulder. "—Ah, our choir is about to head out."

The stadium forecourt had all but emptied. The last to leave was a Twin Rivers chartered coach loading choir members for their trip home. Several waved to Father Vesuvio; others stood silently in line with head bowed. Not content to simply wave back, he strode across the parking lot to chat first with one and then another, among them Harriet White and Phyllis Cobb. Bernard Passmore, first to board, had taken the rear seat spanning the back from which he glowered upon a scene grown suddenly animated with Vesuvio shaking hands, patting backs, and exchanging quips.

Just like Jack, thought Brandy, watching from afar, *always a great mixer and a great actor*.

Vesuvio could switch roles as adroitly as in a play about identical twins where the same man played both the sullen twin and the merry one. As long as the twins were not required on the stage simultaneously, no one in the audience would ever know.

"You blow cold and hot," said Brandy as they watched the choir bus exiting the parking lot, leaving them the last ones there. "One minute you appear to be running from a lynch mob; the next you are hobnobbing." This was meant as mild reproof.

"Some of us priests learn after a while to be unspeakably false," said Vesuvio. "Give me a call this evening, Aloy, if you are so inclined. I will tell you about my meeting with Bishop Norman."

Rain had begun by the time Brandy arrived at St. Norbert's, a journey of twenty minutes. Fifty miles to the west, the chartered St. Callixtus coach unloaded passengers at a highway rest stop offering snacks from vending machines. Rain pelted choir music, held overhead.

Vesuvio had just left Bishop Norman's residence after a meeting of fifteen minutes. An experienced motorcyclist would have said, "Wait till this squall passes." Vesuvio roared through the sodden night, with all its risks awaiting him, intent as a man with a mission that would not wait.

20

Moses with a Deck of Cards

An international Catholic journal had just published an essay by Cardinal Cudahy on the subject of sin, forgiveness, and God's mercy. An accompanying editorial note insisted that it had been submitted prior to the pope's death, and that its publication was not to be construed as an attempt to influence the selection of his successor.

Vesuvio carried a rain-soaked copy with him on his return from his postponed meeting with Bishop Norman who handed him one as if to say, "Bear this in mind."

Vesuvio found another awaiting him in the rectory, printed from a computer on the desk of Margaret Smuggs who had keys to everything in the St. Callixtus precinct. Had he as much as a dead goldfish floating in a neglected rectory flower bowl, Margaret would have known about it in time to suggest that Bernard Passmore rehearse a Requiem.

Vesuvio was used to it, and well beyond paying attention to Smuggs' invasions of his privacy let alone noting her choice of reading matter that ought to especially interest him. Much too much lay at stake elsewhere.

Two lines of Cudahy's essay struck Vesuvio as a bit out of line. One described The Seal of Confession as a *protective bulwark of penitential practice,* and that is was *among the most serious of obligations placed upon Catholic priests.* Vesuvio couldn't argue with that. But to then spell it out to lay people in the last line as emphatically as he did: *I urge all Catholics to acknowledge a priest's commitment to the sacramental seal of absolute confidentiality....* It was as if Cudahy were suggesting that somehow that might not be the case. It just opened up a can of worms and made

Vesuvio feel uneasy. Who was the message really intended for?

Essays such as this from Cardinal Cudahy, while not rare, were unusual, especially for this one's presumptive, authoritative tone, and what Vesuvio and evidently Bishop Norman both detected as a thinly-veiled threat.

Cudahy sounded like St. Paul writing to the Thessalonians, but when it came to intimidation, the Iron Cardinal was by far the better. He was more like Moses descending from a mountain, not with stone tablets, but with a stacked deck of playing cards.

Shortly after his arrival at St. Callixtus, Vesuvio phoned Brandy to begin reading into his ear what he described as Cudahy's pious, self-interested, tub thumping. Brandy put the phone aside as his friend detoured into a volcanic rant.

"Cudahy is a narcissist," said Vesuvio with the conviction of long experience. "—and, Aloy, let us not forget that the Iron Cardinal, stripped of his ecclesiastical fripperies, is no more than a priest, and at bottom no more than a man. All men are brothers. We are all in the same boat, rocking leeward and then starboard, bowsprit to poop deck. People either like us too much, or like us too little when they find out what priests are really about. Jack has managed always to be liked too much. He is like a nun who steals cars; he is funny, but he isn't."

Brandy looked at his telephone in speaker mode, set upon a chair arm. The arm was upholstered. The phone rocked slightly, like a boat adrift in a squall.

"Vincent, you have never before called him 'Jack.' You sound like you have known him all your life."

"Ahem, I have heard you speak of him so much, old friend, I guess he has begun to seem like a lifelong Jack to me as well."

"Sometimes, Vincent, I think that you know more about my life than I do."

Vesuvio laughed. Coming through the phone's speaker this had a stuck-in-the-throat sound. "Well, at any rate, why do you think so many bishops are every bit as fat as our Bishop Norman?"

Vesuvio's seemed like a question leading toward a punchline. Brandy pondered beneath his shirtfront the emerging paunch of older, rail-thin men. Was the answer there? "I am not sure there are so many fat bishops, but why, Vincent?"

As it turned out, the question led nowhere but to a change of subject leading to yet another question. Vesuvio was as adept at feinting, as Jack had always been.

"What do you think, Aloy? Do you see anything above, behind, or beneath our Cardinal's most recent words?"

"From what I heard before you exploded, I say he can write pretty well, just like Crackerjack, but he is a bit florid overall. Takes himself too seriously—sounds as if he is already the pope." Brandy hesitated, evidently aware that he had begun to treat Cardinal Cudahy and Crackerjack as if they were two, and not one and the same person.

Vesuvio laughed knowingly. "Exactly," he said. "If the Iron Cardinal carried a gun, every bullet chamber would be loaded with *latae sententiae*. In effect, he is issuing a not-so-subtle threat: woe to any priest telling tales, for immediate excommunication awaits. This applies to more than the Seal of Confession."

"I do not see it as threatening, Vincent, as long as we do what all of us promised to do long ago at ordination. This gun you speak of, do you think it is pointed at someone or something in particular?"

"Pointed, yes, and also beside the point! Aloy, I think we may be exchanging places, all three of us—Cudahy, you, and I—with you about to become the Grand Inquisitor. We are in a grim game of musical chairs, which you and Jack must have played in your schoolboy days."

"Yes," said Brandy, recalling the game, with a school sister playing a battered piano. "'Pop Goes the Weasel' was one of the tunes. Crackerjack sometimes deliberately missed a chair, I think, just to be the only one left standing."

"I wonder if you've heard of the weasel being a guide to the Underworld," said Vesuvio.

Brandy could hear Vesuvio's fingers tapping out the rhythm on perhaps a tabletop. Vesuvio's unanswered questions added up, while Brandy sat by, wearily listening to what was by now familiar: common parish priests go through life burdened with the sins and crimes of others often at their elbows. The weight grows heavier year by year for men of sensitive spirit unable to bluff their way through or shake it off as a dog might shake water from its fur after a bath in a muddy stream. Still the sickening stench of how people behave will not go away. Still the priest must smile and pretend to know nothing as he greets yesterday's sinners at tomorrow's church picnic.

Had Brandy been able to see into Vesuvio's mind at the moment, he would have been amazed to discover a performing circus seal balancing a red ball on the tip of his nose, imagined in the St. Callixtus Rectory parlor. To a priest of Vesuvio's overheated imagination, this fanciful seal was far from funny, sitting alongside him in the St. Callixtus confessional where Vesuvio had listened to sins and been a dispensary of forgiveness, at least one day a week for the past decade.

"Thousands of confessions—albeit one, two, and three in particular—and one poor seal over the years." Vesuvio closed his eyes and winced as if recalling an especially painful memory. "That is what's below and behind it, Aloy, though above it our Cardinal's essay goes out to the whole world, right over the top of most heads, even some he would gladly chop off."

"I know better than ask you about the one, two, or three confessions in particular, Vincent. You want me to ask so you can tell me that you can't explain. I am wise to you. I should be by this time."

Vesuvio laughed.

Brandy yawned audibly into the phone, their conversation once again stuck in circles, going nowhere. "Riddles, Vincent, you are much better at riddles. All the same, though it is a bit past my bedtime. I will be up for a couple of hours, and my ears hurt from being on the phone so much since arriving home; every St. Norbert's parishioner seems to have a question. Those who do not are either dead or dying. My day tomorrow will be spent between hospitals and funeral homes. –But tell me, how did your meeting with Bishop Norman go?"

"No longer than fifteen minutes, after I waited around almost an hour. I barely beat the choir bus home, as it were. But my meeting proved worthwhile, short as it was. Bishop Norman gave me next week off, Sunday to Sunday—insisted upon it in fact. I did not have to ask: he seemed to know about it beforehand. Goodnight, Aloy. Duty calls us both. With the St. Callixtus choir bus arriving any minute, people will be milling around in and out of the church. I will get back to you again tonight; otherwise, God willing, you will hear from me in a week or so, when I return."

Vesuvio hung up before Brandy could manage to reply. Once again, he had been listening in silence. Though it was well past Brandy's bedtime, his sleep was fitful and punctuated by disturbing dreams.

Vesuvio did not get back to him. Yes, he was right: it was all like a nun stealing cars; funny, but not funny.

21

The Ways of Rabbits

The chartered bus carrying the St. Callixtus choir on its 350-mile round trip, maneuvered its way across the last of Twin Rivers' bridges, into the church precinct.

A few minutes short of its arrival, Vesuvio's motorcycle had blazed past. Choir members had been taking bets from the moment they left the outskirts of North Port City. Everyone lost. Vesuvio was well behind predicted times, though as it turned out, his appointment with Bishop Norman had lasted no more than fifteen minutes. He was also speeding.

In a front seat behind the driver, Harriet and Phyllis Cobb watched as Twin Rivers spun into view with its illuminated twin spires of St. Callixtus obliterating any sense of stature New Town might have claimed.

"That sight always thrills me, our church in moonlight," said Phyllis, yawning nonetheless. "I hope George knows what he is doing when he blows up Paradise. He scarcely knows how to blow his nose in church, let alone protect St. Callixtus from falling debris. But I'm too tired to worry about it now. I swear these coach seats are glued to my bottom."

"It has been a long day," murmured Harriet whose attention was elsewhere, on a red flashlight for emergency use strapped to the underside of the driver's seat, immediately in front of them. An instant later it was tucked between her and Phyllis.

"Don't ask any questions, Phyllis. I will explain later."

Later turned out to be five minutes with the bus pulling into the church parking lot. Headlights of waiting cars gleamed upon the blank windows of Hotel Paradise. For a few minutes past and a few minutes more, it might have been possible to believe that people were still renting rooms there.

Among the cars awaiting choir member arrival was Porky White's, not his squad car but something less conspicuous designated for his personal use.

Harriet ran to him through light beams and shadows.

Meantime the motor coach drove away with its last passenger, Bernard Passmore. Like a mischievous school bully, he had occupied the rear row as if he owned it for the entire round-trip journey. In fact, he owned the bus, the bus company, and signed its driver's pay checks. He was The Bernard Passmore Bus Company personified with his arms draped across a row of seatbacks. He had nodded off. He need not worry about being roused at St. Callixtus when his choir disembarked. He could sleep all the way from there to his capacious front door in New Town. His driver, become his personal chauffeur, would awaken him, gently with properly reverential words, after carrying his trumpet to the front door.

By coincidence Harriet happened to be rousing Porky who had fallen into the half slumber of an alert lawman. "Wilbur, I will be no more than a minute, maybe five. Phyllis and I have to carry some choir books inside."

Phyllis waited near a church side entrance cradling a stack of books.

"Let me help!" said Porky.

"Not this time, Porky. Trust me, maybe ten minutes."

Whenever Wren said such things, calling him *Porky*, he knew she brooked no interference. He settled back into his seat behind the wheel where he had been sleepily monitoring police dispatcher reports. Nothing much was happening. He glanced at his watch. If Wren returned in fifteen minutes, there would still be time to grab a pizza take-out on their way home.

A snoring Bernard Passmore was fifteen minutes from his gentle awakening. Porky yawned. The full moon cast elongated St. Callixtus spire shadows through the locust grove into the hotel alley. A rabbit hopped through them.

Porky liked rabbits. They made him happy, with their nonchalant meanderings in light and shadow, appearing ever so oblivious to dangers that might be near. *The ways of a good lawman were the ways of rabbits*, he mused. Rabbits only needed a sidearm, just in case. If he and Harriet ever had children, he would buy them a rabbit.

Inside St. Callixtus, history was being made. Never in the fifteen decades of that venerable church had two people attempted to create a human tower atop an archive table. Phyllis—wearing the grim, determined jaw of a bulky weight lifter—had planted her feet where Harriet's laptop normally could be found. Harriet climbed up higgledy-piggledy, ankles to head as if in a monkey puzzle tree. Perched upon Phyllis' shoulders, red flashlight in shaking hand playing light beams everywhere except upon the old oak beam, she whispered.

"Phyllis, take one step back and two steps to your left."

There was no need to whisper, but given what Harriet already suspected, anything was possible. Phyllis' laughter had not been foreseen.

"Ha! Ha! Ho! Ho! Ugh! Ha!" echoed from the archive room, punctuated by various oofs, woofs, and giggles of the sort schoolgirls master. The human statue trembled, tottered left to right, then right to left much as an old oak tree had fallen before a woodsman's axe a century and a half before to make the archive beam. For a split second as the statue fell, Harriet's flashlight beam struck home. Phyllis screamed as Harriet, tumbling, rolled across the floor, screeching not with pain, but laughter. Porky rushed in, gun in hand, with Vesuvio a step behind him.

"Don't ask me to explain," Harriet said to Porky. "Father, it's too funny."

It also turned to be too late for Porky's take-out pizza, but the all-night Paradise Café was open. Phyllis drove herself there. Vesuvio followed on his motorcycle. They all ordered eggs and greasy sausages.

"I always wanted to do this," said Phyllis. "All the drunks come here when the bars close. George says eggs and grease are the best ways to deal with hangovers. He should know, and so would you, Father, if he ever went to Confession."

No one was better than Phyllis when it came to subduing whimsy.

At the mention of Confession, Vesuvio grew taciturn and somber. He stirred his coffee with his fork. He had ordered the same as the others but set it aside while folding his napkin into various geometric shapes.

Harriet took note.

Porky ordered a waffle side from the 24-hour breakfast menu. It had to have been a leftover from Sunday past. He used a steak knife to cut it. He attempted to start a discussion about rabbits. Phyllis said her dog had just killed one in their backyard and dragged it onto her deck. She asked Harriet if rabbits carried rabies. In the midst of this, Vesuvio excused himself.

"I guess Father isn't interested in rabbits," said Phyllis.

"He seemed preoccupied," said Harriet.

She glanced at the red flashlight in the middle of the table like a centerpiece. No one had asked what it was doing there. Porky knew better than to ask. He speared Vesuvio's sausages and downed them in two bites each.

"I love you, Wilbur," she said as they were driving home. "I have found just what I was looking for." She kept the rest to herself, for now. She was speaking both of Porky as husband and the oak timber beam's 'knot or not'.

22

Hiding in Brightness

On Pentecost Sunday morning, late afternoon in Rome, a television reporter, the same one who had interviewed Cardinal Cudahy the day before, stood before a Vatican background much like the sepia-toned jigsaw puzzle Aloysius and Jack had been unable to complete. The reporter was not in Rome. He only seemed to be there.

He had news of the Iron Cardinal: "Sources tell us that Cardinal Cudahy has sequestered himself for private prayer and meditation during the remaining five days preceding the conclave. He will be unavailable for further comment on the dramatic scenes unfolding at the Vatican even as we speak. Tomorrow morning may shed further light on this announcement."

The news sent Brandy dipping into his reservoir of homily quotes: "A brighter light can work as well as dark of night when it comes to concealing things." He could no longer recall who said it but thought perhaps it came from Vesuvio. It turned out that he was quoting himself.

While Harriet pondered this latest news of Cardinal Cudahy on a radio in Porky's squad car, Porky pondered his usual Sunday after-Mass breakfast at a café straight ahead. He juggled his preference between an omelet and French toast, between sausage and bacon, and between hash browns and American fries. "You can bet on it," he said under his breath.

"What was that, Wilbur?"

"An omelet," said Porky. "I think I will go for the Denver omelet this morning. Do you remember what I had last Sunday?"

"The Seventh Sunday of Easter," said Harriet. "I think it was a Denver omelet."

"Damn," said Porky. "I will have to try their potato pancakes, new on the menu." Porky was a compulsive juggler of more than beanbags and crime suspicions.

"The Iron Cardinal is not just your usual tough guy prelate sort, Wilbur. If he claims to be sequestering himself, he must be up to something—wouldn't you say?"

"Maybe potato pancakes with a side of ham. Wren, is there something on your mind? You seem preoccupied."

"Ask me after your breakfast, my dear. Ask me about Bernard Passmore."

23

A Barrel of Monkeys

Monday brought Brandy's turn to meet with Bishop Norman on the subject of parish assignments.

Priests as close to retirement as Brandy were usually left where they were until "released" from service. He had been at St. Norbert's on Lake Superior for the past dozen years. He had grown wistful and sometimes silly entertaining hopes that something would intervene between him and the approaching fated day. He might die suddenly; the world might end; Bishop Norman might be made a cardinal and sent off to Rome to oversee the Vatican Bank; his successor would take years getting around to his obscure St. Norbert's corner.

As Brandy said more than once, being a priest was the only thing he knew how to do. What thumb was he supposed to twiddle afterwards? How could there be anything afterward when afterward became an empty pocket where once a few tarnished church keys had jangled?

He had yet to answer the question when, step by step, like a man approaching his own execution, he climbed two flights of blue carpeted stairs to the bishop's office. Somewhere beyond the next landing and a foyer lit by hurricane lamps, in an office with a generous view of Lake Superior, he would be told his days of active ministry were over. *Active* would be the decisive word. He could already imagine it on the lips of Bishop Norman St. Claire, a man whose name had canonized him well ahead of action by any pope. *Active's* two syllables would hang on those august, hierarchical lips, glistening like dewdrops on squash blossoms.

What else? If there were such a thing as a passive priesthood, he had yet to hear of it. He dreaded the word *passive*. Silence was one thing. He had mastered silence, a lesson necessary for his encounters with the earth-shaking Vesuvio. Passivity was something else. Passivity had never taken root in Brandy's soul, nor had *caput* and interminable slumbers when other men were out and about.

It did not matter how old he was. Give or take a year or two, he was already over a limit twice extended *through the generosity of His Excellency, the Bishop*. With every priest in his kingdom half-dead from overwork, *necessity* would have been by far the more accurate word for the bishop's motive.

A grinning monsignor half his age met him at the top step with hand outstretched as if he need be lifted up and required a bit of hectoring. "You should have used the elevator, Aloysius, my friend."

"St. Peter never used one," said Brandy scowling, not so much from his mood but from the glare of those hurricane lamps. The monsignor opened double doors and danced ahead to open yet another set the other end of the foyer.

"Bishop St. Claire awaits."

"So does St. Peter," said Brandy. It was a joke without humor.

Bishop Norman, except for a glistening head grown prematurely bald, bore no resemblance to St. Peter. Squat as a bullfrog, he would have baffled both a portrait painter hired to render him heroic and a Roman executioner brought in to slap him on a cross. He rounded a gigantic desk to greet the priest. The monsignor retreated following a reverential bow.

"Your Excellency," said Brandy, bolt upright for the occasion, and despite his years, rigid as a post.

"Let us ignore formalities, Aloysius. Call me *Norman*." The bishop laid a pudgy hand upon the priest's shoulder. It might have been a ledge from which an enormous ring glistened this side of a pinky finger.

Minutes later with the bishop's hand removed and more formalities ignored, Brandy heard something truly astounding: Instead of being cast off and discarded like last Sunday's parish bulletin, instead of being made passive—whatever that meant—and useless as a plow horse in an age of tractors, at the bishop's "pleasure," he would serve as interim priest at St. Callixtus in Twin Rivers.

Vesuvio had guessed right, if indeed a guess.

"Only for a few months," said Bishop Norman. "I am so sorry to disappoint you with yet more of God's work when you were looking forward to your well-deserved rest, Aloysius—Aloysius, Aloysius?"

Brandy's eyes had glazed over, but he refocused. "Your Excellency, are you sure?"

"Call me Norman, and call St. Callixtus *interim only*. It will be a piece of cake, my boy, and more fun than a barrel of monkeys." He pushed a button on his desk, and then hesitated as those twin sets of double doors opened once again. The monsignor stepped in, and then withdrew when Bishop Norman glanced up and cleared his throat. He cleared his throat again.

"By the way, I hear you were childhood friends with our Cardinal Cudahy, heard it from him in person when I was in Rome a few weeks ago. We talked at length. He sends his greeting, a most peculiar one—I don't know what to make of it. He said to say to you, 'You're *It*'. A private joke, I suppose."

"And a long story."

The bishop sighed. "I would like to hear it sometime. Unfortunately, my next appointment awaits, but with the conclave about to meet, amid rumors of deadlock, it might interest you to know that Cardinal Cudahy could be the next pope. Quite a thing for you to have been childhood friends with the pope, should it turn out that way. I am envious. Quite a thing for me too, were it to happen that among my charges is the pope's childhood friend. I shall have to be at my very best when you are anywhere near, Aloysius." There followed something resembling a giggle and a puppy-dog look, inviting reassurance.

A large table had turned like a rotating bookcase revealing a secret passage.

Brandy, having come before a man who held his fate in his hands, now held that man's fate in his hands, *for a moment*. This was how power felt. This was where the game of tag might lead. Bishop Norman would be envious; his old friend Jack as pope would enjoy a world on bended knee; his friend Brandy could avoid retirement and die at his post with no one daring to intervene; he could make a fool of himself, and be regarded as wise.

"I may have more to fear than you, your Excellency. I once pushed Jack into a mud puddle."

"Jack?"

"The Cardinal."

"And you call him *Jack*!" Bishop Norman nearly swooned. "Jack, possibly the next pope, pushed into a mud puddle. Incredible! —Now I *am* envious. Well, on second thought, I don't mean to say that I would wish to do such a thing."

"It was an accident, and a long time ago, your Excellency. I doubt that the cardinal remembers."

"Ah, yes, a long time ago, out of sight out of mind, as they say. Great men usually forget their ... uh obscure connections to..."

"To..." Brandy made Bishop Norman suffer as long as he could. "To relative nobodies, your Excellency?"

"Yes—I mean no! —Don't be so hard on yourself, Aloysius. I am sure Jack—Cardinal Cudahy—he must remember something about you."

"I was not very good at Pig in the Poke," said Brandy.

Bishop Norman fixed him with a probing gaze. This priest was clearly losing his marbles, creeping dementia no doubt. The turned table snapped back into its original position.

"Most of the bishops would be in Rome right now, awaiting the joyful result, but the Holy See has mandated that many of us—I among them—stay at our posts, a matter of prudence in this age of terrorism. If a nuclear bomb were exploded at the Vatican with all of us there, the entire hierarchy would be wiped out, a disaster unparalleled in the history of the Church. Imagine that, Aloysius."

"Just as it was the day after the first Easter, your Excellency."

"Yes, a disaster," said Bishop Norman, as if he had not heard.

From the bishop's office window high above Lake Superior, ships could be seen approaching the harbor.

The bishop blessed him. "Amen, your Excellency," said Brandy.

"Call me Norman," said the bishop with another sigh. "And more fun than a barrel of monkeys."

Brandy retreated to the foyer. Doors automatically closed as the bishop, rounding his desk, swept up his pen.

"This time use the elevator, my friend," said the monsignor. "Every blessing."

Brandy took the stairs.

"A lot any of them know," he said to his dog Fred tethered to a lamppost beside his car. No mention had been made of his previous service at St. Callixtus, as if it had never happened. Yet it had happened.

"Well at any rate, Fred, old boy, we're not quite caput, are we? More fun than a barrel of monkeys? We'll soon see about that. Still, I wish I hadn't said anything about the mud puddle." Fred, given a firm boost, clambered into the back seat.

Out in North Port City's harbor, a ship's horn blared as a lift bridge descended astern a freighter leaving port.

24

Vodka and Brandy

That St. Norbert's was not to be Brandy's last assignment should have seemed predestined from the moment Vincent Vesuvio predicted it, *if* in fact St. Callixtus at Twin Rivers had been a prediction. Perhaps prophecy was more a matter of insight than of foresight. Regardless, Vesuvio seemed to know everything before it happened, and had a habit of knowing more than he would say.

Brandy's and Vesuvio's new parish assignments went public both at St. Norbert's and St. Callixtus of Twin Rivers on Trinity Sunday, the Sunday after Pentecost: "Father Vincent Vesuvio to the St. Brendan's Chaplaincy at Turning Wind. Father Aloysius Brandy, to be interim pastor at St. Callixtus."

If anything startled Brandy himself, it was the thought of being *interim*. Was there anything beyond an interim?

"It means that he won't last long," said Margaret Smuggs, the St. Callixtus parish secretary. She settled before her desk and reached for a bottle of vodka hidden in a file drawer. Bernard Passmore peered over her shoulder, hands clasped behind his back, as he danced from one foot to the other to catch a better look at her computer screen.

Bernard all but owned St. Callixtus. He could hold it in the palm of one hand. He could put its *for sale* sign on his pinky finger. He could move it from dismal Old Town by snapping his middle finger and his thumb. He could hum a merry tune. Margaret scrolled through a diocesan clergy directory, and finally tapped her finger on the screen. "Brandy—yes, that's our boy," said Margaret. "An old duffer still posing in his Roman collar and looking to die any minute. My god, he was ordained almost fifty years ago!"

Passmore licked his lips. "Nothing to worry about there."

Margaret dumped vodka into a glass of orange juice. "I have to have a drink before starting this wretched day. How about a tipple, Bernie?" Margaret was the only one permitted to take liberties with Bernard's name.

He waved her off. "You know I never imbibe," said Bernard who unfailingly used the most obscure of several possible synonyms.

"Lordy! There you go again, Bernie. Never was such a walking dictionary as you. I say its *drink* and *priming the morning pump*, no matter how much you imbibe it." She poured another jigger of vodka into her coffee cup.

"Piffle," said Bernard. "Just be sure to make it brandy next time, in honor of the old buzzard Bishop Norman has sent here to guard the carcass of this dilapidated edifice."

"Lordy, brandy stinks, smells on the breath. *Dilapidated edifice*, St. Callixtus Church—there you go again, Bernie! I hope you never say the like around our Father Brandy. He might take it personally. If he could listen to the stuff you hear with your itsy-bitsy microphones everywhere, we both would need another job, but next Sunday's bulletin awaits me, with our vacationing Pastor's 'Thoughts for this Sunday of Ordinary Time.' Which Sunday is it? You always keep track. I don't know how you do it, Bernie."

"I ascertain it to be the 11th Sunday, Margaret. As this stinking dump's Liturgical Music Director, it is my charge to keep this derelict church on schedule, and I happened to notice that my connection to the parish archive has been broken. Look into that problem in the archive while I am off to a Chamber of Commerce luncheon and meeting. As for needing another job, have no fear when Bernard's near."

No one could mix metaphor and rhyme as well as Bernard.

"I will need stilts to have much luck with the archive bug. Lordy!" said Margaret as Bernard left the scene.

25

The Bottom is Higher than the Top; Behind is Closer than Ahead

The sudden disappearance of Cardinal Cudahy left a gaping hole in a speculative universe. No one could say for certain what it meant, but everyone had a theory, or if pressed, perhaps two or three contradictory ones: the Cardinal was removing himself from contention; the Cardinal was adopting the humble posture of a shoe-in; the Cardinal was discreetly forming alliances behind closed doors; the Cardinal was in poor health and seeking medical attention; etc.

Meanwhile, the usual helicopters crisscrossed Vatican skies. The usual pigeons perched on tiled rooftops. The usual sea-scented west wind mingled with the mustiness of old stone. A sense of timelessness jostled with a sense of moment.

With the conclave three days away and nothing new to report, the criteria for papal eligibility, easily stated in one sentence, had swollen into a short-course history of the papacy. The world learned of St. Peter and thirty-eight other married popes, not counting those with mistresses. Reporters struggling to fill empty space resorted to Rome's pigeon eradication plan; the mystery of its public bus transportation; piazza statuary; papal artifacts; and notorious, medieval conspiracies. Celebrity newscasters quizzed street vendors about hotdog and umbrella sales. Camera zoom lenses replaced real movement as grand backgrounds receded and then shot forward to the empty balcony from which the next pope would bless a throng, days from now, or it might be weeks.

A chance tourist from northern Minnesota, sipping coke from a can, was questioned for her views, though she admitted having thought the Iron Cardinal a statue, and seemed amused when being told he had gone into hiding. A tall academic on sabbatical claimed to have spotted Cardinal Cudahy beyond a stone wall, pacing in a garden where nuns grew Vatican produce. An impatient world craved news that would not come, especially news of the Iron Cardinal. Church politics, more than ever polarized, placed him in the center of an imagined impasse or an imagined plot. Some thought he may have been poisoned.

On a midweek evening at St. Norbert's, Brandy set aside his newspaper to place a call he did not expect to be answered. The St. Callixtus rectory telephone rang six times. The eighth ring would bounce his call to Margaret Smuggs' voice mail. Without explanation, Vesuvio had cautioned him about leaving messages there. The seventh ring was answered.

"Vincent, have you caught a cold from driving in the rain last week? You don't sound like your old self. I was hoping you would be nowhere near a telephone."

"Not a cold caught, but caught sleeping." This was followed by a series of coughs and unexpected questions, "Rain? What rain? Driving where? Who's calling?"

"You *are* in bad shape. When you are awake enough to remember last week and Aloysius Brandy, call me back. I have news."

Within five minutes Brandy's phone rang. On the other end, a cranky version of Vesuvio vacillated between old habits of civility and petulance and something more elusive. Call it the jittery apprehension of a man feeling his way in darkness not knowing what obstacles lie in his path.

"Brandy, I am sorry. I was half asleep when you roused me."

"Vincent, I am sorry that I disturbed you. Actually, I called by whim after reading about Vatican non-events. Are you so soon back from your respite? Any news from wherever you were, or was it no farther than your sofa? Have you been following the Roman melodrama? It's like a game of tag Jack and I were so good at when we teamed up. Reporters are chasing rumors around the Vatican instead of us chasing our classmates around All Saints."

The comparison seemed to require corroboration.
"Jack?"

"Yes, Jack at All Saints."

"Yes, of course, Jack, but is it not strange to hear Cardinal Cudahy called Jack? If he went by that name, I mean these days, around the Vatican in his circles, Jack seems so devil-may-care. Jack changes the picture. You are for certain the only one still calling him that. That's rich! It would sound to him like hearing in a dream the voice and slap-happy laugh of someone long dead, in this case himself. But to your point, I have been following Vatican events enough to make me wish I were there. You know how infectious pomp and circumstance can be, eh? In this case not much pomp but more circumstance than anyone could imagine.

"But tell me, if you could speak to your old friend Jack just now, after so many years since those games the two of you played, what would you say to him at this time in his life?"

Though he thought the question strange, Brandy had an answer. He had kept it close over the almost sixty years Jack had been climbing the Church career ladder. He had repeated it as Jack went up rung by rung, almost to the top. He had it by heart, and so he could say without hesitating, "'It's a crazy idea. I could never do that.' That is what I would say to him."

"What's a crazy idea?"

"Becoming a bishop, becoming a cardinal, becoming famous, maybe becoming pope. It strikes me as crazy, and you too, I imagine—we have talked about it enough. It's not our way."

"And you would say this to Cardinal Cudahy's face?"

"Of course not. I could say it to Jack, the boy I knew at All Saints. I could have said it way back then. I wouldn't dare say it to the great Cardinal Cudahy. He might order Bishop Norman to force me into retirement, the last thing I want. I have my own career ambitions to consider."

"To continue serving as a priest?"

"There's nothing better." After an interval of silence, Brandy glanced at his phone. "Vincent, are you still there, or have you fallen asleep again?"

"No, I am quite awake, but I sometimes think that I fell asleep years ago, and so this is where we are now: it turns out that the bottom of this ladder is higher than the top. You may not know it, but you have risen above Cudahy. I suppose you have heard that he has secluded himself prior to the opening of the conclave?"

"Of course, Vincent. That news is everywhere. It's pure Crackerjack, sowing distraction and grandstanding—not that I question his sincerity. It's just his way. Your way also, sometimes—forgive me. We're all posers, myself included. I am perhaps too happy to be seen as a sidelined fixture, like the Silent Shepherd in our All Saints Christmas play."

"Crackerjack! It's been a long time since Cardinal Cudahy was called that. I should play the Silent Shepherd these days. You could be the narrator, Brandy. It would be good."

"You silent? Vincent, I can't imagine it. Well, to get to my news, it was too much to hope that I could stay a fixture at St. Norbert's, but at least I am not retiring, and as you probably know by now, if you have read Bishop Norman's communiqué, your predictions came true."

A yawn poorly stifled. "—Predictions? Ah, yes."

"I am bound for Twin Rivers as its interim pastor, and you are off to St. Brendan's Indian Chaplaincy as you predicted. How on earth did you know before I did?"

"It's simple: who commands Bishop Norman? Is that not the explanation? You are *It*, Brandy."

Vesuvio could be as nimble as Crackerjack. It was like being with Jack, secondhand.

"I'm afraid you have lost me, Vincent."

"No matter how it happened, you are *It* because your friend Jack is behind your unexpected presence in these old digs of your reverent apprenticeship. He wants you at St. Callixtus. I can't say more, Brandy, so do not ask me. I am glad you are not here present to draw me out, but you are the one person the man you call Crackerjack can trust, and right now he needs somebody at St. Callixtus he can trust, believe me. Take it on faith, no, take it on the word of someone who thinks being a priest is the best thing in the world, even better than being pope."

"You seem to be saying that you yourself cannot be trusted," said Brandy. "Given your experience on the scene, Vincent, I would think you the one to be depended upon."

"Sometimes experience is exactly the problem, Brandy. Knowing too much can be as dangerous as knowing too little. Whoever said that ignorance is bliss got it only half right. As Adam discovered too late, a knowledge of good and evil has its drawbacks."

"And so, my ignorance is an advantage?"

"Exactly, and now, since I am late for an appointment, I must reluctantly say goodbye. Speaking with you has brightened my day more than you could possibly know." This was followed by a dial tone.

Brandy glanced at an ancient pendulum wall clock in the St. Norbert's rectory—8:50 p.m.

As he thought about it afterward, the whole phone call seemed strange with its twists and turns and its abrupt conclusion, abnormalities he dismissed as stress and fitful sleep or perhaps picking up a cold.

Moody, changeable, and unpredictable, Vesuvio could become aloof in spaces between times, between diocesan meetings, between chance encounters with his friend Brandy, and between phone calls. Brandy had learned he would need to get to know the man again the day after he thought he knew him. Mercurial Vesuvio was never himself, but tonight more so than ever he seemed like a stranger.

Normally Vincent called him Aloy; the only one who called him that; tonight, Vincent had called him Brandy. He was slipping.

"Stress, and an interrupted nap or maybe woken in the middle of a dream," Brandy spoke to Fred while eyeing him closely. "You know about naps, don't you? But I should have discovered long ago the wisdom of letting sleeping dogs lie."

Three hours later, as late as the hour was, a doorbell rang at the St. Callixtus rectory.

The rectory had three entrances, a front door, a back door, and a side entrance opening onto a small garden overrun by daylilies and rhubarb. Margaret Smuggs had keys to all three. Each entrance had a doorbell buzzer connected to a chime over the front. Anyone unfamiliar with this arrangement would have assumed a visitor to be at the front door when he might have been at any one of the three. This inconvenience might have been corrected years ago, except that visitors almost never called at the rear and side entrances. The front entrance was a safe bet whenever the chime rang out.

A large shadow cast from an entrance light lay upon daylilies and rhubarb; a large hand gripped a door handle. Another hand gripped an iron bar. Yet another hand gripped a pistol as the rectory's front door swung open. A hinge squeaked, a floorboard creaked, and a glance back too late took in a visitor already arrived.

Closing of Box Two

BOX THREE

A JACK-IN-THE-BOX

Many a good man has sold his soul
without knowing it.

–VINCENT VESUVIO

26

Church Bells and Fabrications

After a delay unprecedented in recent papal history, a new pope had been elected. All over America, Catholic church bells were ringing, none louder and more vigorously than in remote and generally ignored northern Minnesota. Even a few Lutheran churches joined the celebration. A fleeting whiff of ecumenism was in the air, on ordinary days an element as inert as argon.

This was not an ordinary day.

A seventy-something man robed in white stood with arms outstretched on a high balcony behind a balustrade of sodden flowers. Minnesota's native son, now Pope Vincent, was blessing a worn out, bedraggled crowd keeping vigil beneath dripping and drooping umbrellas. After days of rain and black smoke from the Sistine chimney, it was the end of an ordeal. The Piazza San Pietro lay beneath a layer of indescribable, gray detritus.

In America, people who had never known Cardinal Cudahy were already fabricating memories. Local and national television blazed with documentaries assembled from the new pope's fragmented early years in Minnesota.

Brandy retreated further into his St. Norbert's home, fearful that any moment reporters might descend to ask him about the game of tag. He wanted to pull bedcovers up over his head as he often did as a child. Lying there in self-imposed isolation, he could pretend whatever happened had only been a bizarre dream. Foregoing that, he rehearsed responses before a dozing Fred as television camera crews circled his Iron Range hometown. Surely they would come his way, another fifty miles. If then, what was he supposed to say? Should he mention that he knew the pope as Crackerjack, and that he once pushed him into a muddy puddle?

No one came to his door that day or the next. It was as if his games with Jack had never happened. Brandy, probably the most memorable presence in Jack's life at All Saints, had vanished in a history wiped away like chalk beneath a wet sponge on a school blackboard. He felt both relieved of a burden and saddened.

Reporters stood before the familiar gates of Jack's old home, now a dilapidated and abandoned mansion, as if the new pope himself still resided there and might appear at any moment to give a papal blessing from a rusting jalopy parked in its courtyard. Of course, following great events, there were helicopters like deerflies pursuing sweaty foreheads. Brandy caught an aerial glimpse of the simple cottage where his own family lived and of the nursing home where his mother had died; both glimpses accidental and unnoted in the narration.

All Saints Church's modest spire was circled. He saw it as it might have been seen from Heaven, a dagger broadening earthward. A reporter slipped inside the church where a daily Mass was being said before a larger than usual group of worshippers. Jack's family had never worshipped there, had never registered in the parish, were thought by his mother to be a pack of atheists, and yet now they were said to have worshipped there, and were remembered as devout.

Brandy glanced at Fred asleep on a nearby sofa. There was no one else to ask, "Why are Catholics always described as devout?" Fred slept unperturbed. "Why do we have a corner on devout? Is no one else devout? Is there no other way of being a Catholic?" For certain, both Cudahy and Vesuvio, men with the instincts of prizefighters, had found another way.

Nearby All Saints was the water tower park where young Aloysius had declared his vocation to Crackerjack. Like a river through Brandy's soul coursed Jack's words uttered long ago in twilight shadows: *If you ask me, it's crazy—I could never do that.* Yet, crazy or not, Jack had more than done it, and now he was the first American pope.

27

A Hand in the Doorway

Twin Rivers law enforcement routinely checked the shuttered and abandoned Hotel Paradise, a rookie cop assignment, but with rumors of drug deals and local prostitution in the picture, it held for the novice a sense of adventure soon turning to routine. Though gossip suggested otherwise, nothing ever happened there, and nothing changed from week to week and month to month—and year to year. The Hotel Paradise was not merely abandoned, but in a state of emptiness which could only be described as a void. It was Eden after the Fall, all memory and all past tense, all broken promise, failure, and dilapidated grandeur.

Though late-night patrons of the Purple Palace claimed to see lights on in rooms of its upper floors, its electricity had been disconnected. What they must have seen was a reflection from the Purple Palace's flickering neon signs screaming, *Girls! Girls! Girls!* or perhaps a summer lightning strike, or moonlight forming a prism through Dusty Dwyer's liquor bottles. The Hotel Paradise had become a silent fortress of soiled memory and sometimes sordid lore. Patrolling it could not have been more boring for a team of two deputies with flashlights going floor to floor, past doors hanging by one hinge, porcelain shards of old toilets and bathtubs, while ducking bats sleeping upside down from deadened light fixtures.

All this left them unprepared for a door ajar with a dead hand protruding into the hallway. Within, across the floor, sprawled the bloodied rest of a man dressed in black.

They radioed for assistance.

28

Church Blackbirds

Gone were the ear to the wall and an eye to the keyhole. Old-fashioned eavesdropping had become obsolete, and privacy impossible to find anywhere in the St. Callixtus precinct. The 'wood knot' in the ancient timber high overhead in the church archive room had been identified as a tiny, remote wireless microphone, a type Porky White knew as a *Blackbird.*

Who knew where its chirp went and whether a single bird or a flock? As is the case with mice and cockroaches, where there is one concealed listening device, there is usually more than one.

"You can bet on it," said Porky as he and Harriet discussed his findings on a bench in the canine exercise area at the Happy Pet Clinic.

Following her discovery while perched atop Phyllis Cobb's shoulders, Porky had used a bit of interrogative juggling and dancing to question the manager of a New Town electronics shop. Its owner made a show of searching through his computer files as if his memory would not suffice.

"It wasn't a bad act," said Porky.

"I imagine he scratched his head and wrinkled his brow, old television crime show stuff," said Harriet. "Were there any beads of sweat?"

"Nervous, Wren, you can bet on it. He finally 'remembered' selling a half dozen wireless Blackbirds to 'Mr. Passmore' –*Mr. Passmore*! That's how he put it. 'A half dozen, three years ago, and then a couple recently to replace those gone bad'. But since when does the prominent owner of a top-drawer electronics business–the guy drives a Porsche–call a church choir director *Mister*?"

Harriet made a mental note: *Since when?* "Bud Myerson, right?"

"Right," said Porky.

"Wow! Bud is one of our most prominent parish leaders. He serves on the parish council. We used to depend on him when it came to defending St. Callixtus against those wanting to build a church in New Town. He now belongs to the SNFA and is one of their most vocal supporters. You have heard Phyllis and I talking about those *Sunny New Future Association* signs that keep getting vandalized on the New Town property where the new church would be built if the opposition get their way. A banker, also on the parish council, contributed the land."

"The department gets complaints all the time about those signs. It's kid stuff, mostly involving this boy going by the name of Whisk. We have yet to catch him at it. His foster parents run a gun shop out of their trailer house, undercover and unlicensed. Even if that banker's two acres are worth a million and more, we have better things to do than post lookouts and monitor junior league gunrunners," said Porky.

"Like finding out who killed Phillip Fowler and why," said Harriet reciting from a mental checklist. "And whether that has any connection to Jane Blue's Chicago trips and the beating death of her cousin Melody Stillwater. And do any of these loose ends tie in with Bernard Passmore bugging rooms at St. Callixtus? Anybody going to that much trouble and expense is either hiding something or wants to know what someone else is hiding—or is just plain nosey."

"Maybe all three," said Porky. He reached for his beeping police dispatch phone. As he listened, he tightened his lips. "I will have to cut this short, Wren. We have a problem at the Hotel Paradise." Porky drew a step away from Wren and met her gaze. "On my way," he said, snapping the phone shut.

29

The Small Comfort of Proximity

The next morning, a few minutes before St. Callixtus Church bells announced the arrival of noon, Porky jogged through the locust tree grove to the parish archive. Noting Bernard Passmore appearing to read from a pamphlet rack at the end of the hall, Porky shut the archive door behind him with a bang sufficient to say, *Keep Out – None of Your Business*. This, of course, ignited Bernard's interest. He lumbered down the hall to his office, several walls and windows away.

There, breathing hard, he hooked a tiny speaker onto his ear, and settled back in the parish center's best desk chair, purchased 'personally', with the aid of an invoice forged by Margaret Smuggs.

Without knowing it, Bernard had become an actor in Porky and Harriet's stealth theater where nothing more important than meatloaf was discussed unless calculated to ensnare him. Today something seemed out of the ordinary. This was one of those moments in theater when a main character trips over a backstage prop and knocks himself out. From that point forward, ad lib and improvisation take over.

Porky put two fingers to his lips, pointed to the archive's vaulted ceiling, and then to the honey locust grove, a hundred feet away, beyond the archive's window. Harriet's world at St. Callixtus was about to change forever.

"Wren, the air is especially stale in here this morning. Why not enjoy a fresh breeze out there among the trees?" He need not have winked. Porky's beanbag juggling in front of children and their parents had refined acting skills already honed by his questioning suspects.

Minutes later they stood well within the grove where the air was no better, and the dank, crumbling hotel offered small comfort. Bernard danced from window to window on that side of the parish center offices. Nowhere could he get a good look. He dodged into the archive. Nothing had been left behind.

"Wren, you are not going to like this news. I would have mentioned it last evening, but I wanted to be sure." He whispered into her ear as if the trees themselves might have been bugged.

Harriet trembled as she removed wire-rimmed glasses worn for reading fine archival print. Her eyes glistened. Always braver than brave, she steadied herself in Porky's arms. The locust grove, teeming with its usual songbirds, embraced a silent Wren.

When at last she looked up, still pale and trembling, she delayed the one question that offered a shred of hope.

Instead, as people often do, she recounted last moments with the suddenly deceased, clinging to the last evidence of a life that mattered. "We were at The Paradise Café with him a few nights ago. You had a waffle. Phyllis was there. When she mentioned George and Confession, his mood changed. He folded his napkin every which way—Wilbur, are you sure it is Father Vesuvio?"

"Much as it hurts me to say it, Wren. It is Father Vesuvio. You can bet on it."

She collapsed into Porky's arms. "I don't want to bet on it, Wilbur. I want it to be wrong. O God, how I want to lose that bet!"

30

The Avalanche Named "Catastrophe"

Neither deputy assigned to Hotel Paradise duties had recognized the body, though one was a member of St. Callixtus Parish from the time Father Vesuvio was first stationed there. The victim's face, shorn of its familiar red beard, had been distorted beyond recognition by a single gunshot. A hand and arm had twisted under him as he fell to the floor. When his body was moved, after photographs had been taken, a large bore pistol was found beneath him. He wore a black suitcoat and a Roman collar. A precisely folded suicide note protruded from the coat's lapel pocket. An iron bar lay on a sill beneath a shattered window, the one piece of evidence that did not fit into a suicide puzzle.

Porky and Harriet paced hand-in-hand through the hotel alley, one end to the other and back again. As a lawman, he was in his element. As a husband, he was far out of it, wanting to share details while attempting to be sensitive. Harriet, so often behind the scenes, was completely out of her element. The alley was the worst place to attempt consoling her. Nevertheless, they both persisted, with Harriet at times resting her head on his shoulder.

As they neared the Purple Palace, Dusty Dwyer stepped outside to greet a passenger van carrying four young women to his door. He glanced down the alley and waved.

In the course of Harriet's year in the St. Callixtus archive, Father Vesuvio had intimated things about Dusty that no one else knew, good things. She wondered what Dusty would think when he heard the news. What would Father Aloysius Brandy think when he, the newly appointed interim pastor, heard the news? What about Bishop Norman and the parishioners of St. Callixtus and

St. Brendan's? It was a subsequent stage in the avalanche named "catastrophe." First disbelief, and then wondering what those who did not yet know would think when they found out.

A world had been upended overnight, here, in a hotel whose blackened bricks she could have touched in passing. She and Porky had three times passed the very place where young Fowler's body had been found, beneath the fire escape from which Charlie Cook had dropped Porky's beanbags, just two weeks ago. She had heard about it secondhand, along with all the dreadful things Porky encountered in his criminal investigations over the twelve years of their marriage.

Secondhand was like hearing someone else's account of a house fire in which innocent children had been trapped. Porky had brought home such stories. He had been on the scene. This was different. Father Vesuvio's body, 'pending further identification,' was in a room of a building she could touch. A single brick would connect her brick by brick and broken plaster by stairway and empty elevator shaft to the very spot where his body lay.

Grief, like love, was the mortar connecting souls.

"Wilbur," she finally whispered, "Get me out of here. Take me home." There was neither urgency nor hysteria in her voice. She fled from resignation, a third stage in the avalanche called catastrophe.

As Porky helped her into his squad car and fastened her seat belt, Bernard Passmore finally caught a good glimpse from a chink in a stained-glass window on the parking lot side of St. Callixtus. He had danced to and from every possible vantage point, even as far as the locust grove while Harriet's and Porky's backs were turned.

He had at last confirmed his own suspicions. "Something big is up!" he said to Margaret Smuggs. "Our ever-so-attentive and nosey chief investigator has just driven away with his wife, our pesky Harriet."

Margaret glanced at a wall clock in her office. "He always does that, usually before this."

"This is the first time speeding away with his squad car lights flashing!" Bernard licked lips grown parched.

31

The Spaces Between

Once home in her accustomed world of secondhand report, the world of the St. Callixtus Church historian, Harriet gradually recovered. Over a second cup of tea, she began asking questions. Porky resumed his account:

No sign of a struggle anywhere. The rectory was clean, in Porky's opinion a bit too clean and carefully arranged, though its front and rear doors had been left unlocked. No driver's license or other identification was found on the victim. Vesuvio's fingerprints were not in any of the data bases, local or national. Fresh prints matching the victim's were all over his house, which had been gone over by a parish housekeeper only the day before. The same prints were on the pistol grip. The iron bar was clean, also too clean.

"Our unreliable coroner says it had nothing to do with the victim's death. That puzzles me, though; it doesn't fit into the picture. It is like Vesuvio up and left the rectory, somehow wound up dead in a room at The Paradise in the middle of the night, and the iron bar got there by telekinesis. By the way, was Vesuvio left-handed or right-handed?"

"Left –we used to tease him about it now and then. He would write with his fingers curled pointing down."

"In that case, there could be something wrong here," said Porky.

He need not have spared her the gruesome details behind that statement. Right-handed suicides usually shot themselves from the right side of the head, etc. Fingerprints would be on the left side of the gun. Porky recalled a scene from one of his boyhood detective novels. The murder weapon had been wiped clean, and then with gloved hands the assailant carefully pressed the victim's fingerprints onto the gun. It might have been the first instance where his childhood reading suggested a plausible theory. This thought made him smile inwardly. He had always hoped those novels would someday help him solve a mystery.

"Except in Vesuvio's case, the prints showed up on what is probably the wrong side," he said.

"A perfectionist getting it wrong," said Harriet. She asked about the suicide note.

"Just like the last one, unconvincing."

"Left-handed people often have a leftward slant to their writing," she said. "I would like to see it."

"Putting it all together, Wren..."

Porky looked at Harriet; she looked at him. He shook his head. Neither needed to say murder staged to look like suicide was a strong possibility.

"We're checking out the gun registration," said Porky.

After a deep breath, Harriet asked about his motorcycle.

"It's in the parish garage, but his car is parked in the Purple Palace lot."

"Why there of all places? Everyone will think the worst. It doesn't make sense, Wilbur. If he had wanted to visit Dusty Dwyer, he could have walked there. And why would he be wearing a Roman collar? That is completely out of character. I hardly ever saw him wearing one, except for some occasion when Bishop Norman required it. I suppose the car was planted to make it look like he'd been visiting Dusty, and something went wrong between them."

"A possible frame-up, or maybe something did go wrong between them. Dwyer is on my interrogation list."

Harriet's mind spun through possibilities. "I do wonder about the beard, though."

"Does he shave it off for the summer months?"

"He does that from time to time, and lets it grow back right away. He called it pruning the shrubbery. How did he get into the Hotel Paradise?" Harriet had arrived at a stage called 'questioning the details.'

Porky shrugged, a gesture he had mastered whenever he dropped a beanbag. "I am hoping Sheriff Smoody or some reporter doesn't ask me that."

"Regardless, we had better ask ourselves, and now to the pet clinic. I'll be two hours late, but my boss never asks questions. I think it has something to do with coming and going in your squad car."

On their way, Porky asked who besides Vesuvio had keys to the rectory.

"Margaret Smuggs has keys to everything," said Harriet.

32

Dark Tidings

At St. Norbert's a telephone rang.

A rectory phone ringing midevening often meant someone was dead or dying. Otherwise, for Brandy who had little left in the way of family, it could only be Vesuvio, what he had in the way of a friend, Vesuvio, now 'recovered' from his journey to perhaps no farther than his sofa, with his unique view of news at hand, Pope Vincent.

"Father Brandy?"

"Yes."

"This is Harriet White from St. Callixtus of Twin Rivers—we met briefly a couple of weeks ago. I am the woman doing the church's sesquicentennial history. Do you remember?"

"Not all 150 years, but part of it."

When Harriet did not laugh, he knew this call would be serious.

"Please keep this to yourself. His name is being withheld, pending notification."

"Who? Yes."

"Since you will soon be stationed here, I thought you should be among the first to know that Father Vesuvio is dead. His body was found this morning."

"—It can't be! We were just speaking last evening by phone. Are you sure?"

"I would not be calling you, Father, were we not certain. Did he seem troubled about anything when you spoke with him?"

"Of course, Vincent is forever troubled about something."

"I mean anything personal, Father?"

"No, no, he was the most generous of men. He never thought about himself. It was his way. Dead? God forbid, at this time of all times."

"Why do you say this time of all times?"

"I think it might have been distress about St. Callixtus parishioner's feuding—well, I don't know—if it wasn't one thing it would be another. At the end of the call, he said he had an appointment."

"Did he say with whom?"

"No. He hung up on his end. Not that I would have asked. It was none of my business. Priests are forever expected to run off somewhere at all hours."

"About what time would this have been?"

"Well, as a matter of fact, I happened to notice. It was ten minutes to nine. Did he have a heart attack?"

"The exact cause of death has not been released. Your bishop is being informed, but please wait for an official announcement. I just thought you should know."

"Yes, thank you. Yes—thank you."

For some reason, as if Vesuvio's ghost might be listening, they had been both whispering.

"I look forward to your arrival at St. Callixtus soon, Father."

"Yes, it is soon, isn't it? Thank you."

Harriet switched off her phone. Over the years of her marriage to Porky, she had evolved into a meticulous, detached interrogator. She had withheld painful details, not because she knew that Brandy and Vesuvio were friends. She did not yet know this. Details were central to secrecy surrounding a possible crime scene.

She sat alone outside on a bench in the canine exercise area at the Happy Pet Clinic. The dogs frolicked, chasing each other in circles.

She wept.

Brandy wept.

33

An Incidental Distraction and Small Consolations

It was the business of a priest not to show emotion others might feel in the face of death. Death, after all, was not death; it was not an end but a beginning. Brandy had said so hundreds of times while staring into the face of others' grief. He had gotten quite good at it, when required.

Yet, now alone with his grief, he sat for a time with his face in his hands and did not look up till a beeping phone receiver reminded him that he had not ended a call that would never end regardless. The rest of his life, he would hear the particular telephone ring of Harriet White's call, like all others, and yet like no other.

I just thought you should know, should know, should know... Harriet's words circled in an imagined loop, again and again, long after he had put the phone down. *Vincent dead? How could that be? It cannot be. It is. It cannot be...* Yet it was.

Vesuvio had never been the sort people could set their watches by. He had mastered the art of sudden appearances at the point others had given up hope. Brandy kept glancing at his phone, expecting it to ring again. Any minute, Harriet White would be calling back to say it all had been a case of mistaken identity.

When that failed to happen, he began piecing together the few details she provided. He concluded that whatever calamity had struck his friend must have transpired the very evening he had been on the phone with him. This left the old priest going over the ground Harriet had taken him, whether anything had been said, any hint of illness overlooked, that might have led to his death. He could come up with nothing more than his odd behavior, an apparent cold, and a late evening appointment.

If anything, Vesuvio had seemed uncharacteristically relaxed and sentimental, as if envisioning the stunning fact, not of his own demise, but of a man his friend called Crackerjack becoming pope and taking the name of Vincent. He could imagine Vesuvio laughing till his white teeth flashed within his red beard had he yet been living when the news came, Vincent of all names.

Besides, Vesuvio would have appreciated the irony of it: he could not have selected a better time to make his departure, one Vincent exiting to make room for another. Too soon, Vincent Vesuvio's life would begin to seem like one of those incidental distractions played in movie theaters before the main feature begins. His passing would be all but overlooked in a glut of memories and imagined outcomes swirling around the sudden elevation of the Iron Cardinal Cudahy. Vesuvio would have wanted it that way.

Brandy put his face in his hands again. *A man dies as he desires; his friend swallows the loss in exchange for small consolations.* Someone must have said it.

Fred, who for once looked up, seemed to agree. He pushed a rawhide chew toy across the floor. It lay at Brandy's feet. Fred was turning out to be a stoic.

34

The “Assisted” Suicide Notes

To Bernard Passmore’s consternation, the parish archive Blackbird had begun malfunctioning at times he most needed it. He had berated Margaret to the point of tears through two tugs on a bottle, gin in her left desk drawer; vodka on the right.

“This will never suffice, Smuggs. They are in there right now with their piffle heads together, and I can’t hear a thing.”

“Well, why don’t you just go in there, pull up a chair and ask to join the conversation? What about that, Bernie?”

Bernard raised his large hand. Margaret hunched down and closed her eyes. When she opened them, he had stormed out yelling over his back, “Smuggs, call that imbecilic Myerson at his shop. Tell him to replace the damn thing again, or I will have both of you by the throat!”

“Evil bastard!” Margaret muttered as she chugged another drink. “Put that in your pipe and smoke it—that’s what I say to you, Bernie Passmore. You will get yours one day. Much more of this, and I will be the one to see to it.” She fingered a letter-opener in her desk drawer.

Across the hall, in the archive room where Porky controlled the Blackbird’s chirps using a Wi-Fi disabler, Harriet was speaking.

“Father Vesuvio was such a good man. I suppose he may have had his secrets, but I could never think of him as having a hidden life. He was all dedication and service, a bit eccentric with the red beard and motorcycle and all that, and he hung around with Dusty Dwyer. Plenty of idle speculation about that connection. But it was his way—he was very accepting, a true missionary taking people as he found them. Strippers over at the Purple Palace were as much his flock as any of the holier-than-thou folk who light candles in the church as a public display of piety. You can bet on it, Wilbur."

Harriet and Porky, like many a long-married couple, had adopted each other's verbal tics. She looked up from the suicide note in its plastic sleeve spread out over a parish ledger book. Unfolded, it had begun to refold itself. "You can bet on it," she said again.

"It has no spelling mistakes, and is printed in block letters," said Porky.

"Just like the one left by the young man Fowler, but the slant is wrong for a left-handed writer."

"Another fake," said Porky. "Staged. Two murders staged as suicides, two weeks apart, in a hotel nobody should be able to get into. It makes my stomach hurt."

"We need to compare printing on those two notes. Printing is not exactly the same from one writer to the next. A little flourish here or there on both might reveal something. The killer made a mistake by trying the same thing twice. Try it once, and there is nothing to compare with. Wilbur, I would like to see both of them side by side. This has all the signs. It checks the boxes so far— proper indentations, words meant to sound like what somebody would imagine a suicide note to be in a story, but not a *real* suicide note, a body found in an unlikely place. A car parked to create suspicions. Let's have a look at the other note."

"I'll have it with me when I pick you up after work," said Porky. "And why leave his body in The Paradise of all places?"

"That's the first place I would think of to put a body I didn't know what to do with, if I had an easy way in. Planted there, I imagine, to make it seem like Father Vesuvio had a hidden life—wayward women and drugs, that sort of thing. The secret life stuff people suspect of priests these days, my dear, but Father Vesuvio?"

Harriet, unable to proceed, put her hand to her throat, struggling to swallow between reluctant words. "—I am sorry, Wilbur, but this is all so sad and so soon. Sometimes I hate being analytical. Father Vesuvio with a secret life? I don't think so. Whoever killed him wanted to kill both the man and his reputation. Two birds with one hateful stone. At times, Wilbur, dear heart, you can be so innocent, and I can feel so vulnerable."

Porky took her hand in his, gently raising it to his level standing beside her. He had always been amazed by his wife's steely brainpower alloyed with her tenderness. After some seconds of well-timed silence, he said, "Sometimes, Mrs. White, I think you should wear this badge, and I should work at the Happy Pet Clinic."

"That wouldn't be much fun, my dear. I like being an amateur sleuth, and you're allergic to cats."

"Okay, Wren, so how did the padre's body get dumped there? How did that Fowler kid get in there a couple of weeks ago? The Paradise is boarded up. The entrance my men use to check on things is double locked. We have the only keys. No sign of locks being tampered with. No sign of entry anywhere."

"Simple—there must be a way in that we don't know about—that's the stuff of those mysteries you read as a boy. Not very clever of the author to depend upon something like that, but real life often can seem like a second-rate story written with little imagination. Reality doesn't have to be clever. People confuse realism with cleverness. In fact, if there is one thing that can make novels seem unreal, it's how imaginative they are, the best of them, my dear. Life is seldom very imaginative; it just rolls along. I read years ago somewhere that mystery novels can have one secret passage, no more, but one is permissible—you know the molding in a closet wall that slides a certain way, or the full-length mirror that rotates to reveal a stairway or a hidden room—and one fake hairpiece, and no more than one lie to a reader."

"Maybe there is a tunnel from the Purple Palace to The Paradise. Now, that I can imagine. Maybe that is how those bodies got in there," suggested Porky, warming to the theory. He had read more than one novel with a secret passageway in it.

"Try not to imagine, my dear. It works better that way. Don't let your imagination dictate conclusions, even about secret tunnels."

"Do you think Dusty Dwyer is in on it?"

"No, I still think someone wanted to point us in that direction. That's why Father Vesuvio's car was left in his parking lot. It's too obvious," said Harriet. "What about fingerprints in the car?"

"Not a print anywhere," said Porky. "Figure that one out."

Harriet laughed. "The car must have driven itself there. We have been dealing all along with a perfectionist, usually the first people to make mistakes."

"I am going to question Dwyer anyway," said Porky.

"You might question some of his strippers also," said Harriet. "Just make sure they're fully clothed."

"You can bet on it," said Porky. "Somebody should inform the bishop and that new guy Brandy who was here for the Fowler funeral. I have been wondering about that."

"I have already informed both, of course leaving out any word of suicide or murder. With Bishop Norman I did mention the Hotel Paradise. I hope that was alright. Given obvious public relations implications, I thought he should be forewarned. —It's not every day a priest shows up dead in an abandoned hotel room."

Porky nodded. "From what you say, Brandy is the interim priest as of next month."

"His appointment was announced a week ago in our parish bulletin. As soon as word gets out, reporters will be all over this, even asking him questions. He will be besieged along with Bishop Norman."

"Did Brandy reveal anything?"

"He was cautious and genuinely saddened I think. Of course, I did not share details. And then, the victim's name being Vincent..."

"What does that have to do with it?"

"Our new pope, just elected. Pope Vincent grew up right here in northern Minnesota. There's a coincidence to invite conspiracy theories. Two Vincents on the same day. Some people will confuse the two and think our new pope has done himself in at the Hotel Paradise."

"Church stuff," Porky shrugged, "and out of my line. We're looking for a killer with a grudge and a score to settle."

Harriet smiled as she picked up her glasses. Once again, she had led her husband to a conclusion he could claim as his own. *Yes, a killer with a grudge.* "And, by the way, Father Brandy did mention that Father Vesuvio had a late evening appointment. It sounded routine."

"Nothing is routine when a guy shows up dead not long afterwards. Did he say anything else about it?"

"That is all he knew, but I checked with his appointment calendar in Margaret Smuggs' office. There was nothing on it. He was supposed to have the week off."

"This doesn't make sense," said Porky. "The guy has a week off, and still he has an appointment. It has to have a connection with his murder."

"Maybe or maybe not. You have a week off once in a while, Wilbur, and you're always getting calls from work."

"Okay, but his appointment still sounds to me like a lead we should follow up. You can bet on it."

"I intend to," said Harriet. "You will run into Bernard Passmore on your way out," said Harriet. "You can bet on that too."

Outside, her predictions for once proved partially mistaken. Bernard Passmore had not yet arrived at his parish bulletin board station after berating Smuggs and dancing from her office to his. He watched from an adjacent window as Porky retraced his steps through the locust trees to the hotel once more.

A moment later, Bernard was in the parish archive. "Harriet, is there any word on the whereabouts of Father Vesuvio? Margaret says no one has seen him, and yet both his car and his motorcycle are here."

"His car, Bernard?"

"It's in the Purple Palace lot. I noted its presence on my way here this morning," said Bernard.

Harriet once again removed her glasses to consider a response. “Most observant of you, Bernard. I am sure you will be among the first to hear.”

With Bernard brushed aside, and the door closed, she dialed Father Brandy’s number a second time, then changed her mind before the call went through. She had just discovered something in the parish registers, adjacent a page entry from forty years ago, announcing the appointment of a ‘recently-ordained’ Father Aloysius Brandy as an assistant pastor at St. Callixtus. The entry itself was routine, but a note from Father Vesuvio had been tucked between pages, inserted where her research was certain to lead her as she worked backward through the years. Its date was Pentecost, as it turned out, the last Sunday he served as pastor at St. Callixtus:

> Harriet, in the event something happens to me by the time you come upon this, think of the Song of Six Pence and the Knave of Hearts who stole some tarts.
> I am forced to speak in riddles in the hope that the merciful God who sometimes speaks to us in riddles beyond our vision, grants the same privilege to his faithful.
> I cannot be clearer without betraying the sacred trust a confessional grants even to scoundrels crossing its threshold.
> Nevertheless, averted vision is the best way to perceive something almost invisible.
>
> Pax vobiscum (you and Wilbur). Father Vesuvio.

With Porky in his squad car racing across Twin Rivers, and his Wi-Fi disabler gone with him, the Blackbird chirped once more in Bernard Passmore’s attentive ear. In the parish archive, Harriet sat alone, head down upon the parish register from forty years ago.

35

Two Friends Become One

Institutions of all sorts can project convenient anthropomorphic qualities, but nothing would be farther from the truth than to describe them as grief-stricken. A sudden death of one of their own can be inconvenient; it can require impromptu meetings and snap decisions; it can force a change in plans, and a burning of the midnight oil, but it can never lead to managerial mourning. The institution, whether a university, a church, or a government agency, shakes its collective head and moves on.

Bishop Norman's office had been notified that a body discovered in a routine patrol of the derelict Hotel Paradise had been tentatively identified as that of Father Vincent Vesuvio. Normally this news would have been received with the usual expressions and stoical acceptance: a man larger-than-life turned out to be mortal. How to replace him at the St. Brendan's Indian Chaplaincy, his pending assignment, would be the first concern. The second would be that a tumbledown hotel was an unfortunate place for a priest to die. Priests could die at their rectory, or while divesting after Mass, or in the course of Sunday dinner with a parishioner family. The Hotel Paradise would invite speculation.

On any ordinary day, public relations staff would have gone to the barricades, anticipating an onslaught of reporters with troublesome questions, but this was not an ordinary day. No one at the diocesan level, and no one working for a newspaper or a radio or television station could concentrate on anything local, even with possible local scandal in the picture. The problematic death of an obscure rural priest seemed farther away than Rome where Pope Vincent had blessed a crowd of patient well-wishers huddled beneath umbrellas and unfolded newspapers in a steady rain.

Whatever the outcome of Porky White's investigation, Vincent Vesuvio could not have picked a better day all around to die.

This was not lost on Bishop Norman's inner circle, where someone said, "Well, we can at least be thankful for that."

The first-ever American cardinal had taken the first-ever name of Vincent, after St. Vincent DePaul, a humble Franciscan servant among the poor whose name had long been identified with charitable endeavors worldwide, most notably connected with the society bearing his name (jubilation there as the news arrived).

By his surprising choice, Cardinal Cudahy was presumed to have signaled both a further assault on disproportionate wealth the world over and a renewed dedication to the Church's mission among the poor. Even if the saint had never before been so honored, who could find fault with a choice so bold?

Who but a thoroughly mystified Father Brandy could have seen the connection with yet another Vincent as nightmarish?

Brandy's two friends had become one.

He could pray for them using one name: God would know the difference. Any simplicity created by the new pope's choice of a name ended there. Both remained as Brandy last saw them: one Vincent, a freckle-faced boy named Crackerjack; the other, a man with blazing red hair and matching personality who less than three weeks ago had said, "Some of us priests learn after a while to be unspeakably false."

36

Nowhere and Somewhere

The search for Vincent Callixtus Vesuvio's next of kin came up empty-handed. Here and there a Vesuvio was found, but none who knew him. He seemed to come from nowhere, and then depart as he had come.

While Paradise County Law Enforcement investigated, details were withheld as they always are, and the exact cause of death remained unconfirmed. Despite these attempts at official secrecy, rumor of his apparent suicide rippled from one parish to another and from one priest to another across the diocese to Bishop Norman's office.

Harriet heard gossip and brought it home from a coworker at the pet clinic: allegedly a suicide note had been found.

"We have released no details," said Porky. "I found the note on the body even before the coroner showed up. Aside from the two of us, Charlie Cook, and a couple of rookies who would lose their jobs if they opened their mouths, nobody knows. So tell me, Wren, how did word leak out?"

"Answer that, Wilbur, and you probably will have found the murderer. Someone is trying to spin this story a certain way. It wouldn't be hard: people love gossiping about priests, and once that gets started, it will go everywhere..."

"Well, I hope this doesn't go everywhere: we have found out who owned the murder weapon," said Porky.

"And?"

"Delores Fowler. Figure that one out. I checked at the hospital. She couldn't take a step without falling down."

Harriet hesitated before suggesting that her house be searched.

"For once, I'm ahead of you on something, Wren."

Porky had already gotten a search warrant and been through Delores Fowler's house with a forensic team. They had found a box of cartridges in a bedside table drawer and fingerprints there and elsewhere, including on a home security keypad someone had used to gain entrance without setting off alarms. The prints were being evaluated.

"Mrs. Fowler traveled a lot and is known to be financially well off. It's not surprising that she subscribed to a security service," said Harriet. "I suppose the same holds true for the handgun, living alone as she has been of late."

Porky had also contacted the home security service which kept a time-date log of keypad use. Alarms had been disabled in the early morning hours of the day before the victim's body had been discovered in the hotel room.

"It looks like somebody with the correct keypad code took the gun, used it for the murder, and then left it behind as a suicide prop," said Porky. "If the fingerprints left at Delores Fowler's house happen to match with the ones we found in the rectory..."

"They will match, Wilbur. Of that you can be sure." She smiled. "Wow! This is turning out to be a really good mystery. Put it in a book, and it would be a bestseller."

"I'd rather put it before a judge," said Porky.

The next afternoon he had word on the fingerprints.

"Everything matches, Wren. The same prints left at Delores Fowler's house, those in the rectory, those on the gun handle, those of the victim, all the same."

"That leaves Bernard Passmore out. He didn't take the gun. I'm not surprised. The victim took the gun. We don't know why, but you can be sure he never intended that it be used the way it was. He knew Delores Fowler well enough to have had her home's security keypad code."

"We're back to Vesuvio," said Porky.

"We're back to somebody," said Harriet.

37

The Ways of God

It was not every day that a parish priest took his own life as the Apostle Judas is said to have done. Suicide in some quarters was thought to be the one unforgivable sin. Little could allay the suspicion that a priest who killed himself must have been leading two lives or perhaps three or four, and done something immoral and scandalous, if not illegal, to be blamed on celibacy, as if celibacy were more problematic and prone to waywardness than marriage.

Vesuvio had been by all accounts an exemplary priest, albeit a bee in any bishop's bonnet, but given the tenor of the times, who would believe some dark secrets were not hidden away in sealed files? Overnight, in the thoughts of eager detractors, Vesuvio had become *just another wayward priest skulking around, unable to live with his warped conscience. Awaiting identification? Awaiting exact cause of death? Why bother? Just ask one of Dusty's girls, or maybe more than one. They would recognize him even without his Roman collar.*

All such malicious speculation aside, bankers and jilted lovers were more prone to self-destruction than were parish priests, but priests were a special case. Inevitably people would wonder what had been going on beneath pious noses week by week and year by year. Old rumors reemerged of forgotten tunnels connecting St. Callixtus, the hotel, and the Purple Palace.

"Over the years, many priests might have been traipsing back and forth along those musty passages," declared Bernard Passmore from his sumptuous office chair, his personal version of *ex cathedra*. "Dusty Dwyer can import male prostitutes any time he wants, should his business require it." Bernard, himself from Chicago, knew of such things. The very thought of it made Margaret giggle with delight.

"Oh, there you go again, Bernie, making up such tales to make a mature woman blush."

"Any word about funeral arrangements, Margaret?"

"Not so far. Bishop Norman will probably do it at night when no one is looking."

As it turned out, Bishop Norman was almost that fretful. His office buzzed as seldom before: Pope Vincent on one hand with word of an impending journey to his homeland; a local priest apparently dead by his own hand on the other. Assistants and monsignors scurried about in a fog of apprehension as if a curious reporter might appear from nowhere any moment, or another shoe might drop.

Not a naïve man by any means, Bishop Norman saw the chance of the proverbial chicken coming home to roost, perhaps an entire flock. He also saw a fading opportunity for a transfer and promotion. The chicken coming home would be a reporter noting the coincidence of one of his parish priests ending his life on practically the same day and same hour that the pope took the priest's name for his pontificate.

Bishop Norman's head spun with attempted explanations, some of which were at his fingertips. "Coincidence" was good and serviceable with people in love with mysteries of the sort woven in popular novels like *The Judas Hand*, a bestseller by a Minnesota native.

More pious, biblical, and out of reach was a passage derived from the prophet Isaiah, known to all churchmen helping people grasp misfortune, tragedy, and sometimes mysterious and possibly scandalous coincidence:

"The ways of God are unknown to man."

Armed with this, Bishop Norman would be prepared.

He was a realist. As likely as not, no one would ask. He could relish for once the obscurity geography cast over such far-flung outposts as his northern Minnesota diocese and even farther flung outposts like Twin Rivers and St. Brendan's of Turning Wind. To be sure, this was sensational news wherever Vesuvio was known, yet after all, the dead priest was all but unknown. The world had attention deficit disorder. People would soon forget and get back to their favorite television programs. Bishop Norman closed his office to outsiders for the day and sent word that he was preoccupied preparing for an anticipated visit from the new pontiff.

All this, taken together in usually isolated and sidelined northern Minnesota, hit like a major earthquake whose deep-delved epicenter might have been located in the heart of Father Aloysius Brandy. There, memories of both friends—in fact the only two friends he ever had—Crackerjack and Vesuvio, heaved against each other like two sides of a major geological fault line.

The old priest, attempting to pray for both friends, studied his hands.

They trembled.

38

Two Vincents

When arriving as interim at St. Callixtus, Father Brandy appeared unperturbed.

As he saw it, it was the duty of a parish priest to appear unperturbed, even when events cutting close to the personal grain caused disturbance and bafflement. He had lost a friend named Vincent, apparently by his own hand, and his old friend Jack Cudahy inexplicably had taken the name Pope Vincent. Now, he had two friends named Vincent, one passing out of his life as another metamorphosed into a position unimagined. Here was enough to make anyone appear perturbed for months afterwards, and yet Father Brandy managed not to seem perturbed—not at Vesuvio's funeral Mass, at St. Norbert's when he prepared for his departure, nor at St. Callixtus when he arrived.

The morning of Vesuvio's funeral Mass, no one had been able to think of anyone other than Pope Vincent. Every time the name Vincent was said, all thought focused on Cardinal Cudahy. It might have been his funeral. Crackerjack, not Father Vesuvio, might have been the man laid to rest on Heaven's doorstep in a casket before the altar. His funeral, with Bishop Norman celebrant, became a matter of going through motions with diocesan thoughts elsewhere. It took place midweek with the Bishop flanked by priests of the diocese. The usual arrangements would be safe harbor for an occasion so unusual.

Brandy had been granted his request to do the readings.

An hour afterward, only Brandy would remember much about it. Three weeks later, when he moved into his new home at St. Callixtus, onlookers would never have guessed that his world, having changed forever, was far from becoming familiar.

Ahead of him lay a weekend whose Sunday afternoon reception would have the usual speeches and jokes, all bent on welcoming Brandy into a world where his friend Vincent had once lived and was still of recent memory. He would live in the same house and pace the same rooms trying to fashion a homily. He would nap on a sofa where Vesuvio seemed to have been napping when he last spoke to him. He would gaze out windows where Vesuvio had gazed. He would see himself in mirrors where Vesuvio's face had been reflected. He would take his friend's place at functions. His weeks would end and begin. The liturgical year would move forward through the usual Sundays in Ordinary Time, but the times were not ordinary in any other sense.

Through it all, he would continue to appear unperturbed, wound around and within himself as tightly as an onion in its papery husk. Not a day would go by through all his remaining days without somewhere in his thoughts the flashing eyes, the white teeth, the flaming beard, and the lost companionship of his friend, who like him had always kept going regardless.

Of course, there would be selfishness in it. Vincent would have understood.

For a long time past, each of them had had no one else to turn to. It was the world's way, even for those who made friends more readily than they did. They both had been born into a crowded world no larger than a small classroom among ragtag boys and girls.

At first, that world increased and multiplied as days went on, effortlessly without apparent need for their creation. And then, out of sight somewhere, without fanfare or notice, that world began to shrink, as it does for all, both for the great and for the obscure. Soon hardly anybody at one's elbows could be expected to understand. None were old enough to remember what their elders knew. The past, once so richly populated, had become a foreign country of threatened species.

But for some few, like Jack Cudahy, the world eventually became the whole world, with their names on everybody's lips. Meanwhile, Brandy and Vesuvio, years from knowing each other, right off began to concentrate in smaller worlds requiring attention to detail and duty. The two of them could hustle, as full of business as anyone described these days as a workaholic. They could be every bit as busy as the Iron Cardinal, but theirs were very small worlds. Their labors were known to few, and their names only on the lips of those they served doing the works of days and hands.

39

In Retrospect

One day, a priest named Aloysius Brandy and another named Vincent Vesuvio by chance occupied adjacent chairs at an archdiocesan gathering. Each had already been present a dozen times at ceremonial events swollen for edification of the great. They might even have shaken hands without giving it much thought. Neither cared a fig for such stuff and would rather have been home preparing a pastor's greeting for next Sunday's bulletin, or on a pleasant walk conversing with a friend. Neither knew another.

Out of nowhere, the way an unseen bell will sometimes peal from the other side of distant hills, Vesuvio said, "I have seen you here before."

The meeting had broken up. They went out together into a broad hallway where long tables had been set up. Earnest sorts struggled for position nearest a bishop or an auxiliary while clasping a paper cup of colorful, sweet mints. Smiles went around. Fathers Brandy and Vesuvio, coffee cups in hand, had retreated to a corner without either asking the other if he minded being joined. It seemed so natural, as if they had been doing this through a long lifetime.

"I used to play cribbage with that fellow over there," confided Vesuvio, pointing to a priest in animated exchanges with several others. "I think I beat him once too often by always drawing Jacks, so now he has other games to play—cynical of me to think so."

"It was a popular pastime among my father's friends on the Iron Range," said Brandy. "He died years ago, and these days almost no one knows how to play it."

"The Iron Range, eh? Ever try your hand at mumblety-peg?"

"Would you believe I used to play mumblety-peg with a sixth-grade classmate who is now a higher-up in Rome?"

"Now there's a connection my old cribbage partner would pursue. You're a lucky fish to have that name to drop."

"I don't drop names. Regardless, he would not remember me."

"Sorry, I misspoke ... mind if I ask his name?"

"I knew him as Crackerjack. These days he is known as Cardinal John Cudahy."

"Ah, now there's a powerhouse Jack to draw from the cribbage deck, the Iron Cardinal! Crackerjack! —My name is Vincent, Vincent Vesuvio." He held out a hand to give Brandy's, much the smaller, a hearty shake.

"At All Saints on the Iron Range, Jack and I were both *It* in games of tag," Brandy ventured.

White teeth flashed. A broad grin emerged from within a fiery red beard. In the nick of time in their shrinking worlds, a friendship began for two men who had always had a hard time making and keeping friends. They became Aloy and Vincent, standing alone in a corner. Years passed.

And now at diocesan gatherings Brandy would be alone again in the usual corner.

By the time he took up his post at St. Callixtus, the celebrations and expectations swirling around the new Pope Vincent had subsided everywhere but in the remote country of his birthplace. There, a few reporters still attempted to scratch up crumbs of Cardinal Cudahy's history, surprisingly little of it to be found by even the most diligent researchers. Cudahy's parents were long since dead, their lives no more transparent than when they had settled in the walled mansion compound of Brandy's hometown.

Few records could be located. The new pope's origins seemed as detached and obscure as those of Vincent Vesuvio. Northern Minnesota, having the sort of place Central Africa occupies in some imaginations, little was made of this. Rumor had it that Cardinal Cudahy's main rival for the pontificate had been a Congolese cardinal, equally obscure.

People growing up deep within continents, whether of imagination or of geography, were not expected to have well-articulated family trees.

Closing of Box Three

BOX FOUR

A BOX CALLED A CONFESSIONAL

I sometimes think of religion for most of us as a bicycle with training wheels. We never really learn to ride it until the wheels come off. That is when anything can happen. When the wheels come off, faith kicks in.

–VINCENT VESUVIO

40

A Papal Visit

Vincent Vesuvio had not been declared dead a month when Pope Vincent announced his intention to visit his Minnesota homeland. What was described as a personal pilgrimage would take place in late August. It was now early July.

Though unsurprising, the news immediately upended routines in Bishop Norman St. Claire's world, no longer an all but forgotten outpost of the Church Universal, or so the bishop thought at first. A mixture of jubilation, consternation, opportunism, and panic took over. For a time, the papal visit seemed to become the sole reason the diocese existed. No one could think of anything else. Contacts with the Vatican came by the hour instead of seasonally. Bishop Norman could best be described as beside himself and blowing hot or cold depending on what minute it happened to be and what was the latest word arriving from Rome. The most recent latest words were not to his liking. He seemed destined to play second fiddle to an old priest named Brandy who admitted pushing the new pope into a mud puddle.

In an age when popes travel the globe, of course, the Vatican has its own experienced appointees making travel arrangements and avoiding mud puddles. Where the pope will stop, where he will spend his nights, what he does, and whom he sees must all be planned and orchestrated. However modest and unassuming the reigning prelate may be, his travels inevitably put the entire Church on display. Much of the planning is top-down. A bit of it is trickle-up. Much is prescribed by tradition and protocol. That the pope is both a head of state and the head of a billion-member Church adds complexity and drama at times. History is being made with his footsteps.

The pope's mission can be both diplomatic and evangelical. Popes, for example, never attend public banquets for feasting with dignitaries and exchanging toasts as do other heads of state. Popes never eat in public. Each day will include a Mass and a visit to a school or other place where children will be present. The Church being feudal in its administrative structure, no one will tell the pope what he must do. His preferences will weigh heavily, while occasions will be tailored to highlight local ecclesiastical dignitaries. Cardinals, archbishops, and bishops will be on display. Public officials–mayors, governors, senators, presidents, and monarchs will be accorded their moments with the pope.

This will create the usual photo opportunities, especially valued by politicians with Catholic constituencies. These days, security concerns will be paramount throughout. No one wants to have a pope assassinated on their watch. There will be a culminating rally, a papal Mass involving Catholic youth especially, and a final blessing.

Since little was known about Cardinal Cudahy's formative Minnesota years, itinerary details were expected to shed light upon his childhood and upbringing. Anyone anticipating this was destined to be disappointed. There would be no visit to parental graves, no stopping at a place of birth, no church where a christening or a confirmation took place. One might well have wondered what there was about northern Minnesota that allowed the pope to regard it as home. Since much of his early life was presumed to have been in Bishop Norman's backyard, that prelate vacillated between feeling snubbed and feeling relieved of a burden.

He would be on hand when Pope Vincent's chartered Alitalia flight landed in the Twin Cities. He would stand in a row of greeters on the tarmac behind the archbishop, first in line. Pope Vincent's visit would begin with a Mass at the Saint Paul Cathedral and end with a Mass at the Basilica of Saint Mary in Minneapolis, five days later. The papal itinerary would include the state capitol, a meeting with the governor, and brief stops at Catholic universities. Traveling by car, after an early morning Mass at the Benedictine Abbey at Saint John's in Collegeville, the pope would then visit All Saints School on the Minnesota Iron Range. All this might have been easy to anticipate, but at the same time, left Pope Vincent's youth as much in the dark as ever.

Bishop Norman's index finger traced the pontiff's tentative itinerary with a marching song drumbeat while his thoughts raced ahead to a place he failed to find there, his own cathedral which appeared to have been wiped off the papal map. "Astonishing" was his private word for it. He could not but wonder why the pope was visiting at all when his time in northern Minnesota at this point included only two places.

The visit to his Catholic grade school, scene of his games with Aloysius Brandy, might have been expected; but in a stroke unforeseen, Pope Vincent would travel west from there to stop at St. Callixtus in Twin Rivers. It seemed unlikely that the pontiff would have known his childhood friend was serving as its interim pastor, but as fate would have it—if fate it was—the two would meet.

The tentative itinerary was silent on where he would spend the night. If he left Twin Rivers by two, he would arrive in North Port City at approximately six. *Surely that is the plan*, said Bishop Norman to himself, convinced that the pontiff would hardly overnight at the St. Callixtus rectory on a broken-down bed in the company of field mice and church crickets when a sumptuous mansion suite awaited him at North Port. A note at the itinerary's conclusion offered hope: "Further details forthcoming."

Bishop Norman pressed a button on his desk. "Put a call through to Father Aloysius Brandy at St. Callixtus. I need to speak with him."

By the time Father Brandy was on the phone, Bishop Norman's tone had softened.

"Aloysius, have your heard the latest?"

Once he had heard the latest, the old priest collapsed in a heap on what only weeks before had been Vincent Vesuvio's sofa. As sofas go in church rectories, if anything, it sagged more than most. On an opposite wall was tacked a

St. Callixtus Parish calendar. August seemed not quite far enough away, August of all months, the very month he last saw Crackerjack, ending a game of tag begun long ago.

41

Far from Alone and Far from Lucky

When word arrived of Pope Vincent's impending visit to St. Callixtus, complexities far beyond the poor condition of church rectory sofa springs arrived with it. A lot needed to be done in short order, and so something resembling a countdown before a missile launch began. It is said of the British royal family that wherever they turn up, the smell of fresh paint seems to precede them. Much the same is true of a visiting pope.

His visit hastened greased skids already under The Hotel Paradise. That monumental eyesore had to be eliminated before the pontiff arrived. George Cobb, whose company held the demolition contract, was duly notified. For the first time in recent years, St. Callixtus parishioners were of one mind: The Paradise had to go, the sooner, the better. Neither paint nor locust tree grove nor George's foot-dragging could save it.

Given the prominence of music in any Church affair this notable, one might have expected Bernard Passmore to step forward with an ambitious music program. Instead, he withdrew into shadows as if intimidated by events at hand and uncertain of his next move. An adversary might have been thought to approach.

"I am honestly quite surprised at Bernard's lack of enthusiasm," said Harriet to her husband. "I mean, we will be expected to do something special for the new pope, but he hardly mentions it, and seems afraid. That is very unlike him." She had more in mind than she was prepared to say.

Porky received this news with the distracted attitude of a man who had, as the saying goes, other fish to fry. Two murders weeks apart, so far described as suicides, both of them public, had helped seal the fate of Hotel Paradise.

They might also be sealing his fate as next in line to become Paradise County sheriff if he didn't soon come up with explanations, especially for how the hotel—under his watch—had been the scene of bloody mayhem. What else had happened there that had not yet come to light? The public, voters in this case, could be excused for wondering. Nonetheless, his investigation of both murders was inevitably derailed by security preparations for the pope's visit.

At this point, he considered Dusty Dwyer a suspect for no better reason than that Dusty was a 'shady' character. Harriet counseled otherwise, pointing out that in most detective novels, shady characters turn out to be distractions.

Harriet was convinced that the Purple Palace's owner had balanced the evil of women stripping for money versus women in thrall to ruthless pimps and launched an idealistic rescue mission using the lesser of two evils to pay for it. She awaited the right moment to share further evidence with Porky. A former stripper now working as a Mercy Hospital receptionist was living proof. With further inquiry, she had discovered that Dusty already had three nurses, an elementary school teacher, and a PhD candidate to his credit.

There was nothing obviously illegal about Dusty's activities, but still it was awkward. She could already hear holier-than-thou sorts howling that the end does not justify the means, no matter that they themselves did nothing but click tongues and point fingers. If Porky pounced on Dusty, then she would intervene. Meantime, young women were being saved, at least some of them.

An ambitious project like Dusty's could not stay secret for long. With so many of Dusty's 'girls' involved, word was bound to leak out. After a while, everyone would know. In the cryptic note Father Vesuvio left behind, Dusty Dwyer had to be "the Knave of Hearts who stole some tarts."

Among others who already knew could be Bernard Passmore. A subpoena had been required, but Porky obtained Passmore Bus Company records. He left these with Harriet to examine while he dealt with papal visit security arrangements threatening to overwhelm Paradise County law enforcement resources. She soon discovered that the Purple Palace had purchased numerous tickets in recent years, most of them one-way from Chicago. Almost half remained unused. Melody Stillwater had been far from alone and far from the luckiest.

Bernard Passmore would have known all about it.

42

Smuggs Spills Beans and Drops a Note

Gossipy, chattering parish secretary Margaret Smuggs, swilling booze on the job, accumulated fuzzy information like a dust bunny trapped in a confessional.

Over the months of Harriet's work in the parish archives, Margaret had glommed onto her as a confidant. She would reliably interrupt whenever Bernard was nowhere around St. Callixtus. The chance moment arriving, she would slip into the archive, close the door as if she thought slamming it would unleash a bomb blast, and like a fifty-something schoolgirl perch on a table with her legs dangling.

Today, Tuesday, an hour before noon in an arid July, maturing wheat stood upright and burnished in valleys beyond Twin Rivers, and Bernard Passmore went golfing with a mayor, a building inspector, the local Chamber of Commerce president, and a state representative. Harriet would be in the archive for yet another hour, the same as every weekday for the past six months whatever the weather.

Nonetheless, in strolled Margaret feigning surprise. Not an ordinary liar, she lied in thinly-sliced, sandwiched layers, but as with overstuffed sandwiches, something was bound to slip out.

"Dearie, I thought you had left for the day, as hot as it is. Excuse me, I didn't mean to butt in."

Like many drunks, Margaret reeked courtesy between explosions. She had been commandeered in her 'spare' church time to tally rent receipts for the Passmore Riverside Trailer Park. On top of that, having endured a series of threats and insults from Bernard, she had more blood in her eye than alcohol in her bloodstream, albeit plenty of both. She began with the usual praise preceding hateful harangues, and then...

"I only know what I hear from Bernie—Bernie knows things even Father Vince doesn't know."

"I have sometimes thought that myself, Margaret." Agreeability—as Porky often said—was the green go-light of a competent interrogator.

Margaret sped ahead.

"Well, Dearie, I suppose there's plenty of dirt upright ladies like the both of us can't go into, stuff that goes on behind the scenes in some churches like this one."

"It happens all the time—gossip, Margaret. I am sure you mean *idle* gossip, but be careful what you say in here."

Harriet had been awaiting an opportunity to point knowingly toward the ceiling beam with its Blackbird.

Margaret waved her off.

"Oh, don't worry about that, Dearie. I always turns Blackbirdie off when I come in here with something that Bernie would ring my neck for saying. Of course, he almost slugged me the other day because this birdie never seems to work right, and he says that is my fault, when it isn't. And now he expects me to do his business work on church time, as if I don't have enough to do. But this ain't gossip, and it sure isn't idle. You could never put it in your computer. It might crash on you or have one of those power surges that destroys things."

Harriet, closed her laptop lid, removed her reading glasses, looked up, and arched an eyebrow as if to say, 'Ready when you are.'

"Years ago, Bernie's office was right next door to our one-and-only confessional. That's why Father Vince moved him down the hall. Too close for comfort where he was. Some walls are thin, and Bernie says—of course I shouldn't tell you this—that sometimes before he was moved, he could hear a mumbling of sinners the other side, and then what the priest says in return."

"Absolution and penance?"

"Word for word, because back then before he was moved, Bernie used one of those thing-a-ma-jigs that doctors uses."

"A stethoscope?" Harriet blanched.

"That's it, Dearie! You hit the nail on the head, a stethoscope with a special attachment, so he could hear even better with it. Bernie says he could hear a pin drop in the confessional, and he drilled a little hole though the wall, so he could see who was in there with their sins. He used one of those spyglasses you sometimes see in hotel doors, so you know who's on the other side."

Harriet forced her eyebrows not to rise.

"Then he went and confessed to Father Vince that he'd been listening to everybody's sins and for proof told him one of the biggest ones he heard just the other day, close to the bone. Father Vince on account of the Seal of Confession, could never tell anyone.

"He says Father Vince moved his office out of spite, because priests want to keep all those sins to themselves, and not share them. But Bernie outsmarted him. He went hi-tech with those black, chirpy things. There was no stopping him."

"Blackbirds, plural?"

"You hit the nail on the head again, Dearie. Those Blackbirds he has chirping here and in the confessional, and in Father's office—all wireless. Now, he can just relax in his office and record."

"He records confessions? He's bugged Father's office?" Harriet, hand to her throat , had become the soprano in a frantic recitative.

Margaret rocked from side to side with her palms down supporting her on the table. She eyed Harriet for her next move as a bird-of-prey might ponder a wren.

"No, busy as I am with other things, recording is my job. He expects me to do that, and keep track of his Blackbirds, like the one in here that breaks down all the time. He wants recordings in case somebody won't take his word for it. And when he misses something important, he yells at me.

"You would never catch me going to Confession here. That's for sure. Bernie would know all about it—not that I ever had much to confess, but as Bernie says, everybody has something to hide. That's what he wants to know about, so he can get the upper hand. He knows about the banker who had property that would be a good spot for the new St. Callixtus. He knows about the banker's girlfriends. He knows about wives too, and some that are stepping out on husbands. He knows who sometimes goes in the back door of the Purple Palace to have a squint. Those jezebellies and Dusty Dwyer with his *Girls! Girls! Girls!* sign drive Bernie out of his mind. He can't get the goods on 'em when it's right out in the open. So he found another way..."

"Another way?"

"Chicago, and he gets paid for it," said Margaret before putting her hand over her mouth and changing the subject. "–Who knows what Dusty's real name is? George Cobb stumbled into my office yesterday to ask me if I knew. What that had to do with blowing up The Paradise and cutting down the trees, I would like to know. 'Maybe it's *George*, just like yours,' I said. That really floored him."

"But you were saying something about Bernard and Chicago, Margaret?"

"No, I wasn't. Don't go there, Dearie. I was saying Bernie heard something you better not write about, but lately he's been lording it over me like he thinks I'm his slave, and he is some sort of King Tut. You won't tell anyone, will you? Bernie would kill me."

"He heard something ... Blackbirds?"

"No, before that, poor Dearie, with his stellascope, and the shame is, he couldn't record it. Promise not to tell?"

Harriet raised her trembling hand across her skip-beating heart. "Bernie gets lots of money he doesn't want anybody to know about. It comes in packets from Rome with Vatican Post Office stamps on 'em. They don't come here, but to a private post office box. I have seen some, and even cut a few stamps off because they're so interesting, those Vatican stamps, with pictures of the popes as they comes and goes, and pretty things by that Mike Angel guy..."

"Michelangelo?"

"Another nail smack dab on the head! Bernie expected to have a special invitation for his choir to sing in Rome, in the Cisternian Chapel, and lots of money to pay our way. And now that's not happening, he says, and we won't be going to the St. Paul Cathedral and that Basilica place in Minneapolis either, so he is burnt and angry about everything and blames this new Pope Vincent since everything changed when he got picked.

"You might say the worm has turned. Bernie means to get at him anyway he can, and he says there is ways to teach even a pope what's what. Hee! Hee! He knows who that poor Fowler boy's father is, and why Delores was always going to Rome and places along the Medi ... Mediterrarium. It all came out when she confessed to Father Vince."

At that point, Margaret jumped from her table perch. She had put several new satellites into Harriet's orbit. She squinted and smiled, as if measuring the dazed Mrs. White and seeming to say, *Do something about it, and we'll see what happens. Either way, I won't mind.*

Harriet in a dead stare at sunlight flickering upon the table got the message.

"And so here's the thing, Dearie—I've saved the best for last. All along, he isn't even who he says he is. All the way from his tippy toes to his chinny-chin-chin he's somebody else!"

Margaret's grin was tremendous; her eyes glistened and seemed to enlarge beyond the glittering sequined rims of her glasses. She nodded, folding her arms into self-satisfaction, living up to her name.

Harriet spoke slowly as if silently spelling each letter before she said it. "What are you saying, Margaret? Are you saying the new pope is somebody else?"

As so often happens at moments like this, a question goes unanswered. Bernard Passmore barged into the archive, his golf engagement having been postponed. Harriet drew a deep breath.

"Too hot for golf," bellowed Bernard dripping sweat. "What's that damnable George Cobb doing encouraging trespass? The idiot is talking to that atheist lowlife who dared taunt me when I chased him off. The cur!"

George had been waylaid by a street merchant sitting beneath an umbrella now shifted ten feet onto Hotel Paradise property.

The parish secretary, suddenly become a picture of uncorrupted innocence, waltzed behind Bernard out of the archive to a conference room window where George could be seen purchasing a small black dog with white ears.

Trembling as she gathered up the day's notes, Harriet swept up a slip of paper Margaret had left behind—intentionally or accidentally. Her cellphone rang as she left the church. Porky, on the scene of an altercation in the Paradise Trailer Park, would be late.

Minutes later, Harriet flagged George Cobb as he was driving away.

"George, Porky's tied up, and I need a lift to the Happy Pet Clinic. Can you take me there?"

"Hop in," said George. "I just bought this dog for Phyllis. What do you think?"

George's purchase bounded onto Harriet's lap and began licking her face.

"This is not love at first sight, George. Your dog has seen me before. Every time somebody buys him, they bring him to the clinic for rabies shots. Next thing, he runs back to his owner and gets sold all over again. He has had enough rabies shots for ten lifetimes. If he had many more, he would probably explode. I'm afraid you've been conned, and you're not the only one."

"I paid fifty bucks for him," said George.

"Don't let him out of your sight, and skip the rabies shots," said Harriet.

The note Margaret had dropped came out of her handbag as she reached for her cellphone. "Wilbur, I caught a ride with George. Meet me at the veterinary clinic instead of the church. This is big, very, very big! I may have been a fool. I just don't know."

"Life sure is strange, all sides of it," said George.

"You could bet on it, but I wish I knew what it is," said Harriet, glancing at the note.

From the desk of Margaret Smuggs
St. Callixtus Parish Secretary:

Confidential: MAURICE FOWLER

43

The Silent Witness of ancient Trees

The rivers of Twin Rivers were the North Crow and the South meandering snakelike either side of a northern continental divide.

In naming them, the indigenous Indians knew where they flowed; the pioneer settlers thought they knew better. And so what they called the 'North' Crow streamed south without regard to geography, terrain, and common sense, and the 'South' Crow went north. This could never be corrected.

As Vincent Vesuvio once said to his friend Brandy, *Hell is knowing you can never change what happened* –especially hellish when it turns out to be mistaken.

The Happy Pet Clinic had been built near one of the city's several bridges on the site of what had once been a blacksmith's and farrier's divided stable. Patient horses awaited shoeing and hoof-trimming on one side. Once those jobs were done, they awaited their owners on the other. The lone remnants of this era were black gnats in coiling colonies above the stream and a gigantic, ancient riverside poplar whose delicate catkins had fallen on Harriet's hair and on her bench where wind arranged and rearranged them into furry heaps while Pet Clinic dogs of spring and early summer came and went as had the horses before them.

Harriet, the determined researcher of surroundings, knew that the river poplar could be as much as two centuries old.

She was not given to hyperbole. When she said big, she meant big, when she said very big, she meant very. When she said fake, she meant thoroughly fake. When she said that George Cobb had been taken to the cleaners, she meant he had been swindled. When Margaret Smuggs said chinny-chin-chin as Passmore barged in, she meant either St. Callixtus or the Church of Rome had been misled by someone who was somebody else.

Who was somebody else?

She gazed up into the river poplar whose branches cast shadows like a sundial in the pet enclosure marking time and changing seasons. The spaces between held answers.

It can't be must have been uttered there a dozen times in decades past by people seeking the truth with nowhere to turn but the river and its poplar.

44

Confidential

Margaret Smuggs' tantalizing allusion connecting Bernard Passmore to Chicago had been but one ricocheting shot in a fusillade. Her target had clearly been Dusty Dwyer and what Bernard regarded as his abhorrent Purple Palace strippers. He could not control them through exposure the same way he controlled others. Yet his fastidious hypocrisy urged him on until he found a way to get at the strippers by way of Chicago. Was this what Margaret almost said before theatrically gagging herself? Still, the shot had been fired, and for Harriet it struck home in Melody Stillwater's one-way bus ticket to Twin Rivers, purchased from the Passmore Bus Company.

Harriet decided not to share this with her husband pending further research. She suspected that Bernard had discovered the many bus tickets in his company records and somehow alerted Chicago gangsters involved in sex trafficking. Going forward, every time a bus ticket was purchased, Bernard informed his Chicago contacts and probably was paid so much per head. This in turn led to the beating death of Melody Stillwater, Jane Blue's cousin. Phillip Fowler responded by confronting Bernard, and Dusty responded by no longer using bus tickets. That puzzle piece had been at her fingertips ever since a passenger van pulled into the Purple Palace parking lot the day she and Porky were walking in the hotel alley. Four women got out. The driver was Rita Fajita.

Rita and possibly even Dusty could be questioned, and digital versions of Chicago newspapers were available at the History Center. She might be able to connect violence against prostitutes with dates on Passmore Bus Company tickets. Meantime, there was enough that had to be revealed with Porky all but overwhelmed by papal visit security arrangements.

From her bench in the pet exercise yard she looked up as he peered through a wrought iron fence where pet leads hung. He looked so earnest. Not telling him everything he needed to know was never easy.

He opened a gate and sat beside her.

"What? Who? Wren, you look like you have been trying to bathe a cat by the tail."

"This isn't a cat, but it is a tale, Wilbur.... This isn't sadness. It's anger, and it's awful. That man is awful. That woman is awful. Do you know what they've been doing?"

Porky not only did not know what they had been doing, he had yet to hear who *they* were.

"Bernard Passmore—I am not sure I will be able to sing for him again. I am not sure I will be able to stand the sight of him. The man is a fiend.

"I heard it all from Margaret Smuggs—when she was drunk of course."

Harriet began an uncharacteristically scrambled summary of Margaret's revelations. When she got as far as the stethoscope and the tiny spyglass in the wall before Bernard's office was moved, Porky interrupted her.

Having sometimes wished that wiretapping possible criminals did not require a court order, he was less affected by Bernard Passmore's confessional shenanigans. Briefly, he felt envious. As a lawman, he was fond of confessions, even if he did not understand the Catholic sort, especially with its promise of secrecy that seemed to protect criminals from exposure.

"Wren, *blackmail* and *extortion* are felonies. It won't be the easiest thing to get the goods on Passmore, since his victims have so much to hide. Going to the police and getting into court would bring their secrets out in the open. Other than that, we could nail them both, for *criminal trespass*, but that is small change as charges go. —As accomplice and possible co-defendant, Smuggs might want out, and be willing to turn state's evidence in exchange for a plea bargain. Do you think she would cooperate?"

"I'm not sure. Bernard is clearly abusive. She seems to be somewhere between admiring his genius and revulsion. For all I know she got into a drunken hissy fit and might already regret tattling on him, but at least we have her story: Bernard Passmore is blackmailing half of Twin Rivers. Anybody who's ever done anything he regrets and came to St. Callixtus for forgiveness is now under Bernard's thumb, and it doesn't stop there. While bugging the confessional, he heard something someone in the Vatican wants to keep secret. He's been getting hush money, lots of it, coming straight from the Vatican Post Office. Whatever he knows must be important. The entire Church could be rocked by a revelation big enough to justify paying blackmail on the level he is collecting. Wilbur, what's to be done?"

"*Tax evasion*," said Porky. "Maybe the state or the feds could get Passmore for tax evasion, but that takes time to prosecute."

"Margaret says he mixes the money with church collection money and money from his other businesses, because what he gets from Rome is new bills."

"*Money laundering!*" Porky had several beanbags in the air, each with a different crime on it.

Harriet took a deep breath before adding yet another, the suicide notes she had been studying before Margaret barged in.

"I'm no handwriting expert, far from it, but they have striking similarities, especially the capital E's and a capital F. Odd flourishes used with both letters. They were probably written by the same person, whoever killed *both* Phillip Fowler and Father Vesuvio. I have an idea who that might be."

Porky knew better than to ask. When Harriet was ready to say, she would say. He lowered his head in thought for a moment. He had gathered DNA samples of both victims as evidence. This was standard procedure, along with fingerprinting, an autopsy, and a search for second party DNA that may have been left at a crime scene by the perpetrator. The killer had been careful; nothing of that sort had been left behind, but what was the thread, if any, uniting these two men in a common fate?

"Okay, Wren, so what could connect both Vesuvio and Phillip Fowler? I have twice questioned the young Ojibwe woman Jane Blue. She is shy and evasive, but she knows something. You can bet on it."

"Think about it, Wilbur. She has had a cousin beaten to death and lost the father of her baby. She doesn't have to know more than that to be afraid. Both Phillip and Father Vesuvio must have had serious run-ins with Bernard. We know Father's would have been about Bernard's eavesdropping on the confessional.

Porky nodded. "So why didn't Vesuvio fire Passmore on the spot, and boot him out the door? It doesn't make any sense."

"It does, if you consider that Bernard would have immediately appealed to the parish council, and the Seal of Confession would have prevented Father from providing an explanation. Besides, the parish council is a deck stacked in Bernard's favor; half of them are victims of his eavesdropping, and the rest are SNFA members." "Well, at least with Vesuvio out of the way, Passmore doesn't have to worry about keeping his own butt covered. Now he can pretty much do what he wants."

"Wow! There's his motive, Wilbur."

More than anything else in his detective work, Porky loved a credible motive. Dusty Dwyer dropped several notches on Porky's suspect list making room for Bernard Passmore. "He knows Latin, right?"

"Of course, but he calls it 'piffle' stuff. His favorite word."

"First thing, Wren, can you get hold of a sample of something printed by Passmore, something with a capital E and F? Maybe, just maybe.... And second, I have a plan to catch him in the act. When are Confessions next on the church schedule?"

"Saturday, an hour before the Vigil Mass."

"I'll be there, Wren. I am going to Confession."

Harriet laughed. "Wow! Are you serious?"

"I'm serious, the first in line, but we will need to involve your Father Brandy in baiting a trap."

"We need to involve him regardless. Our new pastor can't be hearing confessions while this is going on. If Bernard pulls the same stunt with him that he did with Father Vesuvio, he will use the confessional as an escape hatch. Father Brandy will soon be tongue-tied by the Seal of Confession.

"And speaking of baiting, my dear, does the name *Maurice Fowler* ring a bell?"

45

Following a Trail through Time

Overnight, word arrived of Delores Fowler's death.

Foregoing work in the church archive, Harriet followed what was more instinct than a hunch to Twin Rivers' Mercy Hospital. One of Dusty Dwyer's strippers, no longer working at the Purple Palace, had found employment as a receptionist at the hospital's front desk where protocols required all visitors to sign in and sign out.

Since the receptionist was among those regularly attending Mass at St. Callixtus, Harriet soon small-talked her way to the past three month's records of hospital patient visitors, almost two hundred dog-eared pages in a registration book with names largely illegible.

"If you came in tomorrow," said the receptionist, "you wouldn't have had so much to look at it. When that one is full, we start a new book and throw the old one out. As you can see, we have two pages to go."

In a nearby chair, Harriet leafed through the book cradled in her lap. She studied the entries from the day before to the first week of the month and from there back to June and May, to the date Father Vesuvio's body was discovered in the Hotel Paradise. Maurice Fowler had signed in on three successive evenings that week using a firm hand identifying himself as the patient's brother.

"You wouldn't by chance remember this man, *Maurice Fowler*?" asked Harriet.

The receptionist smiled. "Normally I wouldn't, but that was my first week at this desk, and they put me on an evening shift. I don't remember him from the first two, so many people come and go, but the last time he came in at the end of routine visiting hours and asked if he could see his sister."

"His sister?"

"Yes, his sister. He said he had to leave tomorrow on a long trip and wanted to say goodbye to her. I waved him through to the elevators, and when he came out, maybe fifteen minutes later, he left this with me as a thank you."

From her handbag, she retrieved a rosary of purple rose beads. "He said it might turn out to have been blessed by the future pope. And one more thing, Mrs. White..."

"What?"

"He had been crying. I will never forget that. He was such a stern-looking man, dressed in black. You wouldn't have expected to see him in tears."

"Do you recall anything else about him? His hair?"

"Reddish gray, just like Father Vesuvio's—poor man—except he didn't have a beard, and he had a bit of an accent, like maybe he came from out East somewhere."

Harriet's next stop was the basement of the courthouse where the Paradise County History Center offered internet access to genealogical records worldwide, almost a billion names in more than sixteen billion records. Among those, she could find no record of a Maurice or Morris Fowler having a sister named either Delores or Dolores. Otherwise, Latter-Day Saints records, and nowhere else, had an entry for the marriage of Maurice Fowler and Delores Blunt, in the County of Devon, Paignton, England, forty years ago this month. Delores Fowler, if one and the same, had died on her fortieth wedding anniversary.

Then Harriet delved further into the immense world of people named Fowler as she studied census records; birth, death, and burial records; obituaries; and searchable, digital copies of old newspapers from major East Coast cities. This consumed yet another morning and a day off from her pet clinic job.

That evening at home, Porky asked if she had finished 'whatever it is you're doing.'

Harriet laughed and apologized for being mysterious.

"I don't like telling the whole world what I plan to do," she said. "It always seems to turn out some other way."

"I'm not the whole world," said Porky.

"You are to me, Wilbur, but I will say this much: I am exploring a connection between the Fowler and Cudahy families, and it is going to take more mornings at the History Center. I hope to finish by the time Pope Vincent arrives here."

Bernard Passmore, ever alert, noted her frequent absence from the parish archive room.

46

Rita Fajita in E-Flat Major

Thursday morning.

Divided Twin Rivers, like ends of a balancing scale, lay before Bernard Passmore in his swollen vision of his own illustrious future grown unaccountably corroded while he had been preoccupied elsewhere. He had just completed his purchase of The Paradise Trailer Park, a riverside slum that would bring in a fortune in monthly lot rent. He had become one of the largest property holders in Twin Rivers. He had built an empire. He could not look anywhere in New Town or Old Town without seeing something he owned.

Still, Bernard's innards felt uneasy. Expectations trivial and great seemed to be unraveling around him. Change, like a contagion, was in the air along with the new Pope Vincent. Bernard was being rebuffed at every turn. This would never do.

Within the week, his plans to bring his choir to the Sistine Chapel had been dashed. His choir had also been denied a role in Pope Vincent's Masses at the Saint Paul Cathedral and the Basilica of Saint Mary in the Twin Cities. A choir was being brought in from St. Paul to sing at a papal Mass in the North Port Diocese, specific location yet to be announced. Much more of this, and he would be out of a job and made a laughingstock. Something had happened beyond Bernard's reach, and Bernard was both fuming and wary as a burglar when alarms go off.

Margaret was subdued and sheepish when he attempted conversation after Father Brandy swept into the office and then out again without saying a word.

"What's that old buzzard got stuck in his gizzard this morning?"

Normally, Margaret would have found an old priest with a gizzard amusing. She stared at her computer screen, shifted in her chair and pretended she had not heard. Margaret was experiencing a double hangover, one brought on by too much vodka yesterday afternoon; the other by too much truth angrily shared with Harriet earlier in the week.

Then, as if on cue, Harriet came out of Brandy's office down the hall, turned left instead of right, too obviously intending to avoid both Margaret and Bernard as she walked the long way around to the parish archive with a Wi-Fi disabler in her handbag. Bernard stepped out of Margaret's office and peered around a corner into the church. Harriet had stopped to light a vigil candle and then another in a rack beneath St. Joseph. Two vigil candles might suggest a crisis. Perhaps Porky had just been diagnosed with a terminal illness. That's why she had been absent much of the week. Bernard could hope.

Back with Margaret, he attempted a droll observation about one of Dusty's strippers. His was not a notably clever twist, but normally Margaret would have laughed or at least snorted her approval.

Bernard took aim again: "The little hussy had the brazen temerity to show up for cantor training after Wednesday evening choir practice. I gave her a not-all-that problematic piece in E-Flat Major with a certain um-pa-pa lilt to it. Any school child might have done it well. She flubbed it. I'll get the whole choir to sing it first thing just to show her how much she flatters herself, the harlot. She calls herself Rita Fajita. It can't be her real name."

Margaret laughed an obligatory laugh, while keeping her head down at her work.

Bernard scowled. "Rita Fajita can take her show elsewhere. Piffle! If she had stayed in Chicago a few months longer, she would never have gotten here. I would have seen to it."

He scrawled "E-Flat Major" on a portable chalkboard used for congregational hymn singing, tucked it under his arm, and stomped out. He licked his lips as was his habit. When he was not bent on humiliation, the other hymns on the chalk board were more to his liking, among them, the bouncy "All Are Welcome."

With his free hand behind his back, he wandered into the church, as he often did, for meditation, not of the devotional sort, but of the sort better described as plotting and scheming in private while apprising himself of his own situation. Life for Bernard was a game of chess with mostly weak opponents. That too seemed to be changing.

Rain began to drum on the old church's metal roof. He propped the hymn chalkboard in its usual place on a pedestal to the right of the sanctuary before circling toward the church vestibule and a favorite observation point, a chink in a stained-glass window facing the church parking lot, the grove of locust trees, and the Hotel Paradise.

Standing there he could feel not like a sneak, but like the admiral of the fleet with telescope in hand. Usually there was not much to see, but from a habit of watchfulness and self-interested curiosity, Bernard would peer through the chink regardless looking for whatever might be afloat as he made his solitary rounds of St. Callixtus.

From the church's bell towers rang out noonday chimes accompanied by distant thunder.

47

Drowning in Memories

Under both umbrella and Bernard Passmore's keen-eyed, squinting gaze, Brandy glanced first at the sky, then at his watch. Somebody he expected to meet in the church parking lot was late by minutes. Rainwater dripped from the perimeter of his battered umbrella; his watch would have become all but unreadable through condensation on his glasses.

Nearby, the parish soup kitchen stirred to life beyond a scrubby vacant lot at his back where the St. Callixtus Catholic primary school had once flourished. Already Twin Rivers homeless and destitute were approaching with the studied nonchalance of people trying to appear less desperate than they were. They shuffled past its door and circled around as if they had taken a wrong turn somewhere and were trying to figure out where they were. Some rubbed their eyes and stared up at St. Callixtus' twin towers before making a rain-soaked dash to the entrance.

Inside, running the day's soup line was Phyllis Cobb with help from Harriet White who was alternating mornings between the parish archive and the Paradise County History Center. Noon was a change for volunteers and the impoverished alike. Schedules were being adjusted. Brandy had decided to open the soup kitchen twice each day, both at noon and at its usual time of 5:30 p.m.

From long experience, bordering on superstition, Brandy knew that if he left his waiting post, whatever he awaited would appear. This is exactly what happened. As he approached the soup kitchen entrance, a Cobb Construction dump truck roared, whined, thumped, and swished to a stop, crosswise in his path.

Bernard cracked open a window transom to let sound in.

At times like this, George Cobb, a hands-on manager, could come up with astonishingly formal greetings.

"Father, I regret that I am late," George said, sounding as if he had just entered a confessional. George jumped out of his truck straight into a puddle. He pretended not noticing that his boots leaked. "I apologize for any inconvenience." He glanced at the mixed-race Indian boy still seated in his truck. "Whisk needed a lift after the police—I mean after school. I will say no more."

"Piffle!" said Bernard, under his breath.

Whisk climbed out of the truck and stood alongside as George tossed a wink in Brandy's direction. The priest, having never managed the art of winking, blinked instead.

"No matter, George. I was just heading to the soup line to see how your wife is doing. We had better get in out of this rain."

"My wife?" said George, as if the fact of his marriage had just then occurred to him. "Yes, of course, Phyllis. Tell her I have Whisk with me. We have sort of adopted him, Father."

"I'll be back in a minute—welcome to St. Callixtus," Brandy said to the boy. He stuck out his hand to give Whisk's a vigorous shake before pivoting and disappearing into the soup kitchen where tables were already filled with women and children. Most of the men stood around cradling steaming bowls in hand.

Brandy returned from the soup kitchen by way of a connecting hallway leading to a church side entrance.

"I see you took the long way around," said George. In the meantime, he had grabbed an umbrella from his truck, one large enough to conceal most of Whisk.

"In more ways than one," said Brandy.

Brandy cast a wary look at the stained-glass window. Except for the distance between them, he and Bernard were eye-to-eye.

"It has only taken me a few weeks here to see a great many things, George. For one, I could never manage without Phyllis and Harriet, but let's get down to the business of those old locust trees before we drown. Over the phone you said they have to go."

"I am afraid so, Father, and with Pope Vincent coming here, it will be a race to the finish line, or words to that effect. The force of the hotel blast could possibly shatter those trees and send splinters flying everywhere."

Temporarily distracted by the thought of his wife being indispensable, George glanced at the soup kitchen entrance as he spoke.

Brandy raised bushy, gray-tipped eyebrows as far as they would go over glasses knocked lopsided by his umbrella.

"The blast," he said, glancing up at St. Callixtus' tall spires, and then down at its dripping façade where a few pigeons sheltered in alcoves. "An explosion?"

"Not exactly," said George, "an *im*plosion, something blowing in from the outside."

"That is already happening here, George. Some parishioners want to close down this fine old church and build another in New Town, but you're not talking about that foolishness." This he directed less to George than to the stained-glass window. "Foolishness," he said again.

"Blowing it in, if it's done right," shouted George, as if the implosive concussion were already upon them, and he had to be heard above it.

"I hope so," said Brandy looking from the church to the honey locusts and then back to the church. The distance between seemed to have shrunk even as they spoke of it.

"I always liked those trees, ever since my days here as a young priest fresh out of seminary. They shielded us from the hotel. Helped us forget that The Paradise was there."

"Phyllis would disown me, Father. She loves St. Callixtus as it is, and not a brick or stone will be hurt as the hotel comes down. That is why, much as it pains me, these locust trees will have to go."

"It pains you, George?"

George recounted a grade school memory, his third-grade year at St. Callixtus Primary. He faced the locust trees first, then after a few sentences, he turned around to look where the school had been in his boyhood. He seemed to see it there on a Lenten afternoon when his teacher, Sister Dolorosa, took her class outside to have a closer look at the trees. "She had us touch the thorns of these locust trees to get us to think about the crown of thorns on Jesus' head that sorry day."

"All exceedingly piffle," sneered Bernard from within the church.

"Do you remember Sister Dolorosa from the old grade school, Father?"

They both glanced in the direction of a vacant, gravel-covered lot where the parish school once stood.

"She may not have been here when I was," said Brandy.

"She was my third-grade teacher," said George, warming to a subject he always warmed to. "Very tall. Taught me the multiplication tables all the way to twelve times twelve."

"Mine, too, now that you mention it, back at All Saints on the Iron Range. I thought mine might have been a different nun with the same name, but twelve times twelve cinches it, the same woman, Sister Dolorosa. It seems inexplicable that we both would have had the same teacher, even though some nuns live longer than certain, nearly extinct sea turtles." He removed his glasses, more to study George for his reaction than to wipe away rain leaking through his broken umbrella.

Caught up in the strange serendipity of it all, George failed to notice that his wet trousers were clinging to his legs.

"More Piffle!" said Bernard, adjusting his gaze as a lightning bolt illuminated the church's clearstory.

"We'd best go inside," said Brandy. The courtyard and parking lot lit up and then darkened with thunder exploding around them.

Lost somewhere in the past, George seemed not to hear.

"Maybe they will both be struck," said Bernard.

Brandy had nodded and raised an eyebrow over twelve times twelve, even higher as George plunged forward with his recollection. Only God knows what might have happened and how drenched they both would be were he to reveal that Pope Vincent had also been in the same third-grade class with the same Sister Dolorosa. The heavens might have cracked, as they seemed to be doing regardless.

Lightning forked over the church towers. Thunder rose to a kettledrum crescendo. Rainwater cascaded from George's construction company hardhat, and from there down his coverall front. He galloped on, though he and Brandy might have died on the spot.

Intimidating thorns long ago sprouted from the trunks of the honey locust trees, circling them in rings. Sister Dolorosa had taken his third-grade class outside on a warm spring day to ponder there the pain of Christ's 'Crown of Thorns' piercing his head, a Lenten meditation. She selected an especially intimidating thorn at just the right level for third-graders and invited them one by one to step forward and tap it gently with a fingertip. "Gently, gently," she said each time, and then when it was over, and they all had done it without anyone bleeding, she said, "Our dear Lord's tormentors were not gentle at all." Not a particularly prayerful or meditative man during the year's other 364 days, George thought of honey locust thorns every Good Friday without fail.

Brandy grabbed him by the coat sleeve, as if to yank him out of a dream. Whisk had vanished, but neither noticed before they found shelter.

Memories, for better or worse, could be more durable than bulldozers and more threatening than thunderstorms.

Some people count sheep on restless nights. George Cobb recited the multiplication tables. Those numbered tables never left him, from a childhood experience with a nun who might have been Moses.

"Yours is indeed quite a story," said Brandy as they entered his office. "And Dolorosa is a most memorable name—Sorrowful Rose, Sister Sorrowful Rose. Quite a name. Most unforgettable."

George thought so. "For some reason, Father, the elevens were the hardest, not the twelves. The times elevens never made any sense. I mean who ever thinks about eleven times eleven?"

They both shook their heads over multiplication mysteries. Rainwater still dripped from George's hardhat.

"Sister Dolorosa was..." Here George fumbled for a word. "*Seismic*—that's it—I think she was seismic."

"You mean psychic, George, able to read thoughts and see the future?"

"No seismic, you know, vibrations in the earth?"

It was the first time Brandy had heard a nun associated with an earthquake. "Take the trees, if you think it's best," he said. "We will have to get along without them." At his desk, he signed the necessary permits on behalf of the parish council.

George said he had always been much better at multiplication than at division. "Not long ago, Harriet White asked me what I recalled about the church's old grade school. I told her that Sister Dolorosa's class is about all I remember. She laughed and said that I made third grade sound like a hangover." George's head spun with that idea.

"Life sure is strange," he said as if Harriet had proven his point. "All sides of it."

"I have often thought that myself," said Brandy. "But to get back to those honey locust trees for a moment, they have been there since I was a young, know-nothing priest just out of seminary." He slid the agreement George's way the other side of his desk. "They were mature trees already. More than I can say of myself at that point. Hardly knew what I was doing back then. Some days I still don't."

They walked out of his parish office and turned left to enter the church as Harriet had done an hour before.

At its entrance, George spoke in the respectful whisper Sister Dolorosa had taught him. "Father, that young Indian fellow Whisk who rode here with me, did you see where he went?"

Father Bandy paused to consider possibilities, but pandemonium arrived first as an answer.

48

Subterfuge and Fists

Bernard Passmore was not a man to be taken by surprise, except when necessary distractions overrode and short-circuited what he regarded as his finely-tuned senses. A Paradise County patrol car, not Porky White's, had entered the parking lot seconds after George and Brandy left the scene. The two officers inside conversed for a few minutes, pointing now and then to the soup kitchen entrance. The one behind the wheel shook his head. They drove away.

In the meantime, Bernard missed creaking hinges. He missed padded footsteps of old sneakers coming his way upon floor tiles. A minute or so later, he jumped much higher than a man of his girth could usually manage. He had discovered Whisk's head beside his, with Whisk on his tiptoes attempting to see whatever he was watching from that splintered church window.

"What're you looking at?" said Whisk as nonchalantly as if Bernard were one of his Paradise Trailer Park buddies staring downriver from a bridge railing.

This illusion ended with Bernard's massive arm around his throat in a chokehold meant to strangle an ox. In this case, the boy's skinny neck saved him while an ox might have died on the spot. Whisk slipped the hold and ran toward a distant side door just as it opened and the pointed shaft of an old umbrella snapped on four switches in a single deft motion. Every light in St. Callixtus illuminated Bernard with his arms outstretched hot on Whisk's heels.

"What's going on here?" demanded Brandy.

At that point, Bernard and Whisk on opposite sides had twice circled the statue of St. Callixtus. "I caught this boy in an act of purloinment," said Bernard, struggling to say anything as he caught his breath. He had stepped into the church's main aisle to hitch up his trousers and tuck in his shirt.

With Whisk dancing beyond his grasp, he had reached for something that was not even a word. *Purloinment* stopped everything for a few seconds. Father Brandy glanced at George. George looked impressed. Whisk kicked Bernard in the shins and ducked behind George.

"You're a little thieving devil," roared Bernard when, in calmer moments, were his shins left out of the picture, he might have said, "Father, this offspring of Beelzebub was intercepted while encroaching upon the Seventh Commandment."

Regardless, Whisk caught the gist of it. "I am not!"

"You are!" said Bernard, limping toward Whisk's human shield.

"Am not!"

"Yes, you are!"

George was reminded of church cantor rehearsals Phyllis described before she quit the choir last week, abandoning Bernard in favor of the parish soup kitchen.

"Enough!" said Brandy. "I will handle this, Bernard." He threw open the church's main doors, and stepped aside, leaving for Bernard a gap wide enough for a funeral procession. "Enough, I say!"

Bernard, unaccustomed to taking orders from 'piffle priests,' had been watching George's clenched fists—not big fists, but still they were clenched. The doors banged shut behind him.

"I will not forget this," shouted Bernard over his shoulder, a promise generally directed at Whisk, at Brandy, at George's clenched fists, and at the universe.

Bernard may or may not have heard Whisk say, "He was spying." He pointed toward the cracked church window.

The priest walked that way to peer through the chink. He could see the Cobb Construction dump truck and the twin rows of honey locust trees whose death warrant he had just signed. He could see the spot where he and George had been standing minutes ago while the trees' history had been recounted and their fate decided. When he stepped away, George stepped into his place to have a look.

A change of subject seemed in order. “Well, as long as you’re here, young man, let us show you around our church. Much has changed since I was stationed here eons ago. I have had to get to know the place all over again. George, will you help me fill in a few gaps?” He glanced at George who appeared to have fallen into a gap all his own.

49

The Fourth Station

George was pressed into service as an assistant tour guide in what soon became a journey through Brandy's memories from his days at St. Callixtus as a young priest. They paused before empty niches while he described statues once there; they pondered discolored sections of floor tile where statue pedestals once stood; they imagined ends of an imagined Communion railing illuminated by imagined angel candelabra long ago consigned to brass recyclers and ecclesiastical landfills. The Stations of the Cross and an alabaster St. Callixtus remained as Brandy recalled them, though the statue now stood opposite the baptismal font at the rear of the church.

"Pope Callixtus I," said Brandy, "the defender of sinners, outcasts, and all who clamor for mercy. Got himself into a barrel of trouble for leaving church doors wide open so the supposed riffraff could feel welcome. Harriet White has the whole story of how Callixtus came to be here from somewhere—I have quite forgotten from where—or how this church happened to be so named, for that matter...." He paused to consider in silence Vesuvio's little-known middle name.

The trio moved on, stopping beneath the Fourth Station, to the left of the confessional, a structure resembling a large cabinet of the sort found in the basements of old accounting firms. From a child's curiosity that had never abandoned him, George opened one if its doors and peeked inside as if it were one of his home's closets or a refrigerator full of leftovers. Normally, floor lighting would have illuminated a padded kneeler. This time, with the door opened no more than a hand's width and no weight on the kneeler, the confessional interior remained darkened, revealing a pinhole of light to the left of where a penitent might have knelt.

Brandy cleared his throat. "George, the Sacrament of Reconciliation will be available this Saturday before the Vigil Mass. Of course, if you have a pressing need, I am available at all times."

"Yes, Father. I mean n-no, Father." George eased the door shut as a slip of paper from within fluttered around his feet.

"The Fourth Station is my favorite of the set," said Brandy. "The wonder is some iconoclast has not demolished it."

George pondered *iconoclast*, hoping he was not being accused, and bent down to see what had fluttered from the confessional floor.

"That's where Phyllis and I sit," said George, pointing to a pew nearest an entrance which in another era had been used by primary school students and the convent nuns coming and going between school and church. These days it provided George a quick exit after Mass.

"This depiction invites us to think about Jesus meeting his mother on his ascent to Calvary. Typically, the Fourth Station shows Mary being comforted by her companions as she recoils and shields her face from the sight of her suffering son. You won't see that here. What do you see, Whisk?"

The boy considered the carving. "She is proud of him and encouraging him," said Whisk. He had noticed Mary's hand on her son's shoulder, her intent gaze meeting his, and words on Mary's lips seeming to say, "Be resolute. Be brave." A small dog stood attentively at Mary's feet.

George was seeing for the first time a scene he had been sitting under for nearly thirty years without ever thinking about it.

As if reading George's mind, Brandy said, "Well done, Whisk. You have seen at first glance what some people miss in a lifetime."

Once again George squirmed, and with life's strangeness again in his thoughts, stared at what turned out to be a receipt from a local locksmith made out to Charlie Cook, probably lost during a recent Confession.

Brandy intoned what might have been a message for the feast day of St. Callixtus: "The Stations of the Cross represent moments in all our lives. As individual waymarks, they serve to remind us of what Christ did, and what we who follow him must do. He gave us a way to understand our lives; the inevitability of pain and suffering; the need for support and encouragement from those who love us in the face of human cruelty and personal calamity. This depiction of the Fourth Station with Jesus meeting his mother has always said to me, 'Take heart, for even this will have a happy ending.'"

They moved on, arriving at the Eighth Station on the other side of the church, nearest the window that had served as Bernard's peephole.

Brandy again leaned forward for another peek though the chink. Once more he saw George's dump truck, the honey locust trees, and the Hotel Paradise. When he stepped back, George took another look.

Through his personal time warp, George saw all that he had seen before beginning the church tour and all that he had missed and ought to have noticed over the years, scenes tunneling backward to the moment he first entered Sister Dolorosa's third-grade classroom. Taking a second look, he noticed a Paradise County patrol car driving across the lot from the street.

"The cops!" George sounded as if he had been caught red-handed in a kid's prank. He jumped back from the window. "Charlie!" he said. "I'll bet it's Charlie, Porky's sidekick, looking for this receipt he lost. It blew out of the confessional."

Brandy took another look through the chink. Behind them a door creaked as Whisk silently slipped out into the rain.

"They cruise through here all the time, George, especially when the parish soup kitchen is open. I have seen them a dozen times in the short while I have been here. I have spoken to them about being too aggressive with our homeless. It's harassment of the poor. They didn't seem to care until I said something to Harriet White, and she spoke to her husband. But that's Porky White's car, here to take his wife to the Happy Pet Clinic where as you probably know she works afternoons."

Outside the church, he asked George what had become of Whisk. George handed him the locksmith receipt made out to Charlie, as if that explained everything. Brandy opened his umbrella and examined the receipt.

"Whisk is like that, Father. He just drifts around. Comes and goes. You never know where he is or where he isn't or where he will show up next. He is like a phantom. His foster parents collect county money for watching him, but they don't do anything. Their trailer house is full of guns—in boxes, on shelves, hanging from hooks. I was in there once when I took Whisk home. It's an arsenal. It's a wonder the kid hasn't shot himself, accidentally of course. I reported that to Charlie Cook, the officer whose name is on this receipt."

"I met Charlie the day of Phillip Fowler's funeral. He asked me why I was here instead of Father Vesuvio. I still don't know the answer to that question. What's his real name? Whisk, I mean. It can't be that. Nothing Indian about it, is there?"

George shrugged. "Your guess is as good as mine, Father, except he is always whisking about. Even sweeps out my construction equipment garages. I am not sure that even Whisk knows his real name. The Indians call him *No-See-Um*."

George believed in the transcendence of first names, one of his many notions bordering on superstition. Had Brandy been at St. Callixtus long enough to know him very well, he would have seen in George one of his favorite homily illustrations: a man of wavering religious faith, believing in things yet harder to believe. George was certain that all men named Charlie or Bob or Sam or Jack or any other first name were brothers and alike in some mysterious sense. He was unlikely to meet another Whisk, but should there happen to be another somewhere in this world, he was certain to be like this one.

He was about to share his theory with Brandy when the priest folded the locksmith receipt into his coat pocket, pointed his battered umbrella at Porky, and stepped resolutely through the rain.

Porky lowered a fogged-up window. Harriet came running across from the soup kitchen entrance.

"One of your men left this in the church," Brandy said, handing Porky the locksmith receipt.

As Porky drove away with Harriet, he passed the receipt across to her. "Completely unauthorized Hotel Paradise key duplication. Wren, what do you make of it?"

Rainwater gushed from beneath the squad car. Harriet was silent until they were on the street speeding toward the veterinary clinic and a block or so distant from the church. Suddenly all of Twin Rivers seemed to have become Bernard Passmore's eavesdropping post. Like a demigod, he was everywhere, peering, peeping, and listening from multiple portholes.

"God forbid! Bernard has added Charlie to his confessional victims' list. This receipt, months old, points that way. Phillip Fowler was still alive that long ago. No hidden, forgotten hotel tunnels in this mystery. Bernard had keys all along. He could open a door and walk in anytime he wanted. And, Wilbur, there is more news! –I took a picture of it with my cell phone, our weekend hymn on a chalkboard, including the key it's in: E-Flat Major. The *E* and the *F* look exactly like those on the suicide notes. Bernard wrote them."

Porky whistled though his teeth. "Fantastic, Wren, though it's still not enough to bring charges. Our prosecuting attorney would get laughed out of court with evidence like this. But I'll haul Charlie into my office for questioning. *Aiding and abetting* is serious business."

"Don't be too hard on him. A devil has had him by the throat, and besides Charlie has a family. Who knows what Bernard told him to explain why he needed those keys?

Who knows what Charlie shared in the confessional—Father Vesuvio was still here when these keys were made—the Seal of Confession, you know?"

"Not a seal when Passmore is in the picture, Wren, more like a killer whale. You can bet on it."

"I won't have to, my dear."

50

Interrogations

Disillusionment and blind rage tore at Bernard Passmore's voluminous innards. He seemed beset at every peephole and porthole formerly peered through with self-satisfaction. He was being blindsided and snubbed by the new pope and ordered about by an old priest defending an Indian half-breed resident of his newly-acquired Paradise Riverside Trailer Park.

"Trailer trash, all of them!" he muttered within earshot of Margaret Smuggs.

"Amen to that, Bernie!" said Margaret.

"And George Cobb and his toady wife Phyllis, I could crush their construction company with just a few words dropped here and there among their customers. They would go down like The Paradise next week, in a heap." His gigantic hands closed around an imagined heap.

George felt crushed for other reasons. Yesterday, after leaving St. Callixtus with Whisk nowhere around, he had crossed the church parking lot and walked down the hotel alley to Dwyer's Purple Palace for his usual two, after-work martinis before the strip shows began. To keep up appearances, he always parked in the church lot. Thanks to his drinking habit, no one looked more like a regular churchgoer than George, or so he thought. This fooled no one, so many Purple Palace customers did it.

Upon arriving at their rural Twin Rivers home, an hour and a half later, George discovered on his cell phone—left in his truck glove box—a message from Phyllis. This was the last of normalcy for the next eighteen hours. He raced back to Twin Rivers. What he had missed was his wife's interrogation by the police, one of them being Charlie Cook, Porky

White's backup and investigative sidekick for the past many years.

With Porky ever more involved in management duties and security preparations for the pope's visit, Harriet had become the power behind a law enforcement throne represented by the large gold star on Porky's left shirt pocket. The Paradise County Chief Investigator's office had moved to a breakfast table in the White's home where business was discussed over juice, cold cereal, and weekend Eggs Benedict. Harriet had handpicked Charlie Cook to keep a lid on it while questioning Phyllis Cobb in a sham interrogation of the SNFA's accusation of vandalism in the vacant lot, "Future Home of the new St. Callixtus Church."

Sham or no sham, between angry tears, Phyllis had fought back. "The new St. Callixtus! Not as far as I am concerned," said Phyllis. "Over my dead body! That is what our dear, departed Father Vesuvio once said—I am sure he is in Heaven, no matter what the scandalmongers say."

This proved to be self-incriminating in a convoluted way.

Charlie asked if she wanted a lawyer. Instead she asked for Harriet White. After an uncomfortable pause all around, Phyllis was asked if she possibly had encouraged vandalism by being excessively vocal near 'young ears.' Was she not an opponent of the Sunny New Future Association? Did she know what it meant to contribute to the delinquency of a minor?

"Whisk's ears, my eye! Whisk has heard things in that dreadful Paradise Trailer Park that would make even you blush. You should arrest his foster parents for taking better care of their guns than of him. You should arrest Bernard Passmore for being a slum landlord, the least of his vices. How he got the money to buy that hellhole I would like to know. The whole place is a contribution to the delinquency of every minor living there, and by the way, instead of picking on Whisk all the time, why don't you go after the same shyster who owns half of Old Town, lives in a palace in New Town, and robs his tenants in the form of exorbitant rent while directing our church choir? Why don't you do something about all the counterfeit money killing businesses in Old Town?" This was all said in the single breath that only female altos and humpback whales can manage.

Charlie fidgeted and beckoned the other officers toward the door in full retreat. One of them dropped a pen he had used for taking notes. Another turned off a recording device in his vest pocket. A video camera the other side of a fake mirror suddenly had a magazine in front of its lens.

"Of course, I know..." shouted Phyllis as half the Twin Rivers police force cowered near a door. "Of course, I know why. Bernard Passmore is all of a sudden the most important man around. This great Passmore even claims that his choir—nothing without Harriet, your boss's wife, my best friend, and the best soprano ever—will be in Rome, in the Sistine Chapel no less, for the new Pope Vincent's coronation, except now it won't happen."

In her heated haste, Phyllis, a convert, sometimes stumbled over Vatican terminology, but papal *coronation* would serve quite well as far as she was concerned.

Then a door opened, and her interrogation ended as suddenly as it had begun. On her way out of the law enforcement center, she spotted Charlie sitting alone in a room with Porky White. Charlie held his head in his hands and appeared to be undergoing his own interrogation.

"No doubt, George, for his complicity in ganging up against me, while you, George, were nowhere to be found when I needed you most. Those SNFA people know no limits; Bernard Passmore is the worst of them," said Phyllis. "I would not be at all surprised if *he* put Whisk up to destroying those despicable new church campaign signs. The man cannot be trusted. He works both ends against the middle. He works the middle against both ends. He discovers ends and middles nobody knew existed. He is a living version of the Hotel Paradise. Everything people gossip about going on in there is comfortably housed in his repulsive physique. Too bad you can't demolish Bernard Passmore with some of your dynamite."

"TNT this time; dynamite is not for the hotel job. At least, that is what it says in an instruction book I've been paging through, *An Idiot's Guide to Demolition*."

"Well, if you happen to have any TNT lying around, put it under Passmore. —George, for god's sake! You're blowing up The Paradise as if you were assembling lawn furniture ordered online. Is your instruction book written in several languages?"

George paged through his book—Chinese, Japanese, French, everything but Latin and Ojibwe. He shrugged.

At the Paradise County Law Enforcement center, gossip centered on the announcement of Charlie Cook's sudden absence on paid leave.

51

Among Field Mice and Church Blackbirds

Pope Vincent's chartered Alitalia flight was a week from landing in the Twin Cities. His official motorcade was scheduled to travel north to Minnesota's Benedictine monastery two days after that. From there, Bishop Norman's role had remained disconcertingly blank. He was not merely left in the dark, but in a state better described as a void. It was as if he had ceased to exist the moment Pope Vincent had been elected.

Day by day, he paced his office, now and then glancing from its capacious windows as if expecting a ship to arrive on the Lake Superior horizon. Ships did arrive at North Port City, iron ore boats and freighters, but none would have brought the Iron Cardinal, now Pope Vincent, once thought to be a friend and confidant. Not even a note in a sealed bottle would come ashore on the beach his imagination combed for a sign that Cardinal Cudahy had not forgotten his loyal services. The great inland sea was as taciturn as Rome's Holy See. Neither had anything to say.

Since his office had no windows landward, he could only otherwise stare at a wall already adorned with a picture of the new pope whose lips were taut and whose eyes seemed to glitter with an intense inner fire. Bishop Norman could not but wonder who, after all, was this Pope Vincent. Even men as great as the Iron Cardinal could change in their moment of utmost greatness, hardening overnight to blast furnace steel. Cudahy now needed no one. Bishop Norman could be cast aside like so much slag spewed from a smelting pot.

When such thoughts became unbearable, he would stride through his office's double doors, out into his bishop's reception area. There is power to be felt in passing through double doors, flinging both open from the center. It is the privilege of the great to have such office doors, and to spread them wide in passing through. It seldom failed to rejuvenate, and yet today he felt no better in his official reception area where laypeople assigned weekend overtime eyed him warily from various distant cubicles.

Would word arrive at the last minute, at the eleventh hour perhaps? Had there been a gap in communication? Was he supposed to have known days ago? Would Pope Vincent's entourage turn east in his direction, to overnight at his diocesan residence, with a Solemn Pontifical High Mass in the cathedral at daybreak? Such questions buzzed around his head like a cloud of gnats. Should he make necessary arrangements without knowing for sure? Should he have the cathedral cleaned, its organ pipes vacuumed, and its candles replaced? Should he assemble his army of priests for a welcoming committee?

Alas! It was not to be, and in those distant cubicles, everyone knew it when official word arrived—not via a cardinal in the pope's traveling party but via telephone from of all people, Father Aloysius Brandy, now stationed at Twin Rivers St. Callixtus.

Receiver in hand with a dozen pairs of eyes directed his way, Bishop Norman temporarily lost his grip on hierarchical composure. He shot well beyond accustomed informality into the linguistic world of Great Lakes seamen and iron ore miners.

"Brandy, who the hell told you to call me with this message?"

A dozen pairs of eyebrows went up an inch, and then a dozen heads lowered behind cubicle walls.

"Your Excellency, it was Crackerjack himself, I mean Pope Vincent himself who left word here."

"Did he speak with you directly?"

"He left word with our secretary Margaret Smuggs."

"A parish secretary? Smuggs? —It may have been an impostor, Brandy—I am sure it must have been. Popes just don't go around dropping messages with parish secretaries named Smuggs. For God's sake! That is not the way things are done when the Holy See is involved."

"I wouldn't know about such matters, your Excellency, but the caller left a signature of sorts, something unmistakable. He told Margaret to inform Father Brandy that he is *It*."

There was no denying *It*.

Pope Vincent intended to spend the night in Twin Rivers with a farewell Mass at St. Callixtus in the morning.

Bishop Norman was flabbergasted. Where were the assembled cardinals and Midwestern bishops expected to sleep? An establishment called the Thrifty Springs at the west end of Twin Rivers and another called the Snooze Inn at the other would hardly suffice. The pontiff himself, in a bedroom of the St. Callixtus Rectory, no doubt in the company of field mice and church crickets?

Bishop Norman's brain marched ahead, galloped, and then began to perform the mental equivalent of a cavalry charge. He could be better than Napoleon when it came to Waterloo. He would snatch stragglers and leftovers to organize a counterattack. He would not be excluded in favor of a woman named Smuggs. He would not have Church hierarchy sleeping in makeshift Turning Wind teepees, a whimsical suggestion advanced by an auxiliary who immediately regretted it.

North Port diocesan office cubicles began to hum. An advance party was sent into Twin Rivers New Town to search out the most commodious luxury residences ringing a crystalline lake and a fashionable country club. Bernard Passmore's mansion of ten bedrooms and twelve bathrooms was one such. Bernard was delighted to oblige, hoping that his choir's date with destiny at the Sistine Chapel would be reinstated, and of course he could make a pitch for the new St. Callixtus. Just in case, he ransacked his wine cellar for the best of his vintages and laid in a case of rare Armagnac distilled in the vicinity of the mountaintop where Noah's Ark was said to have settled at the Great Flood's conclusion.

Mansion by mansion, appropriate arrangements were made for a dozen traveling bishops and three cardinals, in case Pope Vincent at the last minute did not turn east to North Port City.

52

You Will Find What Only You Look For

In Twin Rivers that evening, even as phones were ringing in New Town mansions, Porky White brought home an account of his frustrating trek through a maze of papal visit security arrangements.

Uninvited experts had arrived from national outposts. All looked over his shoulder; all second-guessed him; some, in so many words, suggested he was inept to the point of dimwitted. He had had consultations with the FBI, the Secret Service, the Department of Homeland Security, the Central Intelligence Agency, the Border Patrol, and with military personnel from the various service branches, including the Coast Guard.

"Wren, the Coast Guard! We must be at least fifteen hundred miles from the nearest Atlantic coast and farther yet from the Pacific. The Coast Guard, for god's sake! Next I will be hearing from the National Forest Service."

"Lake Superior is part of the St. Lawrence Seaway. I suppose that explains the Coast Guard."

"Only if they have a cutter or a harbor patrol boat that can travel overland one hundred and fifty miles," protested Porky.

Most perplexing to him, and to everyone involved, was Pope Vincent insisting upon all security personnel being no closer than two hundred yards from St. Callixtus itself.

With yet more in the picture, Porky's mood, already dark, darkened further as he diverted himself with beanbag juggling while Harriet sat by, waiting for him to volunteer something.

He began with three bags, went to four, and then to five. They became a colored blur tumbling over his head from one hand to another, higher and higher, until the arc almost touched their vaulted living room ceiling. Picking up his rhythm, Harriet began reciting *Four and Twenty Blackbirds*, much on her mind of late. When, the third time around, she reached the point where the 'Maid was in the garden hanging up the clothes,' she decided enough was enough.

"You must be practicing for Pope Vincent, or maybe trying to avoid thinking about something. Beanbag diversion, is it?"

The beanbags raced over Porky's fingertips. He said nothing.

"Okay, Wilbur, you cannot keep this up forever. Tell me what happened when you questioned Charlie Cook, late yesterday afternoon. Phyllis spotted him in your office after her so-called interrogation."

The beanbags tumbled into a pile at Porky's feet.

Porky fell into an easy chair. He wiped his face where beads of sweat had formed.

"How long have I been in this law business, Wren?"

"Let's see. You were in it when we first met. That was thirteen years ago. About fifteen years."

"Sixteen to be precise. Long enough to have seen more than my share of pretty bad stuff, the stuff of nightmares, ugly bloody stuff. But even without much blood, this is the worst I have ever seen. Maybe I should have thrown away all those detective mysteries I read as a boy. I should have run away and joined a circus or a carnival. They could always use a juggler between bareback riders and lion trainers. Being a sheriff is the wrong place for me. I don't have the ironclad stomach."

"Wilbur, how bad is it?"

"I always thought well of Charlie. Among guys who have been my sidekick over the years, he has been the best. His head wasn't all that good when it came to piecing things together in an investigation. He was slow on the uptake. He might have played checkers, never chess, but his heart was in the right place, or at least I thought so."

"Wilbur, how bad? Tell me."

An impression of something like grief darkened Porky's features into what seemed almost a shadow cast from within. "Charlie cheated on his wife—had an affair over a two-year period."

"Poor Corrie!"

"It's over now, or so he says, and I believe him. I asked if he had told anyone. He said only Father Vesuvio, in Confession, twice as it turns out—he did not break it off right away. The other woman has a husband and is not about to reveal anything. At least that is what Charlie hopes. I would rather be a circus juggler than a priest, listening to this sad stuff all the time."

"And so, a few days after he told Father Vesuvio the first time, what happened?"

"He finds this note in an envelope under the windshield wipers of his squad car. 'Get me a set of keys to the hotel, or else I will let your wife in on your lovey-dovey nightlife when she thinks you are at work.' That's when he realized how out-of-control this was getting. Fortunately, his police training took over at that point. He kept the note as possible evidence, locked in his desk drawer. The set of keys was to be left in a luggage locker at the bus company depot."

"The Passmore Bus Company depot. About the note, let me guess—hand-printed. All block capitals, same as the two suicide notes?"

"Looks the same to me. I made a copy of it. See for yourself."

Harriet studied up the copy. "WIFE in all printed caps—E-Flat Major. The same unique *E*, the same *F* as Bernard Passmore's on the hymn chalk board. Put that together with the cats Margaret Smuggs let out of the bag. It looks more and more like Passmore is our man, Honey."

"You can bet on it, Wren. We have to get the goods on this guy. We need the smoking gun. Everything adds up, but it's all circumstantial and subjective. Handwriting analysis is not an exact science. I have looked up a number of cases nationwide where it figured in a trial, and it seldom counted for much as standalone evidence. I could never get an indictment from the county attorney with no more than this."

"Passmore killed those men. We don't yet know why, but I'm getting closer. We don't for certain have motives, but at least we know how he got into the Paradise—poor Corrie Cook."

"Poor everyone," said Porky. He picked up his beanbags and began juggling again.

Harriet watched till again he reached five and a swirling blur that had lost all color but seemed no more than a ghostlike mist traversing hands moving as fast as fan blades. Here was an ecstasy of timelessness only jugglers experience and an invisible rhythm only jugglers know.

Meanwhile, mention of Father Vesuvio had turned Harriet's thoughts in his direction. She closed her eyes and daydreamed till she could almost see him returning from an unexpected quarter. She recalled something she read scrawled upon the margin of a century-old church bulletin in the parish archive: "You will find what only you look for," a promise from an unknown someone long passed into eternity.

53

Maurice Fowler

Porky spoke from within the whirling halo of his beanbags.

"I have more bad news, Wren. I'm not sure how to tell you. We did a routine DNA match on Father Vesuvio and the other players involved here. For your sake, I wish I had left it alone—it turns out that Vesuvio is the father of Phillip Fowler and the grandfather of Jane Blue's baby. Delores Fowler of course is the mother and grandmother."

Given his wife's faith in Father Vesuvio, Porky had saved what he regarded as the worst news for last. Anticipating her need for comfort, he let go of his beanbags. Looking from them to his wife, far from disbelief, he saw the confident smile of someone who had just found an elusive puzzle piece and was about to set it in place.

"And so, think about it, Wilbur. Someone in the Vatican is shelling out tens of thousands of dollars to protect an obscure Minnesota priest named Vesuvio. What kind of sense does that make?"

"DNA doesn't lie, Wren."

"No, but people do lie, and when we find out who is lying and to whom, we will have a complete picture, along with motives for these two murders."

Harriet used logic to explore territory beyond the reach of DNA: Vesuvio had been stationed at St. Callixtus for eight years, during which time Phillip Fowler had finished junior high and high school and now and then acted as a server at weekend Masses. Phillip's relationship with Vesuvio had always been nonchalant as Vesuvio's was with him. There was nothing on either side suggesting that a son was with a father or a father with a son. "When young Fowler's body was discovered behind the hotel, Vesuvio was as shocked as everyone, but his was not the paroxysm of grief that might have been visible in a parent."

"Maybe it was a good act," suggested Porky.

"Eight years with two actors, both by all accounts earnest, sincere men. Wilbur, I don't think so, and add to that Father Vesuvio's equally casual bearing toward Delores Fowler. She was just a parishioner, albeit a wealthy mystery woman who traveled a lot and stirred up no end of gossip, none of it having to do with Father Vesuvio. Around St. Callixtus, Delores Fowler was thought to be a widow, and..."

"And?"

"And a man signing in as her brother visited her three nights in succession at Mercy Hospital shortly before she died. I found his name on registration records there: Maurice Fowler."

"The name Margaret Smuggs dropped in your lap last week. So, Delores' brother visited her when she was near death—what is surprising about that?"

"Nothing, except from what I can tell so far by searching genealogical records, he seems to have been her husband instead."

"That could mean Delores cheated on him when she became pregnant by Father Vesuvio years ago."

Harriet winced. "Not so fast, Wilbur. It might mean that the body in the Hotel Paradise was Maurice Fowler's."

"—Coincidentally—or maybe not coincidentally—bearing a close resemblance to Vesuvio, with his fingerprints all over the rectory, and with Vesuvio's car parked in the Purple Palace lot? If that is the case, where is Father Vesuvio?"

"Wow! I would like to know," said Harriet.

"Isn't it easier to believe that this Fowler guy, whoever he was, just came and went, and that Delores Fowler wasn't the widow she claimed to be?"

"Much easier," agreed Harriet, "but for me, believing that Father Vesuvio had a secret life is not at all easy. Anyway, we are getting ahead of ourselves. There's a mistake or a secret somewhere in this picture, and for now, I can't say much more. We were handed an important clue at the very beginning when Bishop Norman switched Fathers Vesuvio and Brandy for young Fowler's funeral Mass. That had the entire parish in an uproar."

"I even asked Charlie Cook to follow up with the bishop, but it went nowhere," said Porky.

"It had to have been done for a reason known to Bishop Norman. It may have had to do with Father Brandy. Somebody wanted him here. I still have a bit more research to do at the History Center; I have a few questions for Father Brandy; and I need a little help from Phyllis. Phillip Fowler worked summers for the Cobb Construction Company when he was in high school. He might have been asked to complete an employment application. Anyway, it's getting late, though. We will need to be well rested for your Confession scene tomorrow evening."

No amount of rest could prepare them for all that lay ahead, the planned and the unplanned.

54

Harriet Has a Drink

The Purple Palace Saturday mornings could be as quiet as a church after a funeral. The detritus of what had happened before would still be around. Whiffs of incense, snuffed candles, and mounds of flowers in the church; in the Purple Palace vapors from empty liquor bottles and leftover beer in stacks of dirty glasses and the saccharine odor of something like old bubblegum mixed with disinfectant as Dusty busied himself washing and organizing.

Now and then one of the neighborhood alcoholics might wander in seeking relief from a hangover by having another drink. This morning Dusty had the place to himself at half past ten when Harriet White climbed onto a stool directly in front of him.

Dusty, who made it his life's point to be ready for anything, was visibly shaken. He ran a finger around a stretched-out turtleneck he had worn all day yesterday and slept in. He glanced at the door to see if Porky might be close behind. He dunked a glass in a tub of disinfectant, wiped his hands with a bar towel, and then opened his mouth for two or three seconds before anything came out.

"To what do I owe the pleasure of the presence of the wife of the chief inspector?" he managed to ask, not without stumbling over an excessive number of prepositions.

"Curiosity," said Harriet. "And if you happen to have any coffee, I will have a cup, with cream or milk if that's around somewhere."

"My pleasure," said Dusty on the slow road to recovery.

Harriet with the cup in front of her stirred milk in with a spoon, and then looked up. "I really admire what you are doing, Dusty. Porky doesn't know I am here."

"What am I doing?" asked Dusty.

"You're rescuing young Chicago women trapped in the sex trade. It's perfectly legal. There's no point in denying it. I won't tell a soul, but words gets around as I am sure you know."

Harriet sipped her coffee. For some reason she wanted a cigarette, an out-of-the-blue impulse known only to tobacco addicts. She hadn't smoked in years.

"I have only one question," she said. "I'm not the law; as I said, Porky doesn't know I am here; I think I am trusted by some of your strippers who attend our church."

Dusty nodded, dunked another glass, and looked up.

"The young man whose body was found in the alley. Did he stop by here to speak with you?"

"Yeah, the day before," said Dusty. "We talked about Melody Stillwater. I told him I didn't know her, but I knew of her. Your husband asked me about her a couple of months ago. I beat around the bush, you might say. I didn't want to get involved. I still don't. Where I come from, in Chicago, we don't use the law to settle scores. We do that ourselves in our own time and in our own way. The Fowler kid asked me if I knew anything. I said I had my suspicions."

Dusty dunked another glass and with a bar rag wiped an area in front of Harriet's coffee cup. "I should have done that the minute you sat down here," he said. "I'm losing my bartender's touch."

Harriet looked at him. He looked at her.

"Your goddam choir director," he said through tightening lips. "I'm sorry I told the kid. There's more you might as well know that connects with this. Father Vesuvio and I go way back, all the way to Chicago when we were kids."

He poured Harriet another cup of coffee.

55

"See, George!"

Phyllis Cobb had heard a rumor straight from what is sometimes called 'the horse's mouth,' the horse in this case being her friend, Harriet White, aka Wren. A better account of this would be to say that Wren planted the rumor with the hope (near certainty) that Phyllis would tell George. From there it would become a feature of an expanding universe. George would blab. Even extraterrestrials—should any be around investigating predictable earthlings and dying of boredom—would become interested in the revelation: Porky White was going to partake in the Sacrament of Reconciliation, otherwise known as Confession.

The moment had been set for maximum privacy—St. Callixtus after the Saturday Vigil Mass when the church was closed to the public for the evening. No one's curiosity would be more piqued than Margaret Smuggs', but first Harriet needed to leak information to Phyllis for word to spread.

"I thought Porky was an atheist," said Phyllis.

Harriet came prepared. "He has changed his mind, at least that is what he says. It might have something to do with the sheriff's election. The race is heating up."

"I thought he was a shoe-in."

"He doesn't want to take chances, wants to have God on his side I guess, even if there isn't one."

Phyllis had memorized the Catholic convert's catechism. "Harriet, if Porky has never been baptized, he can get rid of all his sins in one fell swoop—not that he has that many—of course—I don't mean to pry."

"You know Porky. He never takes shortcuts in his investigative work. He expects that God—if there is one—prefers to go the long way around."

Phyllis went home and said, as if that cinched it, "See, George!" This led to the umpteenth recitation of George's lapses as a Catholic piled upon his string of spousal failures and crowned by this most momentous of moments in the life of Porky White straight ahead, after the Saturday Vigil Mass.

A cradle Catholic, George had his own views of what in his childhood had been called the Sacrament of Penance, now softened to Reconciliation at the time of Phyllis' conversion and their marriage before Father Vesuvio. By the couple's tenth anniversary, everything had softened further.

George saw this as part of a trend, something like slow-cooking of tough meat leading to tenderization.

Speaking of which, he enjoyed his Friday hamburgers more than the same burger eaten any other day of the week. In his Catholic youth, he had exhausted his appetite for the tuna noodle hot dish his mother gathered into a gooey mass without fail fifty-two Fridays out of the year. During Lent and Advent, she had double-downed with creamed salt cod on biscuits. It still made him queasy. The fishy odor lingered for weeks and then traversed the decades whenever he recalled it.

Fridays, in these trendy times, as he sat beside his workmen at a café on the edge of a construction zone, he noticed that the protestants were mostly eating fish while Catholics to a man had cheeseburgers. George's version of the Reformation had begun to look like theology on a lazy Susan. This triggered a memory of another of his youthful mentors, still hanging around Twin Rivers long after the parish school closed for good. Nun-like—in a loose sense—she had once been known as Sister Paulina, but these days she wore stretch pants and preferred to be called Judie. Meanwhile one of his Ojibwe workers was a vegetarian who practiced yoga.

The world was opening up, loosening up, softening and spinning around, all sides of it. In George's view, Phyllis needed to get with it: this was only the beginning. She might nag him all she wanted about Confession, but she would never be up-to-date.

56

The Power of Exposure

Except for the six days of creation, building usually takes much longer than destruction. This equally applies to brickwork and to reputation. Adam managed to wreck both Eden and his self-respect with the single bite of an apple.

The honey locust grove separating St. Callixtus from the Hotel Paradise was more than seventy years old, a year or two either way of the ages of Cudahy, Brandy, and Vesuvio. Among the three men, only Cudahy had grown conspicuously important over time. Among the tree grove, one was conspicuously large and well-shaped, taller by yards than any of the rest. In the end, this made no difference. All fell to an earth making all things equal.

Like grim reapers with chainsaws instead of scythes, George Cobb's workmen, employed overtime Saturday morning, had transformed into memory this natural lifetime of trees and men by the time the clock struck noon. By three o'clock, nary a tree stump remained. The grove had become a smoothed over plain of moist clay and sand with George and Whisk standing in the middle of it, surveying the scene.

Imagination fails when it comes to envisioning the loss of things long taken for granted. St. Callixtus Church precincts could not have been imagined without the ancient tree grove forming a living veil between it and the Hotel Paradise. With the veil destroyed, that five-story, boarded up and dilapidated horror seemed to leap forward into the faces of worshippers arriving for the Saturday Vigil Mass. People who normally parked their cars nearest the trees, drove in and drove away to places yet farther from the church. Children being dragged along by parents looked over their shoulders as if fleeing a nightmare. A parish long divided could at last agree on one thing: thank God Pope Vincent was coming, and on that account, by next week the Hotel Paradise would be flattened and forever erased.

No thought had yet been given to what most regarded as yet another horror loitering beyond The Paradise. With the hotel as much a memory as the honey locust trees, with the space it once occupied also vacant and smoothed over by George Cobb's machinery, St. Callixtus and Dwyer's Purple Palace would be next door neighbors. The new pope would perhaps sleep with Dusty's *Girls! Girls! Girls!* neon sign splashing colored lights on his bedclothes throughout the night. No imagination, no matter how vivid, had yet gotten that far.

Within St. Callixtus and with a Wi-Fi disabler under his chair, Brandy heard a handful of confessions and dispensed as many absolutions before Mass began. Among those waiting in pews were George and Phyllis Cobb occupying their usual place by the Fourth Station of the Cross. On this particular Saturday, Phyllis stayed home till Mass time, but George had spent the entire day at St. Callixtus supervising his tree-cutting crew. With that much out of the way, resembling the scare-a-crow from Oz, he shuffled into church leaving a trail of sawdust. He had expected to stay after, to meet with Father Brandy—to fine-tune plans for Monday's hotel demolition, but Brandy, robed for Mass, came down a side aisle well beforehand to whisper in his ear.

Phyllis whispered in George's other ear. "What have you done now, George? The whole church is looking at us and wondering what you did?"

"Father Brandy just postponed our meeting until morning," George whispered back.

"He probably knows that you haven't so much as showered after a day with those trees. He is probably allergic to sawdust."

"Fine-tune," said George.

"*Fine-tune*, my eye, George," Phyllis added after an unladylike snort, "How do you fine-tune enough TNT to blow up that dreadful Paradise monstrosity?"

"Blow it in," said George. "*Im*plode it. Damn it!"

"Implode, explode, blow out, blow in," said Phyllis. "Who cares, just as long as The Paradise goes away, but your meeting has probably been postponed because after Mass, Father will be hearing Porky White's First Confession. It's bound to be as long as a filibuster. I don't know why Father just doesn't take a shortcut and baptize him on the spot. But as long as you're hanging around, you might follow Porky's example and do the same. I am sure Father would be happy to oblige."

Their whispered voices had grown louder with each exchange. People familiar with the Cobb's incessant bickering were exchanging grins. Those who did not know it was a repeat performance were shushing. A bell rang, everybody stood up, and Mass began and with it a tidal wave of hymn singing, mostly Bernard's. George moved lips from which no sound emerged, pretending to sing as Bernard directed. The shape of George's lips resembled those of a Swiss yodeler on a ski resort billboard.

Since the choir did not sing for Saturday Vigils in Ordinary Time, Bernard cantored from the front, sang, and waved his arms like a man signaling flying craft from a Navy carrier at sea. He became the music and the show, hogging the limelight all the more, trying extra hard in case a scouting party of Pope Vincent's might be among the congregation.

Bernard even decided to solo a cappella the E-Flat Major hymn still visible on the weekend hymn chalkboard. Perhaps that 'miserable stripper,' fancying herself a singer, was among those who heard and despaired of ever sounding so good. After his larger-than-life performance, in his estimation, even the Consecration seemed second fiddle. With Pope Vincent's chartered Alitalia flight just now landing in Minneapolis, this St. Callixtus Saturday Vigil nonetheless turned out to be all about worshipping and envying the celebrated Bernard Passmore.

When the end of Mass rang out in Bernard's operatic baritone, George took the hint to flee before Brandy made announcements and Phyllis could mention Confession again.

Earlier in the day, Margaret Smuggs, who worked Saturday mornings, had mentioned in passing that Father Brandy had scheduled a single administration of the Sacrament of Reconciliation after the Vigil Mass.

A most well-known Paradise County official had decided to make peace with the Church of his wife, not that he had exactly been at war with it. He had just been ignoring it as an atheist for much of his life. His local stature demanded anonymity.

"Porky White," said Margaret. "Now, that should be interesting. I would love to know what's dogging our next sheriff's conscience after so many years, wouldn't you, Bernie? Imagine poor, half deaf Father Brandy listening to forty or so years of our Porky's failings."

Margaret was playing the role of a temptress in sharing all this, fabricating a few things to tease Bernard further. Her goal was to be seen again as Bernard's sidekick, just in case she had betrayed any appearance of her recent treason; just in case he might suspect that after a tumbler or two of vodka and misplaced anger she had spoken too freely to the future sheriff's wife, all for the 'benefit' of her well-researched church history.

Bernard could be easily tempted. He discovered in human frailty a power source whose higher voltages were to be found in those an admiring, gullible public considered most upright. As he saw it, people like Porky were bound to have the secret lives all men harbor, encased in reputations they needed to protect at all cost. They were the pasteboard, Tinseltown heroes whose real lives were a disgrace. Bernard had only to discover what they were up to after nightfall, after the theater grew dark, everyone from piffle shopkeepers and piffle parish priests to self-absorbed clowns wearing crown and mitre, the more important the better. The threat of exposure was a power source beyond even that of nuclear plants.

Atomic energy could illuminate entire cities. For Bernard's purposes, whatever was said in the simple wooden shed called a confessional, and the threat of its exposure yielded far more power. Men, like Porky, comfortably situated with secure reputations, lived in abject fear of life with their mask of respectability ripped away.

57

Alternative Pathways

George, who could not have found his way out of a barn with its doors wide open, claimed to have discovered another pathway to divine forgiveness. Thus, he had joined the 'liberated' masses who no longer knew a confessional from a recessional, a *prie-dieu* from a bill to be paid beforehand and thought an examination of conscience a multiple choice take-home test.

The possible existence of other ways to wipe the slate clean had been given scant treatment in Phyllis' Catholic convert instruction. She was horrified to the point of putting her hands to her ears whenever he attempted to talk about it. Like so many of the 'let it all hang out' generation, she preferred being out in the open, standing in a chronically short confessional line for the whole world to see her in all her disgusting nakedness—not literally of course. In an earlier age, she would have heaped ashes on her head and marched through the streets of Twin Rivers on her way to St. Callixtus. In that other world, she would have carried a placard upon which were written in large letters a declaration that she was no more than a worm.

No one confessed sins more audibly than Phyllis. Whispered transgressions were for cowards. Bernard Passmore could have heard her without the aid of his Blackbird. People in the confessional line would back away to distant corners to stare at floor tiles when she went in and closed the door. Father Vesuvio, and now Father Brandy, might have stayed in the rectory and listened to her sins from an open window.

It riled George when she attempted to discuss his public impenitence. She had never worked up the courage to ask Father Vesuvio what he thought, but she now quoted him as if he still spoke the living truth. With Vesuvio at a 'safe distance,' or as George would say, 'gone to his reward,' Phyllis felt free to make up stuff supporting her side. This might have been just as well since, as Brandy knew, Vesuvio himself seemed to have private misgivings about the sacrament.

That said, George always knew more than Phyllis, and more than any priest, young or old, dared admit knowing. He would dutifully escort Phyllis to St. Callixtus for her biweekly reception of the sacrament. A short stroll later he would appear at his preferred waiting post, the Purple Palace. There, he rehearsed knowing looks, exchanged wordless nods with Dusty Dwyer, grew giddy, and waited for his cell phone to ring.

Phyllis would call when it was all over, after she had confessed enough sins for two lifetimes and said a penance twice that prescribed, including George and his transgressions in her intentions to reform.

George had rituals of his own. After wading into the depths of a second martini, and after consulting his watch and comparing it with the tavern clock, which was always ten minutes fast, he would sometimes argue with an imagined Phyllis, saying things he was afraid to say were she anywhere near: "Sometime let me tell you about Judas," he would say under a breath well beyond sobriety limits; "Let me tell you about fig leaves, and the Potter's Field, and why church candles are made from beeswax." He had memorized it all from Sister Dolorosa's third-grade class.

"Dolorosa who? What's on your mind, George?" Dusty asked while mixing George's third martini. This was somewhat like a priest asking for a bit more detail.

"Pagan babies," George said. For reasons known only to God, George often obsessed about pagan babies as a refuge from sobriety. "We never got to meet any of those pagan babies first hand. They were somewhere in Africa or maybe Mongolia. I always wanted to meet one."

"Yeah, they were in Chicago too —a prostitution ring that got busted with a little help from me. Ask me about it sometime."

George yanked himself out of his inner dialogue in disbelief, then sank back in with another tug on his drink.

He remembered the pagan babies his third-grade class purchased with coins brought to school from raided piggy banks. Pagan babies cost six dollars each in those days. By the time Lent rolled around that year, his class had purchased two, one girl baby and one boy baby.

"Six bucks, Dusty."

Dusty could not resist. "No kidding! George—in Chicago, the Pagan Babies cost way more than that. Of course, those were bigger babies."

George had always wanted a sister. He hoped Sister Dolorosa would hold a classroom drawing for the girl pagan baby, the way she held drawings for pastel-dyed baby chicks the class hatched at Easter. He had yet to see a pagan baby, boy or girl, black or yellow or green as Easter grass, but he had heard and recalled no end of things, visible and invisible, that Phyllis, the convert, would never have imagined.

Among rituals more minute, equally quaint and outdated by some accounts was George's reluctance to cross himself with holy water when passing a font, as if he feared it as much as the after-work showers he also skipped. He would, though, after spilling salt on Dusty's bar, throw a pinch over his shoulder, just in case.

George's cell phone might ring anytime now. He threw Dusty a wink. Dusty nodded, a gesture that seemed to say, "Tell me later. Not now." George would soon stagger down the hotel alley and slide into his car on the passenger side. After Phyllis' weekly confessions, she was the designated driver. If his face had not frozen into a fixed, vodka-induced grin, he would throw her that knowing look.

Tonight was not one of those nights.

As sure as the unlikely has a way of happening, on this night of Porky White's Confession, a straw stack of drink straws harvested over eons—as the proverb goes—broke the camel's back. In this case, George, the camel, had sucked up four martinis as if he approached a desert. Dusty was at the point of cutting him off.

"I am done with it," said George.

"I'll say," said Dusty, hugging what remained of his extra strength Russian Vodka.

"Not that. I have had enough and am going to Confession. There is a special one this evening. It will be very private."

"Sin?"

"No, that is easier to get rid of than Phyllis. I will show her what."

"What was what?" asked Dusty.

"I'm going for it!" said George.

Neither had a notion of what the other was talking about.

Dusty, of course, knew all about confessions, the drunken sort resulting from what experienced bar observers call a 'crying jag.' He had heard his share from men head down over bars in his various joints. He had said as much to Vesuvio.

He had never seen George in his present extremity. George, a local businessman, knew his limit, two martinis as it happened, albeit extra dry.

Dusty glanced up from what had to be George's record-breaking martini, his fifth. Strong drinks were like long knock-out punches in a boxing match. Five would put most anyone out.

George was on his feet, circling, but nonetheless standing. He attempted to hitch up his pants, but instead pulled on his shirt tails. He straightened up to set his jaw, as most drunks will attempt to do from the mistaken notion that bolt upright and jutting jaw suggest sobriety, not *rigor mortis*. He wove his way down the poorly lit Paradise alley. In what had been till yesterday the honey locust grove, he staggered as if dodging zombie tree trunks, one of which turned out to be Bernard Passmore, dressed in black, puffing a cigar.

"Drunk again?" said Bernard.

"Excush me," said George. "Whichswsay is the church, my good man?"

Bernard spun him toward the hotel. George wobbled off toward the street looking for an entrance.

Bernard Passmore ground a cigar butt under his foot. "Our explosives expert. Piffle!" Glancing at his gold "chronometer," Bernard backpedaled toward the church, the man in charge, no matter what the time of day. He had time yet before his appointment with the confessional Blackbird.

Still some distance from his destination, George appeared to be shadowboxing.

58

A Universal Constant

Bernard Passmore's entrances were seldom less than operatic quality, but tonight he felt unaccountably awash with the uncertainties of opening night performances. His confessional Blackbird had quit working, and then started up again as if by whim just as confessions were ending. George Cobb's stumbling into him also may have explained his disquiet; a drunk in the audience, or in the scene, usually spelled disaster of the sort that could knock his baritone into the tenor range, an octave off. Not that he would be singing; with the Vigil Mass over, that was behind him; the night just felt that way.

If not George and a fickle Blackbird, the cause of his hesitations may have been unfamiliar shadows now cast where locust trees had always been. Something ghostlike seemed to materialize in his unobstructed view down the-moonlit alley to where the 'Fowler punk' lay mere weeks ago.

Stark memories washed ashore in a tidal undertow. Beneath Bernard's feet, a world was shifting, becoming even stranger than the strangeness George invoked at every chance. An ending and a beginning wrapped around each other. In the hotel alley, a phantom Vesuvio in black cape and hat bent over Fowler's form. Death-white hands beneath crossed thumbs held a rosary of spaces without beads. Bernard shivered.

He never used first names. It had always been, *Smuggs, do this and that*; always the *piffle rat Dwyer* adored by jezebels and women of the night, and gay at that; always the *pompous, piffle, cooing Whites,* but tonight Bernard called the phantom *Vincent* without thinking about it. He hated the man even in death, because he remained somewhere, part of a light shining in his darkness, making him squint.

He could not imagine why anyone would miss Vesuvio, just another gay priest of a legion, and his buddy Brandy, probably yet another.

Stupidity was Bernard's universal constant.

The Hotel Paradise would soon go the way of the honey locust trees. Bernard would mourn the loss of its durable innuendo and gossip, its ancient secrets, and yellow crime-scene tapes—Sixth through Tenth commandment stuff, throwing in a murder or two or three for the sake of variety, and adding a dash of sodomy when ordinary, nasty sin could be so boring. This loved and hated past might be obliterated in an exceptional explosion, yet tonight Bernard could feel it returning one day to haunt him in the sweaty palm of his expansive hand. He could feel a free man with one sun setting and a captive man with another sun rising.

As it happened, the moon had just slipped behind St. Callixtus erasing his shadow. It could feel like death. Hope, no longer to the west, had pivoted south while Bernard had been looking elsewhere. His all-knowing, all-seeing omnipresence had been shrinking. Pope Vincent's plane had landed with its shadow racing before it in runway lights. A silvery, steaming fuselage now aimed toward the heart of scandals Bernard sowed and would reap as sown.

Bernard barged through the St. Callixtus side door, entering two steps ahead of George Cobb who had been feeling his way as if blindfolded along the church's stone walls. Both men staggered. This race would go neither to the strong nor the weak, but to silence that endureth.

Bernard lumbered toward the parish center office.

George immersed himself in conversation with a holy water font before attempting to shake hands with St. Callixtus.

59

The Unlikely and the Impossible Intersect

The Vigil Mass concluded, St. Callixtus emptied with a gusher, then a trickle, and finally a drip, drip of elderly widows lighting candles or lingering over old rosaries. Father Brandy, his arm aching from so much hand-shaking, stood alone in the church portico. At such moments, he longed for the bygone era when priests could disappear after Sunday Mass, not stand at an exit shaking hands like a man running for elected office. He longed for the old days when the celebrant priest made a beeline through the vestry for lunch, leaving the world outside to its own resources and its non-clergy glad-handers.

The entrances to St. Callixtus, normally unlocked at this time, were locked, except for the side entrance nearest the Hotel Paradise. Lights were turned down. A few candles were snuffed as if by an unseen hand. A Wi-Fi disabler in the confessional had itself been disabled. The stage had been set, awaiting only its actors.

Porky White—in an unaccustomed position for a lawman—entered from the parish center hallway and knelt near the confessional. Harriet pretended to be at work in the archive. Bernard Passmore strode into his office and closed the door. Among the players in this miniature drama, only Brandy was not yet in place. He had puttered up a side aisle, genuflected, and disappeared into the vestry. Minutes later he returned.

Unbeknownst to any of them, the unlikely and the impossible were about to intersect.

As sometimes happens in theatrical comedy, a drunk staggered into the scene.

Conscience had nothing do with this. Remorse had nothing to do with this. Heaven and Hell, damnation and salvation, had nothing to do with this. It had come down to Phyllis' nagging. The weight of George's sins was no more than a bag of feathers compared to the leaden guilt she heaped upon him for his recent failures as a husband. A moralist might have thought him imbued with the fear of the devil chasing his soul. Instead it was only Phyllis attempting to take possession of it, wanting to own it lock, stock, and barrel.

The sight of Porky White kneeling near the confessional could have been enough to turn him on his heels, but those five martinis had left him well beyond the point of no return. Bent on putting it behind him, George plunged right into the confessional before Porky could make a move. He would reclaim at least the lock and stock, if not the barrel of his soul.

The unlikely had trumped the impossible. The charade meant to catch Bernard Passmore in the act of eavesdropping required split second improvisation.

60

The Silent Shepherd Speaks

George closed the confessional door. As his knees settled into place, an interior light went off, and an exterior door light came on. The Sacrament of Reconciliation, while not exactly high-tech, had at least become electrical.

No one could warn Brandy that George Cobb had staggered into Porky White's theater role. On the other side, behind a screen, was not a steady lawman, rehearsed for the scene, but drunken George Cobb on the verge of passing out.

Brandy was not the only character in this play who thought he knew something he did not know: Harriet White thought Porky was in the confessional, as did Bernard Passmore. Phyllis Cobb had been left out of the loop, but kept in the wings as a convincing bystander. When George crashed the scene at the last minute, she was ready to sing the Battle Hymn of the Republic, for she truly was witnessing the glory of the coming of the Lord, or so she thought.

Of the seven people involved in this unfolding stealth drama, only one was beyond reach of impending confusion: Margaret Smuggs had called it a day and gone home to nurse a hangover acquired at her desk.

The remaining six, as much as they had divergent motives, conflicting hopes, and misconceptions—all of them without exception—were wrong beyond the shadow of doubt invoked in trials. When George Cobb shot past a kneeling Porky, all advance planning and subterfuge, every smidgeon of motive, self-interest, and the world's common good turned inside out and backward. For the next fifteen minutes, nothing was as it seemed. The play's characters stuck with their prepared lines, mindless of the fact that this was the wrong play, on the wrong day, in a theater where stand-up comedy was the new feature.

Brandy closed his eyes more firmly than he normally did. He shifted in his chair, not exactly a familiar chair, but one Vesuvio seemed to have kept warm, as if he had just gotten up after sitting there so many years. He said a prayer for Vesuvio's soul, now free from a seal bouncing red balls his way.

He was more than a little taken aback when the man he thought to be Porky White began reciting the Apostle's Creed and stopped halfway through to mumble something about pagan babies. In his forty years as a priest, he had yet to hear a penitent begin with the Apostle's Creed, let alone bring pagan babies into it, and go from there to the mysteries of the multiplication tables.

At his office listening post, Bernard Passmore heard his Blackbird chirp things so outlandish that he began to fear control over Porky White was slipping away: no one would believe what this man was now revealing to Father Brandy. *Was Brandy stupid enough to just sit there listening to garble from a hyperactive sex fiend? What had he just said about pagan babies? Who the hell were they? Had Porky been snatching babies from their cribs at night, or was he indulging in orgies with god knows what sort of loose women, to the number of 144?*

Harriet, the script writer for this pious interlude, listened from the parish archive room. The Blackbird chirps coming her way through a tinny receiver made her husband's voice indistinguishable from that of a talkative parrot. His preposterous sins were so far off script that she could not but admire his creativity while laughing all the while. His drunken slurs were those of Oscar-winning comic actors.

Except in circumstances as exceptional as these, Brandy would never have auditioned for any play, let alone one contrived around a Church sacrament and suddenly become this ridiculous. With George stumbling over something having to do with Nebuchadnezzar and the Potter's Field, Brandy exploded from the confessional with one hand in his hair and another holding his chair as he bounded through a doorway leading into the parish center.

On the fringes, Phyllis grew wide-eyed. What had George confessed leading to this spectacle? Priests as old as Brandy should have heard it all by this time. What had George admitted doing that no man on earth had never done before? Images of sin crying out against nature, quickie divorce, and devils as grinning hyenas swirled before her eyes. She screamed and fainted somewhere beyond Sodom and Gomorrah.

Porky sprang from his vigil on wobbly knees and reached for his service revolver, in this instance no more than a reflex. Harriet had asked him for the sake of reverence to leave it behind in the church archive.

Down the hall, Brandy's voice could more than be heard. It passed through walls of history and of stone, through plasterboard and the hollow-core door of Bernard Passmore's office. It was thunder followed by lightning. It was the voice of God's stand in, the Silent Shepherd no longer silent.

"Bernard Passmore, come out! You have violated the sanctity and sacred duty of this Church. Your time has come. You are fired and forbidden from these precincts until the day you repent. May God in his mercy forgive you."

By this time, Bernard had opened his door, filling its framework. His Blackbird dangled from his ear, detached from its connecting point. He seemed to grow taller and wider. Murder was in his face, now become Cyclopean.

"How dare you, piffle priest," he said. "Have you any idea who I am?"

He raised a gigantic hand toward Brandy. Porky shoulder-blocked the priest to safety, flattening the two of them on the hallway floor. Harriet White stepped in place, gun in hand to answer Bernard's question.

"We know who you are and what you are. —You're under arrest," she said resolutely as if this had all been part of the play, and readied for this dress rehearsal. She stepped close to Wilbur who had come to her side. "I am sure my husband would agree."

"You can bet on it, Wren," said Porky.

Back in the church, Phyllis Cobb regained consciousness amid the resonant sound of George snoring in the confessional, sleeping the sleep of the forgiven and of a baby needing no forgiveness.

From a parish center window often used as a lookout by Bernard Passmore, Brandy watched a Paradise County squad car with flashing lights carrying him away.

The next morning, Margaret Smuggs was fired.

The Silent Shepherd at last had spoken.

Closing of Box Four

BOX FIVE

A BOX CALLED A COFFIN

Not everything unknown is unknowable.
Some things are just never discovered.

–ANONYMOUS

61

Paradise Both Lost and Regained

At long last came the moment St. Callixtus parishioners thought would never come. The imminent arrival of Pope Vincent in a motorcade had greased even the rustiest of gears, dislodging George who as an engineer of destruction might have played Hamlet. *To be or not to be,* by an obscure process of elimination, came down to ... *to be.*

Pope Vincent could not be received with a dilapidated Paradise in the picture viewed the world over on computers, on smartphones, and on TV. A denizen of Vatican Rome, the Iron Cardinal would have toured the ancient Coliseum where lions feasted on Christians ages ago. The rank and randy Hotel Paradise where Christian men, in times more recent, had feasted on destitute young women was not the way to greet Minnesota's pope and the host of dignitaries in his retinue.

A crowd gathered in Old Town as if awaiting an execution at sunrise. Nothing beats demolition, a form of execution, for offering the excitement of vandalism and homicide without remorse and jail terms. Twin Rivers united into a rarely heard common buzz in the emerging shadows of an historic day.

New Towners standing behind yellow crime-scene tapes, affably chatted with Old Town folk. Demolition on this scale led to fellow-feeling and nervous, bubbly bursts of goodwill of the sort one might expect at dawn on Judgment Day. For a few minutes, all were equal: lions lay down with lambs and billy goats; bankers chatted with riffraff; hedge fund managers chatted with hedge trimmers. A world was ending, or at least hesitating between coughing fits.

Harriet White envisioned a new chapter for St. Callixtus' sesquicentennial history, with some such title as *Paradise Lost* or *East of Eden*, except both had been taken. Though there were reporters with cameras on the scene, she had brought her own. A competent detective never relied on others' perspectives.

Porky directed a squad of Paradise County police struggling to keep the expanding legions at a safe distance, though no one knew what a safe distance might be. Some thought perhaps a half mile or so; others, considering a show produced and directed by George Cobb, thought a half foot would be okay.

No one thought the moment would be as George planned it. Naysayers and 'Chicken Little' sorts were certain that halfwit George would bring down the sky upon gullible heads. A few wore protective gear of the sort seen in films featuring asteroid collisions and invading extraterrestrial robots.

A whimsical atmosphere suggested the impending failure of a circus clown. George Cobb was about to make a fool of himself. His project would either fizzle or blow up the entire neighborhood, including both St. Callixtus and the Purple Palace. Some even took bets.

But against all odds, George turned out to be the prophet ridiculed by his own people. He closed his eyes as if he himself were blinded by doubt. Had he not needed both hands to signal, and at least the appearance of bravado, he would have covered his ears and run for shelter.

He gave two thumbs up. After a pause, he gave two thumbs up again, followed by laughter in the crowd as nothing happened. Two or three seconds trickled by. George bowed his head. He might have been the only one to miss an incandescent flash igniting faces all around.

With an exhausted sigh and a few smoke puffs from broken windows, the old hotel folded within itself like a gigantic sleeper sofa. Those hoping to witness a titanic concussion groaned with disappointment even as a cataclysmic spectacle erupted overhead in unearthly silence. A column of plaster dust and pulverized porcelain fragments formed a mushroom cloud billowing skyward, flattening out and spreading in all directions, toward the rivers to the south and New Town to the north. For a time, the sun disappeared above the swelling shadow. Horizons in all directions sank from view as atomic relics of the old Paradise formed a titanic whirlpool pierced by sunlight arrows.

Everything at ground level soon disappeared. Every spectator was left eerily alone. None dared move while seconds passed. A throat-clutching haze gave way to gagging fits. From afar, within minutes, no part of Twin Rivers, New Town or Old, could be seen through the roiling haze. From distant hilltops where farmers watched, the twin spires of St. Callixtus sank from view, the last to drown in George Cobb's silent, man-made sea.

George had imagined dancing in triumph and fist-bumping everyone within reach. Instead, upon opening his eyes he trembled and scratched his head. Ashen white from head to toe, he seemed to have upended a flour canister from a high shelf.

Yet George had done as well as Adam and Eve, though all were amateurs. The Hotel Paradise, having withstood a century's worth of galas, gales, gossip, and suspicions, had collapsed upon itself as tired old suns of distant worlds are said to do.

When he finally recovered enough to see a fist that might be bumped, it proved to be the mammoth fist of Bernard Passmore grinning through a haze. Harriet had spotted him well before this, mingling in a crowd of SNFA supporters as if accepting congratulations.

"Released overnight on his own recognizance," said Porky, "despite my mentioning that murder charges were pending further investigation. We could never get an indictment based on the evidence we have, handwriting analysis and the Charlie Cook mess. We have to get a break somewhere, but with Pope Vincent showing up, I can't put even one of my men on it."

"Bernard has something on the judge, and on the Paradise County coroner, both Catholics," said Harriet without looking the least crestfallen.

"You can bet on it, Wren."

"There is more to come, Wilbur. Something tells me Pope Vincent will bring it. You can bet on that too."

62

Afterthoughts and After Images

A headline in the Twin Rivers Clarion spoke of the hotel's demolition as punctuating the end of an era.

Harriet White thought otherwise, for in its wake were two puzzles looking more and more like one, the murders of Phillip Fowler and Vincent Vesuvio. In crime reports and news stories already grown old, Vesuvio was still listed as 'tentatively' identified, though his funeral had been held, and in the churchyard of St. Brendan's at Turning Wind, his body lay beneath mounded earth where grass had begun to grow. It appeared that Bernard Passmore had written the 'suicide' notes, but what had been his motive? Was it one motive or two? Without what detectives call a smoking gun, and with nothing more concrete to bring against him than flourishes in the printed letters *E* and *F*, homicide charges could not be made to stick. His presence at the hotel demolition said as much. Two question marks, an ellipsis, and a lurking Bernard were the punctuation marks at the end of Hotel Paradise.

As an historian and amateur detective, Harriet knew how easily history can be lost and old crimes buried. Demolition destroys the past in an instant—much of it. The little remaining afterward is where history and crime investigation became the same thing. While compiling her St. Callixtus history, she had unearthed many a story connecting the church and the old hotel in ways visible, long-buried, and forgotten. In a transcendent mind such as Harriet's, past and present became one thing.

With the crowd dwindling at the hotel's demolition site, Harriet cast glances betwixt and between Bernard, the dissipating dust cloud, and Cobb Construction machinery carting away debris, bulldozing and grading what was becoming a vacant lot. Bernard had been joined by Margaret Smuggs, holding a bottle of vodka retrieved from her desk and what amounted to her 'pink slip.' The malice in his demeanor and the hatred evident in hers were enough to bring a reminder from Porky that both were trespassing. Bernard smiled, and Margaret sneered as they were escorted outside the church precinct by two armed officers.

Porky would not miss the hotel as a symbol of lawlessness and rampage, even if most stories were hearsay. Hearsay and rumor could reflect poorly on Paradise County Law Enforcement. With The Paradise blown to smithereens, he would be able to reassign rookie deputies routinely checking the place. Since he was short-handed, this was another plus. The hotel assignment had not helped to stave off the boredom inevitably awaiting guys who got into police work looking for daily shoot-'em-ups. Porky had also become a pragmatic philosopher while managing his Paradise County force.

From the main entrance to St. Callixtus, Brandy watched Cobb Construction Bobcats, dump trucks, and bulldozers. His thoughts were with his old friend Vincent whose body had been found there little more than two months ago. In the way that nature, or the grace of God steps in to shelter and protect from grievous loss, Vincent's death seemed much longer ago than it was. At least now, the Hotel Paradise would not be an immediate reminder the moment he gazed from a window or stepped into the church parking lot. And yet somehow his old friend's body would always be there, suspended in timeless space above what used to be.

Standing on the entrance stairs of St. Callixtus, Brandy also saw something that ought to have been obvious, but that most people beforehand had overlooked. Peering across a broken landscape bereft of its locust tree grove and still littered with broken hotel fixtures and twisted pipes, he saw Dusty Dwyer surveying the very same scene from the other side, sizing it up as Dusty would do. He and Dusty were next door neighbors now.

Dusty noticed Brandy just as Brandy noticed him. Here was another sunrise and another sunset. He waved, and the old priest waved back. Two characters, each of them especially tough and hardened in their own ways, the strip club owner and the parish priest, were sharing the same stage. From this day forward, the play would never be the same.

Within a few hours, George Cobb's machinery had finished clearing the demolition site. A substantial concrete shard had been sculpted into a bench-like shape by the force of the blast. George had it moved toward the boulevard where soon it served as a bench for Brandy to sit while reading his daily prayers, and Dusty one day to join him reading his newspaper, two old men at the end of an era in what would become a tidy civic garden called Paradise Green.

63

Crossings

Unlikely to have occurred to anyone, other than a theologian or a cynic, was the irony of a pope's motorcade passing a roadside sign announcing his entry into Paradise County, 'Eden of the North Country': Eden had no need for popes.

"Your Holiness, we are now in Paradise County!" exclaimed Pope Vincent's guide.

This elicited a smirk. "Paradise is an old story," said Pope Vincent.

"Yes indeed, Holiness."

Pope Vincent and his papal motorcade approached the outskirts of Twin Rivers in a line of traffic not seen since a backcountry forest fire sent hordes of settlers fleeing into the pioneer city hoping its rivers would spare them. Hundreds perished. A nearby settlement ever since has been known as Dire Straits. A bronze plaque on a bridge marked the place where many were trapped. Having researched the route meticulously, the pope's guide pointed out the spot in passing.

Pope Vincent said he had heard the story long before.

"Of course, Your Holiness. You are from this land. Forgive me!"

"Indeed," said Pope Vincent, blessing the spot with a Sign of the Cross from his window. "I grew up here."

The erstwhile guide briefly fell silent. The pontiff seemed lost in thought as befit a man returning home after a long journey with much having changed in his absence.

His Italian guide, a priest, handed him a local newspaper, the Twin River's Clarion with its front-page story of the Hotel Paradise destroyed.

"A fascinating picture taken by a drone, Your Holiness, a fleeting impression only. The story says that no one at ground level could verify it." Pope Vincent's guide spoke in the carefully enunciated manner of one interpreting for a visiting dignitary who does not know English.

"Yes, of course," said Pope Vincent, taking the Clarion's front page in hand and studying the picture closely while reading an account of a 'remarkably coincidental and timely illusion.'

The Clarion photograph revealed a gray, smoldering dust cloud, split seconds after George Cobb's TNT exploded, instantly exposing indentations formed by the collapse of legendary tunnels between St. Callixtus and The Paradise and from there to the Purple Palace. The dust cloud formed along these indentations joined at the hotel's center as it collapsed into its basement. A cruciform shape was unmistakable. Anyone walking the perimeter would have noted this, as George Cobb did once he had fist-bumped Bernard Passmore and everyone within reach. The ashen plaster cloud by then had become the flattened disk slowly overspreading all of Paradise County.

Darkness had settled over the land, and George, whose head was full of indelible Sister Dolorosa impressions, immediately thought of the hour Christ died on his Cross. He could not stand in the precise spot because this cross was made of tunnel indentations and the broken innards of Paradise, crushed into its understory. But in his own fleeting moment of explosive glory, he recalled Sister Dolorosa's story of St. Monica, the mother of Emperor Constantine, returning to Rome with the Holy Cross. "Miraculously," said Sister, "no matter how much wood was taken from it to cherish in grateful prayer, the Cross itself remains whole to this very day." She brought a sliver from the St. Callixtus convent chapel. Encased in a cedar box, beneath a glittering glass was a sliver no bigger than the tip of a honey locust thorn. George never forgot it, though he would never again see it. Today, standing tall beside his demolition cross, he could visualize his finger reaching for the reliquary lid. "Must not touch," said Sister Dolorosa. "Sacred, Sacred, Sacred..."

What George could *not* see would have had him stopping his bulldozers in their tracks as they rumbled forward to erase a vision and smooth out impressions, soon lost forever. The drone's photographs, twenty shots, seconds apart, revealed what Pope Vincent studied as his motorcade entered Twin Rivers. Out of sight above the spectators assembled to witness the old hotel's destruction, out of sight from Bernard Passmore and Margaret Smuggs, from Porky and Harriet White, from Dusty Dwyer and 'his girls,' and from Brandy with his thoughts of Vincent, was the unmistakable, smoky impression of a human body stretching out upon a cross. Seconds later, toward the last of the picture series, the form had already vanished into an opaque haze. The crucifixion scene melted away. What remained of the margins were images of witnesses gaping skyward, disappointed at what a poor show it had been.

As Pope Vincent's entourage crossed the last of Twin Rivers' bridges, flags waved, crucifixes were held high for a papal blessing, small children were hoisted on parental shoulders. The ever-elusive Whisk stood as if at attention beside a white-eared black dog up on its hind legs. Bernard Passmore beamed and waved as if he were the celebrity on display and not a man recently arrested on suspicion of undisclosed crimes.

As the poet Robert Browning observed, "God's in His heaven—All's right with the world!" So it seemed.

After blessing upon blessing, the pope exited his limousine without assistance. With the Clarion in hand, he strode alone toward Brandy, waiting—as requested—at one of the church's side entrances. In every step and every inch of bolt upright man, here was the Iron Cardinal arriving home.

"You're *It*, Brandy," he said with conviction.

"We're both *It*, Holiness," Brandy managed to choke out, in a voice far from his own.

"We're both crazy," whispered Pope Vincent. "I could never have done it by myself..."

A door closed behind them. They were alone. Brandy had never imagined it beginning this way, as if they had been transported by a time machine back to their All Saints School days.

64

A Time to Speak

A vast, empty space of Gothic vaulting floated above the two old friends, united out of nowhere in a world faintly aglow with late afternoon sun through stained glass turning black piece by piece as the day's flames went out. The space was for that moment more substantial than space, and not just space, but light, color, and air, blended into something that could only be sensed by touching something out of reach. It seemed to lower itself over the pope's shoulders like a great stole when he advanced to the altar as if he were a man who had been there many times before. He glanced around at pale, ghostlike statues, half hidden within shadowy niches. In other niches, where statues once stood, faces seemed to stare at him. He seemed to know them all.

Kneeling before the tabernacle in silent prayer beside the new Holy Father, Brandy could not have been more shaken. Here was his old tag buddy Jack from eons ago; here was Crackerjack with whom he had not spoken in more than half a century; here was the man formerly known as the Iron Cardinal, a titan in the Church; here was a memory turned by imagination into something he could never have imagined; yet here Brandy was, and here it was happening, while the entire world looked on in wonderment beyond St. Callixtus' walls.

The world of cardinals, bishops, high ranking diocesan types, prominent state officials, New Town leaders, a governor or two, a half dozen regional United States Senators, national media personalities—all these waited without knowing what was transpiring within St. Callixtus Church between Pope Vincent and an obscure parish priest named Aloysius Brandy.

Bishop Norman, one-up on most waiting outside, said to more than one cardinal, "Believe it or not, they are old primary school friends reunited. Father Brandy once pushed our new pope into a mud puddle." This report never failed to elicit amazement, and here and there an irreverent giggle.

Little wonder, then, with all this guessing and speculation outside a hundred yards or more away, and with everything spinning around in poor Brandy's head, the old priest could not pray at all. He knelt there beside the pontiff waiting for a suggestion that he had prayed enough.

Never, never, in all his wildest imaginings could Brandy have conjured up what happened next. Pope Vincent, while still on his knees with his eyes fixed on the tabernacle, in a voice as if from another world, began reciting a portion of Vesuvio's favorite Old Testament book:

> "There is a time for everything,
> and a season for every activity under the heavens:
> a time to be born and a time to die,
> a time to plant and a time to uproot,
> a time to kill and a time to heal,
> a time to tear down and a time to build,
> a time to weep and a time to laugh,
> a time to mourn and a time to dance,
> a time to scatter stones and a time to gather them ...
>
> ... a time to be silent and a time to speak ..."

Then like a thunderclap at sunrise— "Aloysius Brandy, who do you think I am?"

No question could have been more unexpected. It was like a border control officer asking someone his name, and the man hesitating, appearing to make up something when he had simply been taken by surprise. Brandy hesitated.

"—You are the Holy Father, Pope Vincent."

"And who is that, Father Brandy?"

"Cardinal John Cudahy." By this time, Brandy was getting into the spirit of this exchange, and by all appearances, so was the pope.

"And who is Cardinal Cudahy? Is he not your old friend you called Crackerjack whom you once pushed into a mud puddle?"

"That was a long time ago, your Holiness. We were very young."

"And you have never since told anyone this story?" Pope Vincent's voice grew stern and heated.

"Once or twice your Holiness. I meant no disrespect."

"Did you gossip about it to Father Vincent Vesuvio, and if so how many times? You have been trained to insist that serious sins must be numbered when confessed."

"I think maybe twice."

"Where is Father Vesuvio—he must be near, given the pious shindig going on out there, while the crowd waits for us to finish our prayers."

"I am afraid he is dead, Your Holiness. He died while you were preparing for the conclave."

Pope Vincent feigned shock; then his eyes and voice softened as he looked Brandy in the eye.

"I am afraid you are mistaken, Aloy. I was utterly unprepared for the conclave. I never meant to be there, and as you can see, I have yet in me a bit of life, though far from the life I ever wanted."

Brandy squinted in disbelief.

"Who else ever called you Aloy? Your old friend Vincent is here at your side, beardless as a boy now, but back from the Vatican, another sort of graveyard in its own way, though I intend to rearrange it a bit. Aloy, by the grace of God and the Holy Spirit, how good it is to be home after a long journey!"

White teeth flashed in a familiar laugh. Gigantic hands gripped Brandy's shoulders, lifting him to his feet. They faced each other, Vesuvio's features full of excitement and expectation; Brandy's bewilderment, doubt, and fear, mostly fear of the unknown and of retracing faltering steps down a bleak pathway to yet another beginning and ending.

It must have happened before, many times, the soldier declared dead and mourned, the mariner drowned, the mountain-climber given up for lost in an avalanche nonetheless standing under a porch light knocking on a familiar door. Brandy knew such a story; every Christian knows it: the boulder rolled aside a vacant tomb, and the risen Christ mysteriously abroad, defying the logic of death, teasing doubters. Certainly the apostles must have trembled as Brandy trembled now, afraid to speak lest the spell be shattered into a thousand fragments of yet another wispy dream whose upshot could only lead to a second parting.

"Aloy! Aloy! Have you not heard what I said?"

"I have heard, Vincent —if, Holiness, I may call you Vincent..."

"Of course, Aloy, of course. I traveled from Rome to hear you call me Vincent."

Was it Vesuvio calling himself back to the world of the living? Or was it Crackerjack up to his old tricks, preparing to say the next moment, 'You're *It*, Brandy—just kidding'?

To test the matter, Brandy forged ahead, though his voice had not its usual steady timbre. "If you are truly Vincent, tell me something Jack could not possibly have known."

One of Vesuvio's hands still gripped his shoulder. Brandy could feel it tighten as he spoke.

"Ah, so you test me, my doubting Thomas."

"It is not that I doubt Vincent, but Crackerjack could never be trusted."

"—Fred, you have an old mutt named Fred, your fourth by that name I believe. And for good measure your mother thought Jack's family a pack of atheists, and if I truly were Jack, as pope, I would not sit idly by while you called me a liar."

It could not possibly have been, and yet it was. Breaking through his incandescent disbelief and confusion, Brandy stared into the face of his friend Vincent staring back at him, as alive as Lazarus back from the dead and certain to be asked what he had seen.

"Vincent, then who is it in your grave, and how is it that you are pope?"

After a moment of silence that might have been an hour, with Vesuvio's promise to answer and explain, they stepped from the main entrance of St. Callixtus where a microphone and podium had been placed.

Pope Vincent addressed and blessed a throng now permitted to advance, and Brandy put in his best-ever performance as a silent shepherd standing by. His brain teemed, however, with thoughts of his friend's transformation, from dead to living once again, and almost as amazing, from Vesuvio, the man who fretted bishops and half-deaf old ladies, to one who in every gesture and syllable was a most convincing pope. Galilean fishermen could not have been more astonished when chatty, rough-hewn Peter moved to distant Rome to lead an offshoot sect driven underground by persecution.

65

The Watchers Watched

Celebrity network news reporters and visiting VIP's from church and state, from the American Midwest and nearby Manitoba, withdrew to waiting helicopters and to limousines bound for whatever overnight accommodations had been made in advance of tomorrow's noonday papal Mass.

A principle yet to be identified by sociologists appeared to be at work: the more important the personage, the greater the distance to be traveled between engagements. Despite Bishop Norman's preparations, few stayed in New Town; Bernard Passmore's mansion had been snubbed in favor of distant St. Paul, Winnipeg, and North Port City. Several private jets taxied toward the runway of Paradise County Airport. Trucks and vans loaded with video and sound equipment retreated to park in Old Town's many weed-grown, vacant lots.

Bishop Norman's North Port mansion was fully booked. He could not have been more delighted in his newfound role of congenial innkeeper for hierarchy higher than himself. He brimmed with stories suggesting his attachment to the 'obscure and painfully shy' Father Aloysius Brandy.

Tomorrow's noonday Mass remained a mystery of yet undisclosed arrangements. The air near St. Callixtus might quiet for a spell, but as one reporter described it, "An atmospheric secrecy continues to surround the pope's visit. No one here knows what tomorrow will bring."

Every church entrance had been locked, with no one permitted to enter until one hour before tomorrow's Mass. Once again behind St. Callixtus' massive central doors, Vesuvio and Brandy advanced to the altar where they knelt briefly in prayer before retiring to the rectory.

Engrossed in conversation as they exited the church, they would not have noticed at their backs Bernard Passmore and Margaret Smuggs peering furtively either side of a parish center hallway window. Engaged as Bernard and Smuggs were, neither noticed Whisk watching them from beyond a window at the end of the hall.

"I should never have come back here, Bernie. I shouldn't have let you talk me into sneaking around just to get those Blackbirdie recordings we left behind. I could have told you where I hid them. After the way I've been treated by that old geezer Brandy, I wouldn't be caught dead in this place."

Margaret was as intoxicated as she had been the day she bared Bernard's soul in the presence of Harriet. Had she been less so, she might have held her tongue.

"Well, anyway, there they go, Bernie. Your old friend Father Vince and Alooshias Brandy who had us arrested and fired. There they go, Pope Vincent in the flesh and his buddy. Too bad you killed the wrong man, Bernie."

Margaret held up a passport opened to its picture page.

"Too bad I found this in the rectory when you sent me in there to clean up afterwards, the mess you made. But it wouldn't have made any difference what I found. You had already killed the wrong man."

"Shut up, Smuggs! I have had enough."

"Too bad you killed Maurice Fowler, your golden goose who laid your golden eggs. That's what you did Bernie. Hee! Hee!"

"Shut up! Shut up!"

An instant later, a forearm the size of a lamppost struck Margaret across the throat with force enough to send her sprawling along the hallway where her head crashed against the brass entry latch of the archive door. The door flew open. She lay half in the archive and half conscious, attempting to sit up and speak with blood oozing from her mouth. Twisting around, wide-eyed, she fell on her face.

"Dead," said Bernard leaning over her and checking for any sign of life. "Serves her right." He slammed her head against the floor. "Now I will have to figure out how to get rid of this old hag."

Grabbing her by the feet, he pulled her down the hallway to his office and closed the door. Having ducked out of sight, Whisk took a further glance from his window spying post before darting away.

66

A Hand Once Vesuvio's

In the St. Callixtus rectory, after a moment of exuberance of the sort felt after a fiery performance, Vesuvio had grown somber.

"To answer the question you asked before we stepped outside, your old friend Jack is in my grave. I took his place in Rome, another grave as far as I am concerned. More than once recently I have envied him."

"What was he doing here? What on earth were you doing there?

Vesuvio hesitated. As is often the case with a question anticipated and an answer rehearsed, he was suddenly at a loss for words.

"Let me guess," said Brandy. "I'm not as naïve as I look. You dropped a number of hints before you became Pope Vincent. We both know of a priest here and there who keeps a mistress. I suppose now and then one fathers a child and becomes a cardinal. If anyone could manage such tricks, I am sure Crackerjack could. I can imagine that, but I can't begin to guess why you would trade places with him. You must have known each other and never mentioned it. Cardinals don't go around asking obscure priests to impersonate them."

"And obscure priests don't go around interrogating popes! Bear with me, Aloy. The world is upside down and inside out. I can't prevent you from putting two and two together, or in this case one and one. I will explain as best I can, but because some of what I know I learned in the confessional, I cannot explain everything. That is just as well. As you yourself once said, sometimes it is best not to look too deeply into things. Do you recall saying that?"

Brandy nodded. “I have often felt that way, but you are using my words against me.”

“I have no choice!” said Vesuvio, his voice rising. “I can either tell you something, or tell you nothing, and we can spend the rest of the evening playing cribbage or Pig in a Poke.”

Brandy seemed to consider that as an option. “Even before you became pope, you had a way of being mysterious.”

They were bickering. For a few exhilarating moments it felt like old times between friends. This could not last.

Brandy was like a man running hobbledehoy with a shoe on one foot only. One second he was with his old friend Vincent; the next with the pope. He vacillated between familiarity and trepidation. Immobility at last won out.

Vesuvio talked well into an evening gradually darkened with a waning moon settling behind clouds. From beneath the creaky parlor floorboards where they sat, a cricket began to chirp. A mouse scurried through a wall. Fred stood up, stretched himself, turned around, and went back to sleep. A hallway clock chimed the quarter hours. Vesuvio would pause for moments while his elevated eyes seemed to study a geography of ceiling plaster cracks. He might have been talking to himself, unwinding a story he had gone over in his thoughts many times, and had yet to comprehend. Brandy, shifting now and then, occasionally nodded, and remained silent.

Cardinal Cudahy had a passport bearing another name. He had used it in traveling anonymously from Rome to Twin Rivers. Simultaneously, Vesuvio had traveled to Rome, to Cudahy’s capacious apartment in a neighborhood just outside the Vatican known as the Borgo. There, he found everything he needed to impersonate the cardinal from his zucchetto to his red hosiery and his ring.

“When I finished dressing and viewed myself in a mirror, Aloy, the transformation had even me convinced. I looked every inch the cardinal.”

Despite his mood, Brandy managed to look fascinated.

Cudahy had also left maps and instructions for entering the Vatican and getting wherever he needed to go should that prove necessary. They were in touch with each other by phone on a daily basis, but since Cudahy had announced his intention to sequester himself, there was little for Vesuvio to do but read books and watch Vatican news coverage on television, much as Brandy had been doing in the St. Norbert's rectory.

Then came a day without word from Cudahy at Twin Rivers. The following day he failed to appear back in Rome as expected, and then came a messenger with the notice that the conclave was about to begin. His presence was expected. In the company of two of Cudahy's attendants, who seemed not the least suspicious, Vesuvio made his way to the Sistine Chapel. On the way, one of them remarked that he seemed to have lost weight, from fasting he assumed, without saying.

And so Vesuvio found himself helpless in an undertow of events.

"When it was all over, Aloy, I did not know what to do, but I suppose that is usually the way in the first hours and days anyone is elected pope. There are always people on the scene steering you this way and that. You always feel that you are about to make a fool out of yourself, not much different, really, than when we were first ordained."

Vesuvio thought Cudahy would yet return, and they would manage to exchange places as they had done before. He would once again be Vincent Vesuvio; Cudahy would be the pope. Days went by before word of the 'suicide' of an obscure northern Minnesota priest drifted back to Rome, as far as a papal throne the new Pope Vincent refused to occupy, opting instead for a simple acacia wood chair.

"Of course, I knew it had to be murder, for Jack loved his life too much to do away with it, least of all now, when there was a chance he might become pope. I also thought I knew the one who had killed him, mistaking him for me. His murderer had every reason to want me out of the way. I knew too much. It's ironic that mistaken identity on both ends led to my brother's death and my becoming an accidental pope. While arising from one and the same deception, how far distant can two consequences be?"

The one thing Cudahy had not shared with Vesuvio was his intention to kill the extortionist and murderer of his son. If he succeeded, he would free himself forever from a scourge that, were he elected pope, would give Bernard Passmore control of the entire Catholic Church. He would be forced do Bernard's bidding, or the Church would be faced with a scandal like none other in modern times: a pope who had been secretly married for forty years and who had fathered a son.

The one thing Vesuvio had left out of his story so far was that he and Cudahy were brothers. He looked at his old friend, bent beneath the weight of revelations. There were some things demanding silence every bit as strong as the Seal of Confession. One of these was compassion. Brandy would have been better off not knowing, leaving his memories of Crackerjack as they were. Still, he had to be told.

Vesuvio abruptly stood up and walked to an entryway closet where his motorcycle jacket and leather leggings still hung.

"You haven't gotten rid of these?"

"I had not the heart to—not yet," said Brandy. "It's been hard enough as it is taking your place here."

"It wasn't supposed to happen this way," said Vesuvio, laying a hand on Brandy's arm. It was, though, the pope's hand where once it had been Vesuvio's.

"You really are a sentimental guy, and I am quite shame-faced, old friend."

The supreme leader of the world's billion-plus Catholics apologized to a priest whose congregation numbered less than two thousand, and who could not have replaced a wonky candlestick without his parish council's approval.

"Forgive me, Aloy. I have not been a very good friend, to leave you thinking I was dead when I wasn't."

Brandy, a paragon of stoicism and forgiveness, but never much at acting, said there was nothing to forgive, yet it had the hollow sound of a line poorly rehearsed.

"It's hard to be angry with you for being alive."

A world had shifted beneath the feet of two men who never climbed the Church ladder, cherished their mutual obscurity, and had often spoken of careerism dismissively. That one of them by sheer happenstance now perched upon its topmost rung seemed a madcap prank of the sort Crackerjack might have engineered. "I never meant to win," Jack might have said. "I never meant to play this game."

Now Vesuvio was saying it, not in so many words, with his eyes not mirthful as Jack's might have been, but remorseful and apologetic.

Not even death could have divided Brandy and Vesuvio as much as Vesuvio's white zucchetto, removed now and resting like a doily on an arm chair. Their friendship would never be the same. Both men knew it, but neither had the heart to say *It's over*, this obscure life they shared and cherished as outsiders in a remote Church corner.

"And don't call me Holiness, Aloy. I insist upon being Vincent where your lips are concerned. Not *Pope Vincent*, but Vincent, the old Vincent. I hope you can still think of me that way."

Brandy must have looked doubtful.

"You can't, can you?" said Vesuvio. "That is what has happened, isn't it? The old Vincent, it turns out, is dead after all."

He flung himself into the arm chair. His zucchetto slid off to the floor where Fred sniffed it, and Brandy jumping to retrieve it, held as if it were a chalice.

"Many an old dog has worn such a headpiece, Aloy. By the way, if you happen to outlive me, and Vatican fools mention canonization, tell them I was no saint. Promise? Meantime, forgive me."

"There is nothing to forgive," said Brandy for the second time in minutes between what might have been the crowing of a cock in a tale about Saint Peter.

"Oh, there you are mistaken," said Vesuvio. He hesitated as if before diving from a cliff. "There is much to forgive. I am ashamed, for I have deceived you from the get-go about my brother."

"Your brother? Who is that? I do not understand."

"Yes, my brother, Aloy. I do not accidentally resemble your old friend Jack Cudahy. I am his brother. Did you hear me? I said I am Crackerjack's *brother*. You knew him as Jack; the world knows him as Cardinal John Cudahy, the Iron Cardinal; I knew him as Maurice, Maurice Fowler. Years ago, I was Vincent Fowler."

67

A Class Reunion

Had Harriet been eavesdropping on Vesuvio's remorseful confession of a secret long kept from his friend Brandy, she would not have been surprised: She had already arrived at the truth. It might be better said that, as often happens, the truth had come looking for her in the form of further revelations from Dusty Dwyer and the happenstance of an unusual first name. Dwyer's contribution had come during her second cup of coffee last Saturday morning at the Purple Palace bar. The unusual first name turned out to be Lozira, that of Maurice and Vincent Fowler's mother.

All this she dutifully shared with Porky, in her usual Socratic way, gently nudging him with obvious dots to connect on the way to a conclusion he could claim as his own.

Harriet's exploration at the Twin Rivers History Center had led her far into uncharted territory inhabited by Maurice Fowler. She knew enough to perceive in some hinterland of thought the border between accumulated facts and guesswork, the horizon line she could move toward but never reach. She could not know everything, but she knew a lot.

She had poured over census records, birth records, newspapers, and associated family histories published both in books and in digital databases, establishing that Charles Christopher Fowler and Lozira Cudahy had two sons, Maurice and Vincent.

Every diligent family historian learns to value unusual names. The name Lozira was one such. In the entire world there might not have been ten women so named. This had made everything easier for Harriet.

Jack Cudahy, Father Brandy's boyhood friend, in fact was Maurice Fowler. The priest Harriet knew as Vincent

Vesuvio was Vincent Fowler. This much was indisputable. Both men lived under aliases. They looked enough alike to be mistaken for twins.

Jack had been the star performer in an All Saints School Christmas play. In those bygone days, as Harriet knew, a small-town weekly newspaper routinely reported such things including the names of their parents when children were mentioned, in this case Charles and Lozira Cudahy.

"Wow!" said Harriet, abandoning the muffled tone favored in research facilities. When others working nearby glanced up, this became an under-the-breath, yet breathless, whisper: "The Cudahys of Father Brandy's hometown were almost certainly the Fowlers of everywhere else."

The whereabouts of Maurice's brother at that time might have remained a mystery, except for Harriet's lingering at the Purple Palace longer than she had planned, and the coincidence that both Dusty Dwyer and a boy he knew as Vincent Vesuvio had been enrolled in the same Catholic boarding school in Chicago. They had been on the same baseball team; they had sung together in its boys choir; they had been blessed by a visiting pope; they had become friends. As Dusty had said to Harriet that morning, they went "way back" together.

Eventually, young Vincent shared a secret he was not supposed to tell anyone: his real name was Vincent Fowler; his father was the famous and infamous Gus Fowler.

"Gus?" Harriet had said.

"Yeah, everybody called him Gus," said Dusty. *Charles Christopher* didn't sound right for a big-time mobster like Gus, if you know what I mean..."

Gus at times was a hunted man, pursued by rival mobsters and the law. At other times he was a kingpin eliminating rivals and flouting the law. Either way, he amassed enormous wealth. During a period when he was lying low, he settled in Brandy's Iron Range community using the alias Cudahy. He was savvy enough to know that his sons might be kidnapped or harmed to get at him. He gave them both new names.

Young Vincent, in a bragging way, shared some of these details with young Dusty whose first name—proving that God has sense of humor—turned out to the same as George Cobb's.

"No kidding, Wren!" said Porky at that ironic point in her story.

Harriet continued: "The rest could be found in newspaper accounts, the last of which reported the infamous Gus Fowler's disappearance. He was never found. His body might have been buried in a landfill or perhaps he had concrete shoes somewhere in the depths of Lake Michigan.

"By the time they were no longer in danger, both Maurice and Vincent had gone to school, worked, and acquired public records under their aliases. They both decided it was simpler to keep them, and detach themselves from their father's past, but because they looked so much alike, they could not detach themselves from each other.

"This must have been especially hard for Father Vesuvio. No wonder he grew a beard. When his brother became the celebrity Cardinal Cudahy, his picture was everywhere."

"I've seen that before," said Porky. "One of my men has a brother with a criminal record. Every time his picture shows up in a news story, people think it's him. Drives him crazy."

"It's quite a coincidence, really, that four men who knew each other as schoolboys should be reunited late in their lives by the same series of events. Father Vesuvio and Dusty, Father Brandy and Jack Cudahy. It's almost like a class reunion," said Harriet.

"Are you saying that Cardinal Cudahy was murdered in the Paradise Hotel?" Porky asked, though he knew the answer.

"That's what I am saying," said Harriet. "He was the father of Phillip. That is why the DNA matched. And this sheds some light on two mysteries: The iron bar on the hotel room windowsill and the gun registered to Delores Fowler and taken from her home while she was in the hospital. Bernard planned to use the iron bar to disable the man he thought to be Father Vesuvio. Then he would shove his body off the fire escape just as he may have done with Phillip Fowler."

"I think Phillip was killed somewhere else and his body dumped in the alley. His jacket on the fire escape was pure theater."

"Regardless, it worked for Bernard. It was pretty clever: Hit your victim over the head and set it up to look as if he had hit his own head in a suicide leap from the hotel fire escape. If you think about it, it worked the first time. Bernard still has not been arrested, and with nothing more to go on than those printed suicide notes, as you yourself say, we do not have much of a case."

"It helps if you have a medical examiner who ignores the obvious," said Porky.

"And is Catholic and probably under Bernard's thumb."

"Okay, so what about Delores Fowler's gun?"

"Maurice Fowler knew the keypad passcode, went to her home, and took it, possibly intending to kill Bernard."

"A cardinal killing someone?"

"It would not be the first time in Church history, and Cardinal Cudahy had plenty of motive—extortion and revenge. He may have known that Bernard killed his son. He also may have had his gangster dad's killer instincts."

"I'd be on the front page of the New York Times and on every supermarket tabloid, arresting a cardinal for murder."

"Don't get carried away, Wilbur. Nobody knew Cardinal Cudahy was here. As far as the world was concerned, he was in Rome. He would have had a perfect alibi. But before Cudahy got to Bernard, Bernard got to him, thinking he was Father Vesuvio. There was probably a struggle, and Delores' gun wound up in Bernard's hands. This changed Bernard's suicide script. We may never know for certain what happened. I would have your forensic team take a closer look around the rectory, not just its front door, but the rear door, and its side entrance leading into a weedy garden. In the detective mysteries you read years ago, all questions were eventually answered. In the end, everybody knew everything. It doesn't usually work that way with real mysteries. Some things are known to some people; other things to others; nobody knows everything."

"It makes my stomach hurt," said Porky.

"Not to make that any worse, Wilbur, but thanks to Phyllis Cobb, I have had a look at an employment application completed by Phillip Fowler when he began working summers for Cobb Construction. For his parents, he lists Delores and Maurice Fowler, and next to his father's name, he wrote, "Deceased." I doubt that he ever knew that his father was very much alive as the famous Iron Cardinal John Cudahy. It makes sense for several reasons why his mother would have kept that from him."

68

Cain, Abel, and Mother Goose

Left to themselves in the St. Callixtus rectory, Vesuvio had at last broken through the tangled network of layered lifetimes, his with a boy named Maurice Fowler and his with Brandy, strung across each other like the cross-stitching of an ancient tapestry.

"As Jack Cudahy and Vincent Vesuvio, my brother and I went our separate ways. Jack climbed the Church ladder in leaps and bounds. It was like that Mother Goose nursery rhyme—Jack be nimble; Jack be quick ... Jack jumped over every Church candlestick. Jack grew a reputation; I grew a beard to avoid being mistaken for him."

"But why did you trade places with him?"

"He had lost his son, and Delores was dying. In the event he was elected pope, with all the notoriety that brings, a trip for personal, secretive reasons would have been impossible. As you yourself once described him, Jack was quick as a whistle. All his life he had outrun the truth. He thought he could do it this time. In the end, though, life catches up with even the swiftest of runners. Jack lost everything most dear to him—but I can't reveal more. I acted from compassion, though, in effect, I killed my brother. It's an old story, as old as that of Cain and Abel I suppose, though it is not always easy to tell one brother from the other. There is a bit of both in the best and worst of us. In view of all that has happened, ask me whether I am the Cain or the Abel of this story, and I would not be prepared to say."

Brandy looked reproachfully at Vesuvio. "Yes, you and Jack are brothers. I can see it now, but, Vincent, so were we in a sense, or at least I thought so."

"Indeed, Aloy! Indeed we are, and I hope we will remain so. No one is more dumbfounded by this turn of events than I am, and no one more deserving of a fuller account than you. Once I was elected pope in Cardinal Cudahy's stead, no one would dare call me an impostor. As a precaution, I chose the name *Vincent* because I had been responding to that my entire life. I thought I could manage the bluff for as long as it took, and then I learned it would take forever because my brother was in my grave..."

Word was already spreading about the profound personality changes come over the former Iron Cardinal since he had become Pope Vincent. The flames of Pentecost, long simmering within, had begun to express themselves in hair growing somewhat redder, an emerging beard, and a jocular laugh some took as a token of creeping senility in what once had been a formidable brain.

Vesuvio knew what any informed Catholic would know: the reigning pope is also the Bishop of Rome: an ordained priest cannot be pope, unless consecrated a bishop first.

He was left with indulgent grins and feigned amazement when he ripped off his disguise in a private assembly of the most prominent cardinals. He produced a passport nearing its expiration date and a celebret almost as old signed by Bishop Norman's predecessor. The cardinals examined both, passing them around as if they had been issued by administrative authorities from a distant planet. The passport picture showed a man with a red beard, younger and heavier set than Pope Vincent—who hadn't eaten in days. A call went through to Bishop Norman. Word came back that Father Vincent Vesuvio was dead. The bishop himself had said his funeral Mass.

It should not have surprised Pope Vincent to discover that they began humoring him as one would humor a mad king. They thought some slippage had occurred within the fearsome Iron Cardinal's brain.

The cardinals questioned him the way a youthful Jesus might have been examined by Elders of the Temple. Tones were patronizing; eyes moved askance; chuckles were muffled, whispers went around. He was still after all the pope, to be both feared and respected. Pope Vincent had become as delightfully crazy and good at making up stuff as when Brandy first dubbed his brother Crackerjack.

Regardless, even if some smidgeon of inconceivable truth were to be found in Pope Vincent's ravings, this man claiming to be a dead man could not simply be pulled back into the shadows and proclaimed a mistake for the entire world to make what they would of it. That prospect led to confusion and wrangling. A diagnosis of madness seemed the safer course: Pope Vincent was out of his mind and revealing preposterous imaginings. He needed to be humored until psychiatric help could be brought to bear.

At the heart this strange scene, however, Vesuvio was still Vesuvio just as the young Christ was still the Son of God. Neither could brook nonsense and derision from the anointed experts of either Vatican or Judea. Vesuvio was still the man to strike fear into the hearts of bishops. The assembled cardinals were still bishops. He was still the volcano, the Torquemada to make Torquemada tremble. He finally had had enough of Inquisition and pop psychology analysis. Old men trembled in their red shoes and socks when he stood up from his acacia throne.

As Pope Vincent of the world's billion Catholics, he ordered them to make him a bishop, which they did more or less on the spot while adhering to prescribed ritual. As far as they were concerned it was all pantomime to pacify a crazy man till help could be found, and yet they had the power and the glory, no matter what they meant by it.

Thus, the priest of Rome became the Bishop of Rome. In the aftermath, all marveled that the first-ever Pope Vincent seemed to have returned to his senses. A miracle had occurred.

"That is about as much as I can share with you, old friend," said Vesuvio. "I can't prevent you from filling in some gaps on your own if you choose to, but it looks to me like that mongrel of yours wants to take a trip outside. Do you suppose the three of us can slip out the back door for a few minutes, without the whole world knowing?"

69

Words in the Heart of Darkness

St. Callixtus precinct lay engulfed in darkness not experienced since pioneer days of candles, kerosene lanterns, and shadows dancing on walls.

The moon had vanished beneath a thick cloud layer. Security beacons formerly illuminating portions of Hotel Paradise had gone the way of the demolished hotel. Out of respect for the pope, the Purple Palace had closed for the first time in memory. Its *Girls! Girls! Girls!* sign no longer blinked and flashed.

Equally out of the ordinary were the church's darkened façade and twin towers, for decades local nighttime landmarks.

"It's dark as a coalmine out here," observed Vesuvio.

He had been holding Fred's leash, while enjoying the possibility of being the first pope ever to be walking a dog, by day or night. As it turned out, he was talking only to Fred, Brandy having gone into the rectory for a flashlight.

When Brandy returned, they heard a faint sound in the distance that truly might have come from a coal mine, the clink of something like a shovel point striking against stone. Fred barked and shot forward, breaking Vesuvio's grip on his leash. Seconds later, a distant voice familiar to them both could be heard cursing.

Meantime, Porky at home with Harriet during a respite from security duties, turned to juggling for stress relief while he summarized security arrangements in place for the night.

He had set up a patrol zone around the church, the rectory, and the parking lots, a circle with a quarter-mile radius including the Purple Palace which Dusty Dwyer had closed for the day.

Porky dropped a beanbag. Harriet picked it up.

"The first thing you told me about juggling was that it is not about beanbags or balls or oranges. *It all has to do with the spaces between them.* It's about concentration on spaces between and counting, like an airborne rosary; sticking with the rhythm, and not letting the beanbags become a distraction."

"Thanks for reminding me, Wren. Right now, I have a few too many distractions." He dropped another beanbag.

"We should not think in terms of your favorite detective stories. This is more like a Jack-in-a-Box, or a box of *Crackerjacks* with a surprise tucked inside, or maybe no surprise, and that is the surprise—when there isn't one."

Following Harriet's suggestion, Porky had spoken to Father Brandy about sending a forensic team into the rectory for a more thorough check. "It's almost two months ago now. I doubt that they will find much."

"The prints you found around the rectory belonged to Maurice Fowler. If your forensic team finds any traces of blood, it will be his blood."

"Okay, Wren, how is it that Margaret Smuggs knew Maurice Fowler was where Father Vesuvio ought to have been? Was there a Blackbird in the rectory?"

"That's one possibility. Wilbur. Another is that she got in there right after the murder and before your investigative team. She discovered some sort of ID, most likely a passport. He couldn't have travelled internationally without a passport. Where is his passport?"

"I would like to know," said Porky. "We combed the place after the body was found. Everything we came up with had the name Vesuvio on it."

"Well, Margaret found something, enough to convince her that somebody in this picture—either Cardinal Cudahy or Father Vesuvio— wasn't who he said he was. It all points in the same direction—to Rome and to Maurice Fowler, aka Cardinal Cudahy. How Maurice happened to be in the rectory instead of Father Vesuvio is a question I have yet to answer, but I think his murder was a case of mistaken identity."

"And so the killer got it wrong—it's plain as day, Wren!"

Harriet smiled. Having stood up and walked to a window whose curtains had yet to be drawn, she spoke with her back to him.

"Let's say it's plain as night with everyone in the dark. Yes, the killer got it wrong; Father Brandy got it wrong; and we got it wrong at first. Bernard Passmore thought he was ridding himself of a pesky priest. Father Brandy on the phone that same night thought he was talking to Father Vesuvio who had come down with a cold. I needn't repeat what we thought until Margaret squealed on Bernard, and I dug into those ancestral family history and census records. There never was a Jack Cudahy as Father Brandy knew him. Maurice Fowler was real. Cardinal John Cudahy, or Jack, as Father Brandy knew him, was no more than a character in a play. The actor all along was Maurice Fowler. There is much more. Do you see it, Wilbur?"

She had drawn the curtain over the window as happens when an act ends in a play. She turned to face him.

Porky rubbed his forehead.

"Okay, Wren, I'm on it, but we won't be prosecuting anybody in this picture. Rome is too far away, almost everybody is dead, and there is no law against living under an assumed name. But, tell me, what is the motive? I need to hear a motive. Was it money?"

"Thanks to Gus Fowler's shenanigans, the Fowler family had more than enough of that. Maurice was in life for the game. He thought he could get away with anything. As John Cudahy, he darted and dodged all the way to Rome. He was the ultimate impostor. He wanted power and glory of the sort he discovered on the school grounds and on life's playing grounds, all the way to the Piazza San Pietro. He wanted to be on top, and he almost got there."

"So why did Passmore go after Vesuvio?"

"My guess is that, despite the Seal of Confession, he thought sooner or later Father Vesuvio would turn him in. Father Vesuvio himself seemed to be worried. I suspect he had already been threatened, which is why he left the note behind in the parish records. It began, remember, 'In the event something happens to me...' Well, something did happen, but it happened to Maurice Fowler instead. As Cardinal Cudahy, he was involved in a scandal big enough to shake the Vatican to its foundations. What if as pope, word got out that he had been secretly married for forty years, and had a son? Wow!"

"Double wow!" said Porky. "So Bernard Passmore found out while eavesdropping on confessions."

"You see how it all fits together, don't you, Wilbur? The fortune coming Bernard's way, paying for his silence, was enough to purchase Twin Rivers, money mailed from the Vatican Post Office, under special diplomatic privilege bypassing all customs inspection."

"Old Chicago gangland money, if old Gus passed it on to him. Wouldn't you say, Wren?"

"Possibly, but Maurice also married into money. The British Blunt family from which Delores descended owned a network of mines in the west of England and had invested deeply in the South African diamond trade."

"Mobsters, diamonds, scandals, murders, mistaken identities—someday I am going to write my own detective novel," said Porky.

"Add riddles, Wilbur. A good detective story has to have a riddle. And this has one. Father Vesuvio left it in the St. Callixtus parish register: *The four and twenty blackbirds baked in a pie*; when the pie was opened, the confessional was violated; Bernard Passmore is the *King in his counting house counting out his money*, and Margaret Smuggs *the Queen eating bread and honey*, but when she was demoted to *hanging up the wash*, she blew the whistle on the King; Dusty Dwyer, with his sex trade rescue mission, is *the Knave of Hearts who stole some tarts*. It makes sense. Father Vesuvio was trying to warn us while also warning Father Brandy without revealing more than he could, given his role as a confessor. That's a pretty good riddle, isn't it?"

"I guess so." As a lawman, Porky favored facts over riddles. "Another question, the one I asked you before. If Maurice Fowler was the guy whose body we found in the hotel, where is Father Vesuvio?"

"Actually, Wilbur, two questions with perhaps the same answer. Where is Father Vesuvio, and who is Pope Vincent? Wow! I think I know."

At that point, a beeping police dispatch phone intervened.

"Wren, there is something strange going on at St. Callixtus. Its exterior floodlighting is off. It's black as pitch in the precinct, and there's a dog barking and a commotion of some sort." Porky headed out, with Harriet a step behind.

Seconds later, they were in a Paradise County squad car with its rooftop harness lights flashing blue and red as they sped across the first of two bridges between their home and St. Callixtus. Police dispatcher reports crackled from the radio, hit and miss, and insistent. Porky fixed his gaze straight ahead. Street lights glided into view and then receded. Some of his own officers on foot manned the second bridge-approach with flashlights. Porky slowed and lowered his window as they neared the security perimeter.

"Sir, there has been an incident, somewhere in the cleared area where the Hotel Paradise used to be. It's dark in there without the hotel security lights and the *Girls! Girls! Girls!* sign. The church lights went out about twenty minutes ago."

"I'm on it," said Porky. He hit his squad car's siren and accelerated with his window still lowered. "Keep your head low, Wren. I just heard two gunshots."

The two became four in echoes off the stone walls of St. Callixtus.

Over his dispatch radio came a report shouted. "One man down, maybe two, in The Paradise area!"

Porky hit his brakes in the church parking lot, loose gravel spraying from his squad car's wheels. His headlights, and those of several other police cars, had by then illuminated the vacant Paradise site with a dozen crisscrossing beams, speckled and sprayed with flashing blue and red lights.

"Stay here, Wren! Stay down!" shouted Porky as he bolted from the car.

Elongated shadows of crouching officers with drawn guns moved in from several directions toward the leveled expanse where the Hotel Paradise had been but yesterday. The hotel's history had reached a final scene unfolding in shouts, echoes, and darkness pierced by light in which two figures, one in black and the other entirely in white, bent over two sprawled bodies.

Of the two, the one in white had to be Pope Vincent. The other, just then making a Sign of the Cross, had to be Father Brandy. Given these calculations, Harriet ignored her husband.

With equal disregard, Brandy and Pope Vincent ignored a command to freeze.

"Hold your fire!" shouted Porky. "Everyone stand down!"

"It's the Pope!" shouted a breathless Harriet. She laid a restraining hand upon the outstretched arm of an officer holding a gun.

What followed was the strange scene of some men upright, holstering their firearms, as others knelt in the presence of their pope in a personal audience like none other.

70

A Rosary of Joy, of Sadness, and of Relief

A lifeless mound was what remained of Bernard Passmore. Nearby lay Whisk, otherwise known as No-See-Um. An old revolver of a type not used in police work for many years lay between them across the wooden handle of a bloodied garden spade.

Brandy ministered to Bernard who, having overheard ever so many confessions in recent years, had passed well beyond confessing. Pope Vincent knelt beside Whisk. Among those on the scene, Harriet had moved nearest to him. Looking up at her, he held two fingers to his lips and whispered, "Whisk is still alive, but with a serious head wound. For all I know, Harriet, he may be dying. Could you fetch me some water? I doubt that he has been baptized, and so I will do it conditionally."

Whisk as Whisk, Harriet as Harriet, from a man she had yet to meet—Harriet immobilized, held her breath as words no one else could say pulled Father Vesuvio alive from beneath an avalanche called catastrophe, and an instant later magically turned him into Pope Vincent. Death and life danced in a circle. In the space between, Whisk was dying, but Vincent Vesuvio lived once more.

A plastic bottle of water soon found its way to Harriet and from there to Pope Vincent.

At that point, several reporters had arrived on the scene. Cameras flashed as police, establishing a cordon, pushed the reporters back. Sirens announced approaching ambulances and yet more police cars. Soon the entire parking lots of both St. Callixtus and the Purple Palace were full of cars, ambulances, fire trucks, and network media vans disgorging cameras and sound equipment. Porky would afterwards wryly observe that everyone showed up but Coast Guard personnel in a cutter.

Everyone included Dusty Dwyer, conversing with the pope as Whisk was wheeled away on a gurney. A papal hand was seen upon the strip club owner's shoulder, then a blessing, and then again two fingers to lips. The Seal of Confession was not the only seal of secrecy in the picture as St. Callixtus' façade and its twin towers again lit up.

From that direction, shouts were heard. Another body had been found. Uncertainty and confusion, already everywhere, tipped in the direction of Pope Vincent, soon surrounded by police escorting him and Brandy to the rectory whose doors front, back, and garden side were guarded along with windows all around. Meantime a SWAT team under Porky's direction entered the church. Harriet reluctantly waited in his squad car. After fifteen minutes that seemed to be an hour, an 'all clear' was sounded. Porky slid in beside her and took her hand.

"It's Margaret Smuggs, dead as a stone in Passmore's office. From what I can piece together, he had switched off the church floodlights and was attempting to dig a grave for her in the Paradise lot, when out of nowhere Pope Vincent and Father Brandy showed up looking for Brandy's dog. Passmore in a blind rage came at the two of them with his shovel. He might have killed them both, but then Whisk stepped into the scene and shot him with a handgun from his foster parents' home arsenal. According to Father Brandy, Passmore—wounded—flipped around and struck Whisk in the head with the spade point. We'll know more by daylight. Are you all right, Wren?"

Harriet winced. "Poor Whisk. Except for that, I have never been better, dear Wilbur." One by one, tears fell on the hand he held, a rosary of joy, of sadness, and of relief that in the spaces between at least, God was in His heaven, and once again, all was right with the world.

71

Afterthoughts and an Accidental Pope

By the light of day, continuing as daylight circled the globe, a single photograph represented the chaotic story unfolding overnight at St. Callixtus in Twin Rivers, Minnesota: Pope Vincent, bottled water in hand, baptizing the heroic dying boy who had saved his life and that of an 'unidentified priest' standing by.

Reading the story in the Twin Rivers Clarion, during breakfast with Porky, Harriet noted that at least a local reporter had identified Father Brandy, though misspelled his first name.

"It is one of those photographs that will forever show up somewhere, on calendars, in history books, in memories. The more I get to know Father Brandy, the more I think he would not want to be identified in any of those places."

"You can bet on it," said Porky as he speared a second waffle brought to their table at The Paradise Café.

"There is a good one of you also, Wilbur, that shot of you leading a SWAT team into the church. You look so determined and brave."

"I was scared out of my shoes," said Porky.

"Wow! So was I," said Harriet. "I thought maybe there was a killer in the background we had missed all along, maybe a thug pimp from Chicago out for revenge."

For reasons of safety and to preserve crime scenes intact both in the church and out in the Paradise lot, the papal Mass had been moved to mid-afternoon at St. Stephen's Cathedral in North Port City. Pope Vincent was already *en route* there. Bishop Norman was both exuberant and panic-stricken to the point of personal involvement in replacing cathedral candles and supervising floor polishers.

Bernard Passmore had managed to achieve what he most wanted to avoid: Sensational circumstances surrounding Pope Vincent's pilgrimage to his homeland would make old St. Callixtus a pilgrim's destination the world over, assuring the old church's preservation for generations to come.

THE BLOODY RETURN OF THE IRON POPE would be the storyline in screaming headlines around the globe.

Pope Vincent would forever be Cardinal John Cudahy.

Brandy's old tag friend 'Crackerjack', would rest forever beneath a stone in St. Brendan's churchyard, bearing the name *Reverend Vincent Callixtus Vesuvio*.

The body within would forever be that of Maurice Fowler.

Porky White would be elected sheriff in a landslide vote.

A statue of No-See-Um would be erected in Paradise Green. Thousands of pilgrims and tourists would have their pictures taken standing alongside it.

Dusty Dwyer had become one of the few laymen on earth to have been personally blessed by two popes, once as a Catholic choir boy and once as a strip club owner. Years hence, a fund in his name would be established to support the rescue and recovery of women trapped in the sex trade.

Bishop Norman soon received a promotion, appointed archbishop of a major Texas city, in the heartland of cheroots and Texas Hold'em poker. The 'Iron Cardinal' had not after all forgotten him.

Year by year, Harriet White would add a few pages to her St. Callixtus history.

What could not be written there would be kept safe and secure with Harriet, Brandy, and Dusty Dwyer, each of whom knew parts of Vincent Vesuvio's story.

As the years went by, Brandy in front of his old TV would continue to follow Vatican twists and turns while Pope Vincent raced through Roman streets on a motorcycle. With Vesuvio in charge, it was bound to be a dizzying ride with observers on their toes, eyes rolling, and sometimes Curial heads as well.

Motion sickness became a daily hazard in the Holy See.

Brandy, ever the silent shepherd, with a name no one could spell, had grown accustomed to Vesuvio's bittersweet humor and zig-zagging ways long before the rest of the world. He smiled quietly from time to time when his old friend Vincent, red-bearded again, appeared on international TV to say things popes in memory had never before said.

Vesuvio had become the surprise in the box of Crackerjacks; Crackerjack the surprise in a box called a coffin.

Jack was no longer *It*, and one day only God would know.

Brandy sometimes prayed over the grave of his old friend Jack in the churchyard of St. Brendan's at Turning Wind. Out there on the fringes of the reservation, he occasionally saw a striking Indian woman with an infant who missed being a pope's grandson, but at least was his grand-nephew.

By coincidence, the one and only time he heard from Pope Vincent, a letter arrived as he returned home. It began, "Dear Aloy," and ended, "Your old friend, Vincent." Between the beginning and the end, Vincent described his frustrating struggles with a Church whose corruption some days seemed universal. “It’s like trying to rearrange a cemetery,” he said.

Years hence, a rare autumn snowfall lay upon the Piazza San Pietro as Pope Vincent’s funeral procession brought him to the undercroft of St. Peter’s, the final resting place of recent popes.

Among the throng present, only a silent, tearful Harriet White knew him as Father Vincent Vesuvio, an obscure parish priest who became an accidental pope.

Closing of Box Five

Acknowledgments

I wish to thank my wife Kate whose encouragement and support was a constant presence through the four years I wrote and re-wrote this novel. I am certain she has read it in its various forms at least a dozen times. Since its completion, she has worked tirelessly at editing and formatting to bring it to its present published state. It is not an exaggeration to say that *An Accidental Pope* is as much her work as mine, for from beginning to end, through bad days and good, whatever the writing weather, she has always been at my side.

Otherwise my writer's guide in these pages has been the masterful Sinclair Lewis whose depictions of the everyday life and easily missed drama of the American Midwest have never been equaled.

A special thank you to Sister Karen Hilgers, David Sjoblad, David Casper, and Father John Padberg, S.J. who read and commented upon an earlier version, and to Father Ulick Loring who listened patiently to fragments of this written in England. I also wish to thank Vivian Dudro, editor for my novel *Everywhere in Chains*, whose various suggestions for that novel have been applied here. Finally, thanks also to John Herreid for reading *An Accidental Pope* and for his support and encouragement managing the Ignatius Press Novels Blog, an important forum for Catholic writers.

I also wish to thank a handful of readers who even in their silence provided a sense of direction and purpose.

The least thing a writer needs is applause.

March 2018, Victoria, Texas where this novel at last earned the words THE END.

About the Author

James Casper was born and grew up in southern Minnesota. Apart from living in various Minnesota locales, he has resided in Boston, St. Louis, eastern Tennessee, and London, England where portions of this novel were written. He and his wife of twenty-four years have traveled extensively. Rome is one of their favorite places. He is happiest walking from lock to lock along the Thames in England.

Website: FarhavenPress.com

More by James Casper

Everywhere in Chains: Secrets of the North Shore is a moving story about a young girl whose real father's whereabouts is kept a secret to "protect her" from the truth. Ultimately, she is reunited with him, along the way proving that the path to healing takes a lot of courage and strength. The story provides a way forward for families who are victims of priest sexual abuse and for those who have a loved-one in prison.

The Far End of the Park
Explore a year of turmoil, revelation, and change in the life of Jude Henley. Here is a story that will make you laugh, cry, and remember what it felt like to be growing up.

And finally, if you like this book, please leave a short review online at Amazon or elsewhere. Your reviews really do help others decide if the story behind the cover might delight them, so it means the world to authors if you have something good to say. Thank you, from the team at Farhaven Press, Kate, James, and Henry the bulldog.

Made in the USA
Las Vegas, NV
22 August 2021

28662890R10187